£3.25

# *The Patchwork Tea Cosy*

THE old lady poured out a cup of tea, put the cosy on the pot,
She warmed her hands upon the cup, which now was nice and hot.
It was obvious that the cosy was very, very old,
But every little patch to her had a story to unfold.

The big red square had been a skirt in which she'd spun and twirled,
Excited when she came of age and round the dance floor whirled,
The dark brown piece from trousers her little boy once wore,
He'd waved goodbye in uniform, and seen his home no more.

The bright green scrap, like sunny grass, scattered with flowers gay,
Had come from a dress her mother loved. She'd long since passed away.
Here and there a splash of blue, reminder of summer skies,
But more than that, the very hue of a loving daughter's eyes.

The sombre shades of heavy tweed, and a snippet the colour of heather,
They'd been wearing those when he proposed, and they made their pledge together,
A recollection there, in each faded square, keeping warm a pot of tea,
And as she sips the cosy brings alive a lifetime's memory.

— *J. O. Coatsworth.*

# People's Friend Annual 1992

## *CONTENTS*



BACK COVER Langdale Fell, Cumbria.

# Dreams Are For Sharing

BOB and I are so please you'll be godmother to our baby," Wendy's old school friend said excitedly over the phone. "And who do you think I've asked to be godfather? You'll never guess!"

"I can't imagine, Sue," Wendy told her. "I suppose Bob's young brother would be ideal — but he's a bit too young. Is it your cousin from Australia?"

"No. I thought it would be wonderful, since you used to be such good friends, if Graham Berry would —"

"But he's up north!" Wendy gasped, shaken as memories came flooding back.

Just about the last person in the world she wanted to meet was Graham, especially now.

"Yes, but he might enjoy a visit home to see everyone. So many of our old school pals will be there and," Sue chuckled, "it might make some of them think twice when they see how successful he is. Remember how they used to tease him for being a swot?"

"I remember," Wendy said tautly.

Then, her voice shaking a little, she managed to say lightly, "I suppose if he comes he'll bring Rita?"

"Well, of course I've asked him to. We'll see if she's just as beautiful, just as perfect as he says she is.

"I knew you'd be pleased," Sue babbled on. "You and he were always such good friends in the old days — proving that two people can be good mates without being sentimental!"

At least it was certain now, Wendy thought wryly, that not even Sue had guessed the truth.

"Yes," she said with a laugh, "just like twins — that's what Graham used to say. Well, you've certainly given me a surprise."

"Of course, he might refuse, or he might come and we'll find he's changed — might have become an awful stuffed shirt. Rita might have changed him — she sounds a bit forceful."

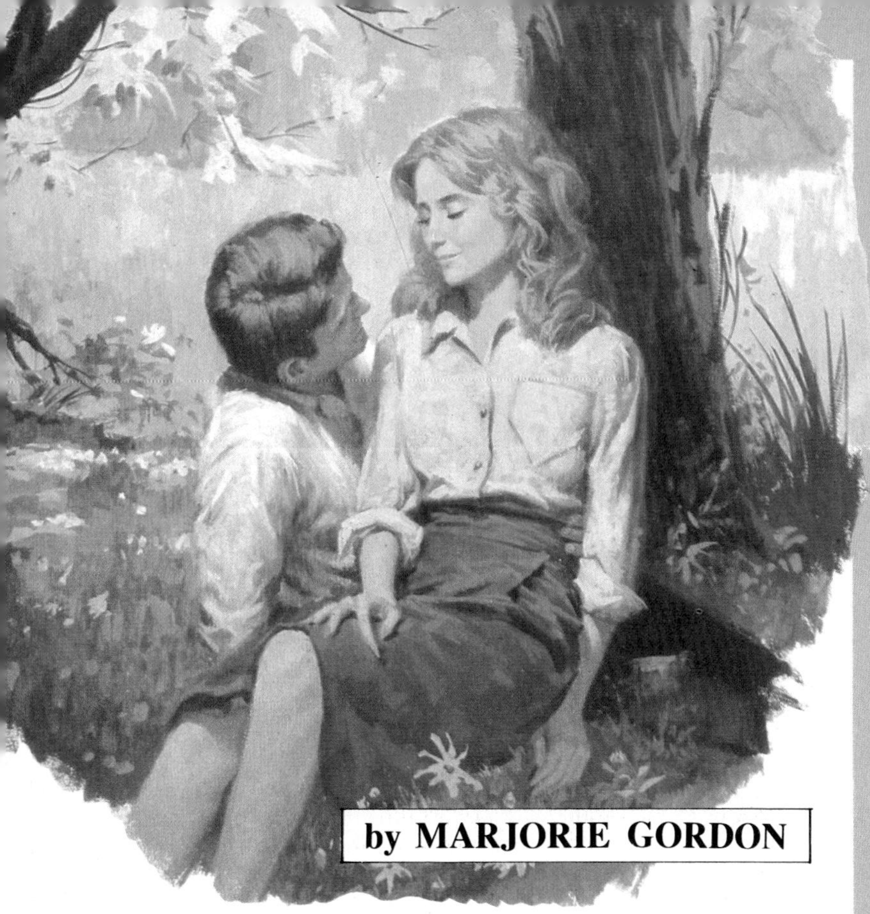

by MARJORIE GORDON

WENDY had had as much as she could take.

"Let's hope the sun will shine for the christening and the garden party after," she said, changing the subject. "I've got a super new dress but haven't found the right hat yet."

"You will," Sue told her confidently. "But, Wendy, before I ring off, you won't really resign, and move away, will you?"

"Oh, yes! I need a complete change of direction, or whatever. I've got all my feelers out and will let you know when something turns up. Must fly, 'bye, Sue."

She rang off, before Sue could say any more or ask questions, before she, Wendy, could blurt out the truth, her humiliation, her failure.

She shuddered. How was she going to bear to meet Graham Berry and the wonderful girl he'd raved about?

Though hating herself for the thought, Wendy couldn't help hoping that he'd turn down the invitation to be godfather, even though he and Bob had become close friends at university.

Wendy remembered the postcard she'd sent from Italy — a picture of the Grand Canal in Venice — in answer to his ecstatic letter.

"So you've met the perfect girl you were looking for," she'd written curtly. "I'm heavily involved with *IM*perfections. All the best, Wendy."

She knew she'd hurt his pride, for she hadn't heard from him since.

And that, though she missed his letters, had been a relief.

By the time she went to bed that night, Wendy had convinced herself that Graham wouldn't come back, that he wouldn't be staying in the big, cold, gaunt house facing the park, with the uncle and aunt who had brought him up when his parents died in a car crash while on holiday overseas.

He knew that her home, where he'd always been so welcome, had been sold up years ago when her father had been moved 400 miles away to manage a branch of his company on the south coast.

No, of course he wouldn't come. He wouldn't want to put the clock back.

But if, by some horrible twist of fate, he *did,* she would see to it that she only met him and Rita at the christening.

Somehow she'd dodge the party in Sue's garden, and get back here to her flat, in the big block near the school where she taught the very young pupils.

Every day, after Sue's call, she played tennis on the school courts before going home, in a frantic endeavour to work off some of the tension.

IT was on the Wednesday evening, 10 days before the christening, that one of the junior school teachers came hurrying over to the courts.

"Wendy!" she cried. "Shall I phone the police? There's a man leaning on your car. He was seen looking at all the cars and then —"

But Wendy was away, running towards the car park, sure that all her fears were about to be realised. She had no doubts that the man was Graham.

It was just what he would do — and she had to face him.

For a few seconds they just stood facing each other speechlessly.

Graham, Wendy realised in that one swift look, had changed. He looked older, though he still had the same glow in his brown eyes, the same unruly brown mop of hair.

Perhaps struck by something in her expression, he said, "I thought I'd give you a surprise, as I did Sue and Bob. They gave me your address, and said if you weren't home I'd probably find you on the tennis courts."

Wendy heard herself mutter chokily the first inane words that came into her head, "So you're going to be godfather."

"That's right. Let's talk about it. We're going to the Blue Cockatoo. All of us — Bob and Sue as well."

At that, Wendy recovered herself. Shuddering inwardly, she thought that about the last thing she could face was dinner anywhere with Graham and Rita, even with Bob and Sue there. She'd still be the odd one out.

"I'm sorry," she said quickly, almost shouting, "but it's impossible. I've got a date for tonight — unbreakable."

She paused nervously, then she added, "I'm frantically tied up with a lot of — of plans at the moment."

"But — but —" Graham began, as she got into her car.

"I'll see you both at the christening," she said.

"I couldn't do it! I couldn't do it!" she cried to herself, as she drove off. "I'd break down. It'd be the last straw!"

Back in her flat, she flopped down into the rocking-chair in her living-room, and gave way to tears as she hadn't done since Graham went away.

SEEING him standing there, with that little-boy-baffled look on his face, had brought everything back — all those far-off days at school, when Graham was always being ragged about being a "swot" because he was so studious, read so much, determined to do all he could to win scholarships for his engineering training.

He was teased unmercifully, because with his physique he could have been wonderful at sport. But Graham took no interest in any game involving running after or with a ball.

She, Wendy, had been teased for, of all things, actually wanting to be a teacher, for dreaming of being the head of a big school.

Like Graham, though, she'd always been fascinated by nature, the lives of birds, animals and insects. She'd enjoyed pottering through the countryside on her bicycle. It was on one of those outings that she'd seen Graham, watching an ant-heap.

After they'd talked for a while, he'd asked her solemnly, "Do you think there's anything really wrong with us?"

"Wrong? What do you mean?"

"Well, the way they all go on at school as if — as if — well, as if we're nutters having ambitions and studying."

"Ah!" Wendy, looking at a hazel tree just in front of them, had a flash of inspiration. "Maybe we are — nuts, I mean. And, Graham, don't you think it's fun, being a nut!"

They'd laughed, but from that moment they'd been friends. Wendy, who at that time was reading "Anne Of Green Gables," told him about Anne, referring to everyone who was on her wavelength, as "Knowing Joseph."

"That's good," Graham had said. "*We* both know Joseph. We're the lucky ones."

"Let's always know Joseph. Let's always be nuts!"

So they shared their dreams, their books, their outings into the countryside.

It had been a long time before Wendy realised Graham didn't share one of her dreams, the one that mattered most.

Oh, why had he come now, when everything else was wrong, too?

Suddenly, her doorbell rang over and over, and a voice called through the letter-box, "If you don't let me in I'll break the door down and end up in jail!"

So Graham had realised she'd been fibbing about a date. Remembering the Graham of old, and thinking of the neighbours, Wendy knew that he was quite capable of staying there until she did open the door.

Quickly mopping her eyes with some cold water, and dabbing some powder across her reddened cheeks, Wendy took a deep breath and opened the door.

Graham strode in after her, and stood beside her in front of the fireplace.

"Just tell me what I've done! What's the matter with you that you treat your old pal like this?" Suddenly his tone changed. "You've been crying . . ."

"Yes," she stammered. "I — I've had rather an awful disappointment, and it's shaken me!"

"Tell me."

"I — I can't."

He took her arm and said in a firm voice, "We'll go to our favourite tree. You can tell me anything there. Come on, you needn't change." He laughed a little uncertainly. "You look great in your tennis gear!"

"No, I can't," Wendy replied just as firmly. "Anyway, you can't just leave Rita."

"Unfortunately," Graham said, "Rita wasn't able to come. It's a pity, but she has this high-powered job in public relations, and goes to lots of conferences and things, all over the place."

"I see. She must be disappointed."

"Yes. But forget about her. We're going to sit on our old tree-trunk, and you're going to tell me what's gone wrong, just as you always did."

So, Wendy thought, he wasn't going to talk about Rita.

EVENTUALLY, after two cups of coffee, Wendy changed and they set off across the southern tip of the park into the wood. On the way, Graham chatted easily about being godparents, about the ceremony, the party afterwards.

It wasn't until they were sitting on the old tree-trunk, with the early-evening sunshine gleaming through the trees, that he said, "Tell me what's biting you. Please," he added pleadingly. "Something unpleasant at school, with staff or —"

"No," Wendy said quickly. "Nothing like that. It's just that — well, you wanted to be a fine engineer and you are, with a splendid job."

"And you wanted to work your way up to be the head of a big school," he remembered.

"That's right." The words suddenly rushed out. "I've failed. I've been — oh, so humiliated. But why should you —"

"Hush," Graham said gently. "Of course it matters that you were humiliated. What happened?"

Touched by his concern, it was as if the years rolled back. She poured out her heart about the interview she'd had for an assistant headship, about the questions, the comments.

"What it all added up to," Wendy wound up bitterly, "was that I'm OK as a teacher of very young children, but haven't got what it takes to be a head, or even an assistant head — for the paperwork, for handling all the staff."

"All very nice, but like a slap in the face with a piece of wet fish," Graham said.

Her lips trembled into the semblance of a smile.

"That's better," Graham encouraged.

He added thoughtfully, "You know, I can understand your feeling miffed, but, well, when you think about it, doing the actual teaching is the most important part of your job.

"And you've reminded me that a while back it was made clear to me I'd never make management material, or director material."

## *Woodland Path*

A WINDING path that undulates
Up hills and down the dales,
That wanders, lost between the trees,
With charm that never fails;
It skirts the ponds where tiny fish
Break glistening surface free,
Where woodland creatures scurry by,
Each squirrel knows its tree;
The path passes by the kingcup fields,
Pursues its way in peace,
Is trodden underfoot by men
Who come to find release.

— *Margaret Comer.*

"You! Weren't you furious?"

"Frankly, no. I'm happier and better at the job in overalls with dirty hands. I'd go potty in an office having to tell staff what to do."

Wendy looked at him, astonished. "I hadn't thought of that. I suppose it *is* one way of looking at it.

"I do remember now, the interviewers were awfully nice about my handling of the very young children."

"So there!" he said cheerfully. "By the way, what about — er — boyfriends?"

"Oh, here and there," she told him lightly.

"No-one special?" Graham persisted.

"Once," she managed to say calmly, "but it didn't work out."

At that he stood up. "Look, Wendy, I rang up Sue and Bob and suggested we postponed our date at the Blue Cockatoo.

"I don't feel like a restaurant. I want us to talk a bit more tonight, though. Remember how we used to rustle up snacks in your attic at home?

"Could we go back to your flat and rustle up something quick and easy. I've got — well — a sort of career problem, and we could talk about it in peace."

"Oh, Graham." Instantly she was all sympathy. "I'm so sorry, and here I have been babbling on. Yes, of course, I'll rustle up an omelette, and I've loads of fruit and cream and cheese — still like different cheeses?"

"You bet!"

THEY walked back hand in hand, as in the old days. Then they concentrated on the meal, while he told her the firm had asked whether he'd consider returning south, at any rate for a few years, to help with a new project.

"But haven't you got used to the north?" she asked, thankful that she, at least, had planned to move away. "And, of course, there's Rita. Would she like it here?"

"Wendy," he said suddenly, with a strange expression in his eyes, "do you remember your reaction all those years ago, when I told you I dreamed of meeting a perfect girl, having a perfect marriage and wonderful kids?"

"Indeed I do," she retorted. "And I hurt your feelings very badly."

"I can still hear the scorn in your voice as you told me such a perfect person, such a perfect life, if it could ever exist — which you doubted — would be as dull as dish-water. The sentiment reached me even in your curt postcard from Venice."

"I'm sorry," she said, "but —"

"So was I! I was ecstatic, having just fallen madly in love with a beautiful, wonderful, perfect female.

"But you were right. That perfection in itself can be — well, the perfect person doesn't know Joseph!" Graham finished.

"Do you mean that you and Rita — ?"

"I mean that for a while I've been feeling a bit uneasy about everything," he admitted. "We had a sort of commitment, nothing definite.

"Then I had the letter from Sue, and asked Rita if she'd like to come. I knew from her reaction that it wasn't going to work for us.

"What I'm trying to say," Graham wound up, "is that Rita doesn't know Joseph. Besides, Rita wanted a perfect male — and who knows better than you, Wendy, that I could never add up to that!"

"I suppose you did have to *meet* your ideal," Wendy said thoughtfully, "before you could find out whether she really was the one for you."

"I knew you would understand, you always did. And, Wendy, maybe you had to go all out for that promotion to assistant head, to find out your real work is in the actual teaching."

"As yours is in the nuts and bolts, the grease and the gears!"

"Hurrah!" Graham cried triumphantly. "We've both learned something. Lift your wine glass, Wendy, and let's thank our stars and drink to them for keeping us both still knowing Joseph."

"And nuts!" Wendy reminded him with a twinkle. "We'd better make sure our god-daughter grows up knowing him and being nutty!"

Perhaps, she thought, deep down in her heart, maybe she could nurse a tiny hope for the future. □

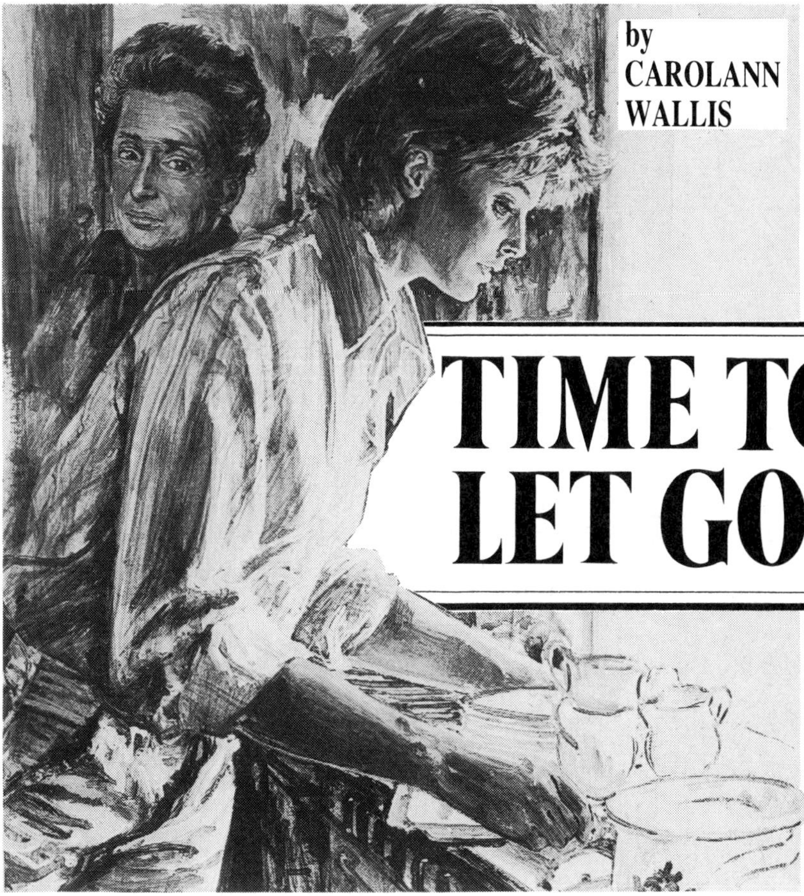

by
CAROLANN
WALLIS

# TIME TO LET GO

IT was finally Mike who broke the stunned silence. Helping himself to another bowl of cereal, he pushed his glasses higher up his freckled snub nose and said nonchalantly, "Well, I think it's embarrassing."

"Mike!"

Laura absently removed the bowl of cereal from under his spoon and wandered over to the sink with it.

"Mu-um!"

Mike's deafening wail acted as a kind of starting gun that galvanised the family into their usual rushed morning exit.

Steve kissed Laura absently somewhere beneath her left ear. "Sorry — I've got to go. I'm taking the car in for its MOT before I start."

He gave her a helpless, don't-look-at-me-for-moral-support look, waved vaguely towards the group at the table and vanished.

As soon as the door banged behind him, Lucy stood up, cramming the last of the toast into her mouth.

"I'll cadge a lift from Dad," she mumbled. "I've got an early lecture."

"But I thought —"

Laura sat down again opposite Gran, and watched Mike munching his way solidly through his cereal. His twin brother, Ben, waited for him patiently, having already picked his way through nearly an eighth of a slice of toast.

Twins, thought Laura for the millionth time, are like chalk and cheese. Mike was a tough, macho man, and Ben was a romantic. She worried about both of them equally.

Mike stood up, swigged the last of his glass of milk, and looked at his gran disapprovingly.

"Come on, Ben. Let's go."

That was an order, so obediently, Ben picked up his satchel and trooped after Mike. But he hesitated at the door.

"I think it's nice, Gran," he said, with his heartbreakingly sad, wise smile.

"So do I, Ben, love." His gran blew him a kiss across the cluttered breakfast table.

LAURA leaned on her elbows among the dirty breakfast dishes and the silence. She looked at the woman sitting opposite her, at the bright, blue eyes, the head of thick, grey hair, at the face which looked so like her own.

As if in an enchanted mirror, she looked at her mother and saw herself in 25 years' time. It wasn't a bad sight, she had to admit. Her mother was still an attractive woman.

That brought her mind to the problem she'd been trying not to think about.

She lit a cigarette. It was early and that meant she couldn't allow herself another one till after lunch, but this was an emergency.

"Tell me again, Mum. You've met a man and you're —" She tapped her cigarette ash into an ash-tray, concentrating on the procedure as if it were vitally important, playing for time.

What did you call it at 65? Dating sounded ridiculous. Walking out together? Courting? Too old fashioned . . .

"— seeing each other?" she concluded lamely, trying hard to suppress a smile at the sudden, intrusive thought of her mother's legendary short-sightedness.

"I don't know why you're so amused." Her mother glowered at her cigarette smoke.

"Oh, Mum, I'm not!" She waved away the smoke from her cigarette and covered the older woman's hand with hers. "I'm not laughing at you, honestly I'm not. And I'm sorry about Mike's rudeness. I'll speak to him tonight about it. You know he didn't mean it — he's, well —"

"He's Mike," her mother finished for her, and they laughed

together, shaking their heads at other memories.

"I know," Laura said. "He's just at the age when he walks out of the room when the soppy bits come on television. He's no time for romance, I'm afraid."

"Well, maybe Mike spoke for all of you, just the same," May said. "Maybe all of you think it's embarrassing."

"Of course we don't, Mum! I'm just worried about you — anxious, that's all."

"Why?"

Laura shrugged. "Well . . ."

She ran her fingers through her hair. Suddenly it seemed as if someone had changed the script in a drama she'd played for years.

After her father had died eight years ago, she'd helped her mother sell the house, supported her through that first lost year and acted as mother to the child her own mother had become. The older woman had been so vulnerable, and so terribly lonely, even with the two-year-old twins clambering on her knee, even in the middle of their noisy, rambling house.

Laura felt a lump in her throat, suddenly remembering the heart-breaking way her mother had coped. It was a kind of lonely bravery, so that no matter how much Laura tried to offer comfort, there was always a place she couldn't reach, a place where the real hurt and pain survived.

The bad times had passed and Laura believed her mother had stopped hurting. Now, she suddenly realised that maybe she didn't know as much about her mother as she'd thought.

Maybe she had never stopped hurting, maybe that cold, lonely place was still there. Maybe that's why she had turned to this man . . .

"Tell me about him," Laura said, smiling at her mother, feeling suddenly strange and shy.

"I've got a better idea. Why don't you meet him? See for yourself? You'll like him — I know you will."

Laura nodded unconvincingly. "I'm sure I will."

THEY met in Polly's bookshop," she told Steve that night in bed. "Ted was buying books for his grandchildren, and she offered him advice. They never looked back."

She sighed. "She's such an innocent, Steve."

She plumped up the pillows and lay back staring at the ceiling. "I mean, he might be a real rogue, after her savings. You read such dreadful things —"

Steve squeezed his arm behind her head, drawing her close.

"She's hardly got savings to speak of, love. And anyway, she's no fool," he pointed out. "I don't think she's quite such an innocent as all that. Give her credit for some sense, Laura. It's time to let go —"

"Let go? How?" She turned to stare into Steve's eyes. "We're responsible for her. We have to take care of her just as we take care of Lucy and the twins —"

Steve kissed her. "I know, and we will. But there's no sense jumping to all sorts of daft conclusions.

"She's made a friend, that's all, and we're going to meet him. We'll take it one stage at a time, right?"

"What did you mean 'let go'?" she asked after a minute or two. "She needs us, Steve, all of us."

He sighed. "I know she does, love, but maybe not the way she once did. Maybe it's time to take a step back.

"She's got to live her own life, Laura — yes, even to the extent of making her own mistakes," he insisted as she tried to argue.

Laura switched off the light, then giggled. It sounded the same conversation they'd had umpteen times over Lucy. She had been a headstrong, difficult 15-year-old, anxious to grow up too quickly. Now, at 20, she had almost finished college and, though she had boy-friends, she'd no plans to get too serious.

"I've got my career to think of. I want to travel, see a bit of the

The Wonder of Water . . .

**_FALLS OF BRUAR_**

*Situated near Blair Atholl on the A9 Perth-Inverness road, the Falls of Bruar are particularly worth seeing after rain. They consist of three falls, with the top fall itself threefold, being the longest with a total drop of 200 feet. Larches were planted on the banks of the Burn of Bruar after Robert Burns wrote his "Humble Petition Of Bruar Water," addressed to the Duke of Atholl of the day. If you follow a path up beyond the falls for about another mile, you can cross the burn by a bridge and descend the opposite bank.*

world, enjoy being selfish and independent before I make any commitment.

"You're only young once, Mum, you know," Lucy had lectured Laura, brandishing the dish-towel. "I don't want to rush things."

That little speech, made as they dried dishes together last night, had left Laura open-mouthed. It contained everything she'd ever tried to tell Lucy all through the stormy years.

Maybe that was the whole point, Laura thought now. Lucy had worked it out for herself.

She smiled in the dark. Lucy was all right.

TED MORTON was a handsome man, Laura had to admit. Tall, distinguished looking and with an enviable suntan.

"Ted comes from Perth — the one in Australia, that is," May explained.

"You're a long way from home, Ted," Steve said as he handed him a glass of his best whisky.

"I certainly am, Steve. I'm here for just two months, visiting my youngest daughter who lives not far from here with her family."

He took a sip of his drink and nodded approvingly. "It's my first visit, but I've found everyone very friendly."

Laura smiled, trying to look more relaxed than she felt and trying to pretend that Ted wasn't under scrutiny. That was difficult, she admitted, catching sight of the twins, perched on the settee, polished and rosy, staring at every move Ted made.

They chatted casually, feeling their way around.

When Laura slipped into the kitchen to check on the meal, Lucy came after her.

"Isn't he gorgeous, Mum? Couldn't you just fancy him yourself?" she squealed, dancing round with the oven gloves.

He was very nice, Laura had to admit by the end of the evening, and he and her mother were obviously very happy in each other's company.

Yet there was an edge to the atmosphere she didn't quite understand.

It wasn't until Steve had left to drive Ted home, and Laura, Lucy and May were in the kitchen washing up together that she understood that edge.

"Ted goes back in a month's time," May said. She handed a dripping plate to Laura. "He wants me to marry him and go with him."

Laura rubbed at the dinner plate, stunned.

It was Lucy who spoke first. "And will you?"

So casually, Lucy thought, as if it were the most natural thing in the world for Gran to meet a man and follow him halfway round the world.

"It's a long, long way away," Laura said gently.

Her mother scrubbed at a pot. "I know."

"The world's getting smaller all the time," Lucy announced cheerfully, putting her arm around her gran and planting a kiss firmly on her cheek. "We can all come out and visit you at Christmas — it'd be wonderful to eat turkey on the beach!"

LAURA glanced at the window. The blinds were undrawn, and the window, which earlier had offered a view of the garden, now showed only a dark mirror which reflected back to her the image of her bright kitchen and the three women together.

For a sudden moment she caught her breath — three women of different generations caught in a moment of just being together doing ordinary things. The preciousness of it all made her sigh.

She was so aware that everything was changing. Lucy was growing up, and would be leaving home soon.

And now Gran . . . It was nonsense, of course. She couldn't go all the way to Australia by herself, with a man she barely knew. But whether she stayed or went, nothing would be the same.

"I think," she said carefully, "we should talk about this in the morning. It's late."

Her mother nodded, kissed her good night and went upstairs.

Lucy nibbled a piece of cheese and watched her mother carefully. "Aren't you pleased for her, Mum?"

"Oh, Lucy! I know it must seem like a huge adventure to you, but she hardly knows him. I can't see that she can seriously consider leaving her home at her age."

"Surely you don't get too old for romance, Mum," Lucy said. "You're beginning to sound like Mike!"

She put her hands behind her neck, lifted her corn-coloured hair high and then let it cascade over her shoulders again, an easy, casual movement. "I think I'll go to bed."

Laura hugged her. Life was so simple for Lucy.

Alone in the kitchen, Laura sat down at the table, her head in her hands. It would be difficult, but she could sort this out.

Her mother would see sense if she were handled tactfully enough. She and Ted could remain friends, but give each other a little more time. Next year, perhaps they could meet again.

Yes, that would be the best way, Laura decided. She heard the sound of tyres on gravel as Steve drove the car in, and stood up.

She looked at her reflection in the kitchen window and stared for a moment. Caught in the middle, between Lucy and her mother, she suddenly felt like the only grown-up.

EVERYONE was late next morning. There was no time for breakfast, no time for talk.

Laura was glad of that, because she wanted to prepare the ground carefully.

She made a pot of coffee and set out two mugs.

"I'm glad everyone's gone," her mother said. "I love them all dearly, but I treasure a few moments like this, when we can talk. Don't you?"

Laura nodded. She hesitated, searching for the right opening, rehearsing in her mind what she would say, but nothing sounded right.

It was May who spoke first.

"I need your advice, Laura." She smiled, cupping her hands round her mug of coffee. "I don't know what to do. If things were different — if we were younger, if we had more time —"

She shrugged. "But Ted and I, we both know we have to make a decision."

"Mum, you've plenty of time. What's a few months, a year —"

May shook her head.

"No." She sighed. "Oh, maybe once I would have agreed with you. But when your father died I realised that the only time you can count on is now.

"There was always so much that had to come first — his job, the house, then the children. Oh, I don't regret the way things were."

She sipped her coffee. "Maybe we lived too much in the future, planning ahead. But you can't bank minutes like pound notes, Laura," she said. "They just get all used up."

Laura put her hand over her mother's, but the older woman stood up, and wandered over to the window.

"We see things the same way, Ted and I. We've both had plenty of time to be alone, time enough to know it's not what we want.

"I do care about him — so much, Laura. I feel whole again — I feel as if I'm *me* again." She sighed. "Maybe that's why I'm afraid of what you're going to say to me. I know you'll be right, and maybe tomorrow I'll be glad you talked me out of this. But just now —"

Suddenly realising her mother was crying, Laura got up and put her arms around her.

Over her mother's shoulder, she looked out of the window, suddenly remembering how she'd felt last night, seeing the three of them together, caught as if in a picture which only showed her the way things changed, minute by minute.

Wasn't that what her mother was saying now? And it had taken her mother a lifetime to learn it.

I'm so lucky, Laura thought, that I know that now. You can't bank minutes like pound notes, her mother had said. They've got to be spent positively and with faith, she realised.

Steve had known all of that, when he told her to let go.

She looked at her mother. It would be easy to persuade her to be careful here, to take her time and wait a bit.

But that would be wrong.

Ted had unlocked that cold, lonely space inside her mother, and she'd always be grateful to him for that.

People would say it was crazy, foolish, that Laura was mad to encourage her — they were wrong.

Laura's smile as she spoke was tremulous but her voice was steady.

"The world's getting smaller all the time," she said. "And I really do fancing eating turkey on the beach at Christmas, don't you?" □

# A Family Tradition

by
**BEN MATTHEW**

EDWIN GROVES heard the accident before he rounded the bend in the lane that ran past his driveway. Fighting his fear he cycled slowly round the corner. He could see one of the vehicles in the ditch. The other was out of sight.

Forcing his legs to work, he went on and was relieved to see his father's car already there.

"Edwin! Thank goodness!"

With barely a glance at his son, Dr Charles Groves issued quiet commands. Because he was there, because the injured people needed help and it was expected of him, Edwin obeyed his father.

Only when the ambulance had left the scene and his father had continued on his way to his next case did Edwin give way to the nausea he had been fighting to control.

His home was only a hundred yards away, and he managed to reach his room unobserved. There he flung himself on to his bed and buried his head in the pillow.

The last half-hour had confirmed what he already knew — he could never do as his father wanted and become a doctor. But how could he tell his family?

As far back as anyone could remember, the eldest Groves sons had gone into medicine. Even when his Uncle Herbert had had a daughter for his first-born, Harriet had followed the tradition and was now a respected gynaecologist.

If only he knew what he wanted to be. If he could go to his father and say, "I don't want to be a doctor! I want to . . ."

His mind become a blank when he thought of the future.

Edwin washed and went down for dinner. He was one of a large family — five younger than him — and they were all gathered round the large dining-table.

Nathan Groves, his elderly grandfather, greeted him with a smile.

"Well now, I hear you acquitted yourself very well at the accident.

We'll make a fine doctor out of you!"

Edwin managed to eat some of the food in front of him, then rose and made his excuses.

"Some studying to do," he murmured.

His grandfather nodded approval.

"Good lad! We can't do with you failing those 'A'-levels."

It was those words that gave Edwin the idea. If he did fail his "A"-levels he could not go on to study medicine. It was as simple as that.

Edwin was not quite 17. He was a good scholar and found work easy. He found *not* working much harder and soon he was one of a group of idlers who skipped classes on the least excuse. Later, he was to look back on the rest of that year with horror, but at the time all he could think about was *not* having to explain why he was letting his family tradition down.

He needed his "A"-levels to become a doctor and if he didn't have them, there was nothing anyone could do about it.

Soon he was joining his new friends in the evenings. Edwin didn't enjoy the discos and clubs, but he was not proud of himself. He wondered how his father didn't come to hear about his exploits, but Charles Groves was a well-respected member of the community and Edwin guessed people were reluctant to be the first to say anything.

His teachers were puzzled, but Edwin did just sufficient work in school to stop them contacting his father — silently resolving not to put it into practice when the examinations came.

EDWIN was on holiday when the results came through. Two low passes and three failures. It wasn't until he was standing in front of his father that he realised what he had done.

Charles Groves looked up at him and Edwin saw the lines of tiredness, the puzzled hurt in his father's eyes as he asked the silent question, "Why?"

"I'm sorry, Dad! It was my own fault —"

"I've heard rumours, son! I ignored them. I thought I could trust you!"

There was more and, knowing how hard his father worked and how his mother struggled to keep the family well clothed and well fed, Edwin hung his head.

"I'll get a job, Dad! I'll find something —"

"No! I'm not having a son of mine walking away a failure. If you *couldn't* do it, if you found the work difficult, I would accept it and help with whatever you wanted to do. But you have a good brain and you will go back to school for another year! Understand?"

Edwin had never heard that note in his father's voice before and he could only nod.

"I'll not let you down again," he promised in a low voice.

In the kitchen his mother held him in her arms, but she couldn't disguise the hurt in her voice, her eyes. Edwin saw that she, too, had lines of weariness on her gentle face, saw her hands were work stained.

His father was never one to seek for wealthy patients. He served his patients untiringly and his mother supported him in any way she could.

So Edwin went back to school and worked hard to make up lost ground.

Most of his erstwhile friends had left and he avoided the others.

One lunchtime he saw them coming towards him, and although he didn't allow himself to be upset or goaded by their taunts, he preferred to avoid them.

At the time, he was just passing the imposing stone entrance to the cathedral, and, acting on a sudden impulse, he went in.

Edwin had been in the cathedral before, but mostly on school projects, to sketch the stonework, to examine the stained glass, to trace the architecture. It was the first time he could remember just being there, for no particular purpose.

For a while he wandered round, but slowly he became aware of the majesty of his surroundings, the arched stonework, the intricate carving, the soft sunlight filtering through the stained glass.

He was aware of a strange sense of isolation. Although other people were there, walking round and talking in hushed voices, he seemed apart from them.

All too soon he had to leave the cathedral to the other visitors, but in the following weeks Edwin went back as often as he could. He began to know every part of the building. Almost as soon as he entered he would feel the peace, the serenity, calming him, filling him with quiet wonder.

He sat for long periods, not praying, but letting his mind fill with thoughts. He thought about his parents, his work, everything that mattered to him. He began to love the holy place.

Then, just before Christmas, his mother was taken ill. The weeks that followed were a fight to keep her alive, and when he went back to school after the holidays there was no time for visiting the cathedral.

Edwin spent his lunchtimes working and left to catch an early bus. As the eldest, he found himself caught up in household affairs but when the day came that his mother was home with them again, he knew it had all been worthwhile.

Sadly, Edwin's grandfather passed away soon afterwards. Edwin sat beside the old man's bed, keeping a vigil through his last night in the house, and when his father told him it was not necessary, the boy smiled.

"I want to, Dad. I think Grandad would like me to be here. There's nothing to fear here."

Gently he laid a flower on his grandfather's folded hands, and seeing how his son cared, Charles Groves went quietly away.

BERYL GROVES improved only slowly. So in the summer, Charles Groves rented a cottage in the dales, complete with a daily help, and took his family up into the lovely, wild countryside for a month.

Edwin spent hours with his younger brothers and sisters, but when he could he would walk far into the hills, wondering how such beauty had its beginnings. How people could fight, kill, when all this loveliness was there for anyone who had eyes to see. His family noticed how much of his time was spent in thought, but wisely left him alone.

The postman came early to the cottage and it was Edwin who opened the letter from the school. The results were all anyone could have wished from him. But the sense of elation was missing. Now he would have to tell his father, make a decision.

Impulsively he picked up an apple from the dish, pushed the letter into his pocket and went up the hills behind the cottage. There were little signs of life. The sheep ambled about, the birds welcomed the day and in the distance the sound of a tractor hummed over the still, morning air.

Edwin climbed until he was level with the old man on the tractor. He sat on a log and munched his apple, marvelling at the straight furrows the old man left behind him.

Then the farmer called a halt. He came and sat beside Edwin, and pulled a pipe out of his pocket, filling it with slow, practised movements.

"You a visitor?" he asked.

Edwin nodded. "Only one more week," he said sadly.

"Mmm, well, make the most of it. Not many places like this around." The old man pulled on his pipe and looked over the valley. "This is my life, on the land I love."

Edwin looked at the half-ploughed field. It was an awkward,

triangular-shaped piece of land.

"Tell me," he asked, "how do you plough such a straight furrow?"

His companion smiled, and was a while before he answered.

"See yonder spire? Well, laddie, I keep my eyes on that for the first furrow and know I'll not go far wrong. Ay, and that doesn't only apply to ploughing.

"Keep your eyes on the church spire and you'll plough a straight furrow through life. Not always easy, mind you, but there's always one around if you look hard enough."

Soon the old farmer was back on his tractor, but Edwin's eyes were on the spire. Slowly, as though the sun was rising, as though his eyes were just opening, he began to understand.

He thought about his grandfather and the peace he had found in the darkened room as he sat beside him. Edwin had no fear of death, he could comfort the sick and dying. He could care for people's souls, but not their bodies.

He recalled the hours he had spent in the cathedral, how he had sat letting his thoughts wander at will. Had those thoughts become prayers in that sacred place? Had he been unconsciously asking for guidance, for the sign that had now come to him?

The sun glinted on the distant spire, and Edwin sprang up. He lifted his arm in a gesture of farewell to the old farmer as he turned and ran down the hill, covering the ground in great leaps and bounds.

★ ★ ★ ★

Soon he was again standing in front of his father, but this time there was no hesitancy, no shame.

"Dad, I must tell you. I don't want to be a doctor. I couldn't —"

"Edwin! Is that why — ?"

The boy nodded.

"I want to go to college, but theological college, Dad. I want to enter the church!"

"Are you quite sure about this?"

"Oh yes, Father! I've never been so sure about anything. Some day I'll tell you. How things came to me, but about not being a doctor — you don't mind?"

Charles Groves stood up and came over to Edwin. With an arm round the boy's shoulders he led him over to the window.

"I feel ashamed that my own son did not feel he could talk to me. You know, I never wanted to go into medicine, but my father expected it and I did as he wanted. I vowed then that if I had children they would choose their own paths.

"What happened to that vow? It must have got bogged down under the pressure of work, of the family. Can you forgive me?"

Briefly father and son held each other close. Then Charles pushed Edwin away.

"Go up to your mother now, son, and tell her. She'll be so proud. And, Edwin," he called after him as he reached the door, "you've chosen well!" □

by
LINDA
LEIGH

# *With A Little Help From A Friend . . .*

THE bottom had dropped out of my world, and my mood was as grey as the weather. I struggled against the wind and rain which were more suited to November than August, muttering about bosses who wanted letters to catch an early collection, juniors who went sick, but most of all young and upwardly mobile accountants who were going to work in Düsseldorf.

I was so lost in misery I barely heard the voice.

It spoke again, more insistently. "Say, honey, is this the way to Westcliffe?"

A car was level with me. I turned to answer the driver, forgot all my manners and stared.

She had short blonde hair, an apple-blossom complexion and the twinkliest blue eyes I've ever seen, but that wasn't what held my gaze. She was wearing a spangled ballet-type dress, sparkling tiara and she had two beautiful gauzy wings.

"What's the matter, honey, ain't you ever seen a Fairy Godmother before?"

Her blue eyes danced and her half a dozen chins wobbled as all her 16 stone shook with laughter.

"Fairy Godmother?" I gasped.

"Well, who else would dress like this?" She shook with laughter again. "Well, anyway, honey, I'm awful late. Is this the right road for Westcliffe?"

"Yes," I said. "Take the second exit at the next roundabout and keep on the main road — you'll soon see it signposted."

"That's great. Thanks, honey."

"If you're a Fairy Godmother," I asked, conscious I was being ridiculous, "why don't you just wave your wand and magic yourself to Westcliffe?"

She gave me a long, speculative look, then reached into the back of the car.

"My wand's broken." She showed me the three pieces, one of which had on it a beautiful shining star. "Guess they'll fix it for me at Westcliffe."

I doubted it. I'd often been to Westcliffe but I'd never seen or heard of a wand-wright or mender-of-magic, or whatever such people are called.

"Well, I must be getting along. Thanks for your help. Have a nice day!" she said.

"It might be nicer if you granted me a wish. It's the normal procedure, isn't it, if someone gives you some help?"

It was her turn to stare.

"What are you after, kid?" she asked. "It looks to me as though you've got it all, already. Good figure, good looks — what else do you want?"

She didn't wait for me to tell her but went on, "Whatever it is, honey, just go for it!"

She disappeared, not in a shower of magic dust but with the tortured scream of tyres trying to cope with an 80-mile-an-hour start.

WHO could she have been, I wondered? My best guess was that she was a Stateside Roly-Poly. The next time the "Roly-Polies" appeared on television I'd look out for her.

Perhaps she did have some magic about her, though, for somehow I didn't feel nearly so downcast, and every time I thought about our encounter I had to smile.

Her "go for it" stuck in my mind, but how could I "go" for Alan if he was in Germany and I wasn't? Obviously I had to find some way of getting to Germany, too. We didn't have an "understanding" or anything like that, but given more time together I'd been hoping we would.

Alan called into my office just as I was locking up.

"Hello, Alan," I said. "I just heard about your promotion this afternoon. Congratulations. I'm very sorry you're leaving, but I do wish you every success."

I didn't mean a word of it. Well, the part about being sorry was true!

We arranged to meet later for a drink then he went to the Managing Director's office. He was talking to the MD's secretary, Trish, when I left.

Trish had only been with the firm a few weeks. She and Alan already knew one another. I hadn't had much to do with her, but she seemed nice and she was very efficient.

"I won't go back," I heard her say.

"Think about it," Alan replied. "There's not much point in cutting off your nose to spite your face."

I didn't hear any more, but I did wonder what they could be talking about.

Alan was able to give me an idea of when he'd be leaving when we met that night. He'd be sharing his time between Germany and Britain in equal proportions for the first six months, then increasing his time in Düsseldorf until the office opened officially in nine months' time, in May.

I HAD to wait for ages in Trish's office a few days later, until her boss had signed some papers. It was the first time I'd really talked to her and I found her very likeable.

The conversation got around to the new office.

"Do you think they'll let anyone here apply for a transfer?" I asked.

"You fancy it, do you?" She shot me a keen glance, and I knew *she* knew it was Alan I fancied rather than the job.

"Maybe," I tried to sound casual, "but they probably want secretaries who are more experienced than I am."

"Don't let that stop you!" She smiled. "Nothing ventured, nothing gained, remember."

"You aren't interested, then?"

"No, thanks!" She was very definite about it. "I've already worked in Germany. I don't want to go back."

She realised that didn't sound very encouraging. "For personal reasons," she added, colouring.

I made up my mind then to "go for it," as Fairy Godmother had advised. Trish seemed to think it was worthwhile trying, and if she wasn't applying it lessened the odds.

As the weeks passed I did a lot of Company "homework," finding out all I could about the firm, apart from my own particular section. I studied their expansion programme, trying to understand their reasons for choosing Düsseldorf, and the difficulties and advantages of opening there.

I did "homework" in another direction, too, hoping it would help give me an edge later on.

I remembered Fairy Godmother saying, "Good figure, good looks! What else do you want?"

I hadn't thought I was particularly attractive, because I have a beautiful, glamorous sister who's a model, and next to her I feel buxom and frumpy. Now, however, was the time to get rid of my inferiority complex.

Under her guidance I changed my hairstyle and make-up, learned to make the most of my eyes, and how to make a few good suits and dresses go a very long way by the clever use of accessories.

When Alan came back after a six-week stint in Germany, he could hardly take his eyes off me.

"Nicky, you look wonderful!"

We spent more time with each other now when he was in England, and because of the work I'd been doing, I was able to hold up my side of business discussions even better than before. I was so pleased with myself that if I were a cat I'd have been purring.

Cats have claws, though, and mine were soon to show.

Waiting again for a signature from Trish's boss, Mr Soames, I accidentally knocked some files off her desk. Whilst picking them up I came across a "Teach Yourself German" book.

I was nothing if not direct. "Why are you studying German, Trish?"

She went very red and barely met my eyes.

"Oh, yes," she said uncomfortably. "I've been meaning to tell you, Nicky. I may apply for a transfer to Düsseldorf after all."

So much for not wanting to go back, for "personal" reasons!

WHAT made things worse, much worse, was that just before the interviews, and my application was one of those being considered along with Trish's, I found her in Alan's arms, in the stationery room. The door was open, but they obviously didn't hear me approach.

"I never thought I'd feel like this," Trish wailed. "If I don't get this job I don't know what I'll do!"

Alan put his arms around her.

"Don't worry," he said. "I'll do what I can to help."

I crept away.

Was Alan the reason Trish now wanted to go back to Germany? It was no secret they'd known each other before Trish came to the firm, but there'd been no indication they'd been anything other than



▶ over

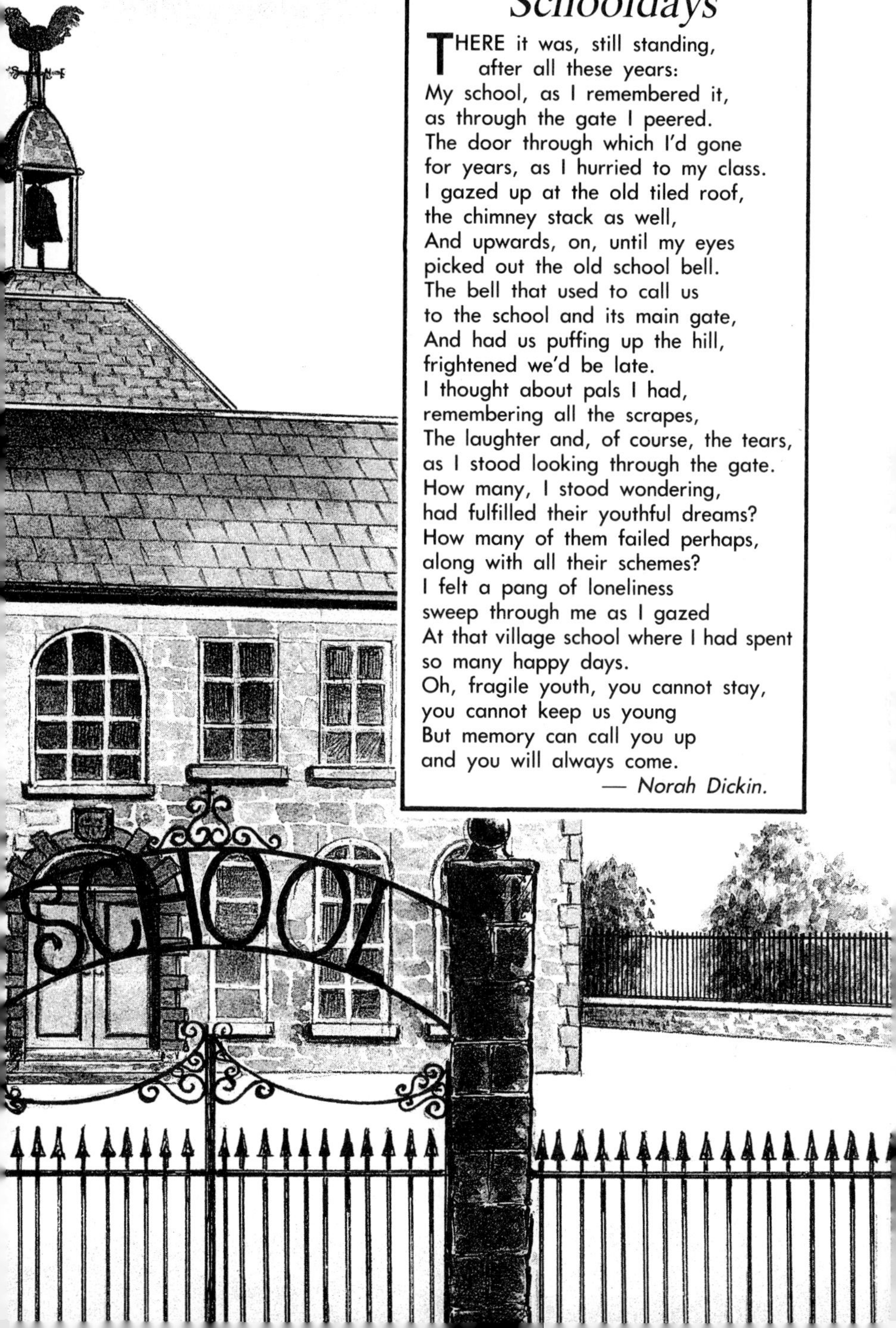


# *Schooldays*

THERE it was, still standing,
after all these years:
My school, as I remembered it,
as through the gate I peered.
The door through which I'd gone
for years, as I hurried to my class.
I gazed up at the old tiled roof,
the chimney stack as well,
And upwards, on, until my eyes
picked out the old school bell.
The bell that used to call us
to the school and its main gate,
And had us puffing up the hill,
frightened we'd be late.
I thought about pals I had,
remembering all the scrapes,
The laughter and, of course, the tears,
as I stood looking through the gate.
How many, I stood wondering,
had fulfilled their youthful dreams?
How many of them failed perhaps,
along with all their schemes?
I felt a pang of loneliness
sweep through me as I gazed
At that village school where I had spent
so many happy days.
Oh, fragile youth, you cannot stay,
you cannot keep us young
But memory can call you up
and you will always come.

— *Norah Dickin.*

friends. This was like a bolt from the blue!

I couldn't believe it. Alan had seemed so genuinely fond of me and lately we'd become very close. I felt frozen inside, desperately afraid and wildly angry, all at the same time.

I kept out of the way of both of them for the next couple of days, but Alan caught me up just as I was leaving the office on the evening before my interview.

"Good luck tomorrow, Nicky," he said. "I'll keep my fingers crossed for you. It'll be wonderful if we can work together!

"I wish there was some way I could help, but the decision rests with Mr Soames and Herr Burgener," he went on. "I'm sure you won't need help, anyway!"

He smiled encouragingly and kissed me lightly.

How could he be so hypocritical? He would try to help Trish, but he could only cross his fingers for me!

I heard Fairy Godmother's voice saying, "Go for it, honey!"

All right, I thought, I'll show them both! If I didn't get the job it wouldn't be for lack of trying. I'd give Trish a run for her money!

I MADE a special effort and knew I looked good the next day. I felt confident, too. I'd learned a lot over the past nine months, and I also had my little "edge" I'd told no-one about.

Trish looked as though she hadn't had a wink of sleep, and when she saw me her composure wilted visibly. I should have been pleased, but found I felt sorry for her.

There were four of us being interviewed, together initially, and as we went in Trish murmured, "Good luck, Nicky."

I felt very mean, suddenly. After all, the issue meant as much to her as to me, and I hadn't wished her good luck.

As the interview progressed, it was obvious that Trish and I were in the lead. I could see Trish's boss, the Managing Director, was impressed with my general knowledge of the Company's products, and my research into the Continental openings.

Trish put up a good show, but she hadn't expected me to know as much as I did and it disconcerted her.

Occasionally Herr Burgener lapsed into German, and he did so once again.

"Machen wir jetzt eine kleine pause und trinken eine tasse kaffee?"

I seized my chance before anyone else could do so. "How would you like your coffee — black or with milk and sugar, Mr Burgener? I'll bring your coffee," I answered in German.

"I didn't know you already spoke German," Mr Soames said.

"I know the firm's arranging for an intensive course in Germany," I said, "but I've been learning at night classes since last September."

Trish and I had to go back individually for a further interview during the afternoon, and were told they'd let us know as soon as possible.

There was a defeated, desperate look in Trish's eyes. She reminded me of a frightened animal who knows the hunter is closing in. My interest in the chase was fading fast.

AS soon as I got home, I ran a bath and stayed in it for ages, trying to soak away the tiredness and a vague feeling of guilt.

Why should I feel guilty? I asked myself. I'd done nothing wrong!

Mother hammered on the bathroom door. "Come out of there, Nicky. Alan's here!"

What did Alan want? I wasn't even sure I wanted to see him! I was going to enter a convent, or emigrate, or *something*.

He swung me up in the air, damp dressing-gown and wet hair notwithstanding, and kissed me. His delight was obviously genuine. "Darling, you've done it, you've got it! We're going to be working together!"

He kissed me again, and I clung to him.

"Trish?" I asked, rather nobly I thought, but I could afford to be generous. "Is she very disappointed?"

He shook his head. "She's going, too. They've decided there'll be enough work for two people. You'll both be told officially, tomorrow, but I couldn't wait. I had to come and let you know."

I was still musing over the prospect when he said, "Trish'll be able to straighten things out with Helmut, now.

"She was engaged to him. They had a frightful row, unfortunately, then both of them got on their high horses. Neither of them would admit to being in the wrong. In the end the engagement was broken off.

"Trish came home, but she's learned where her heart lies. She should have gone back ages ago."

I knew where my heart lay, too, and from the way Alan was holding me, so did he. But what about that incident in the stationery room?

As if he could read my mind, Alan continued, "We didn't say anything in case people thought I'd pulled strings to get her the job, but Trish is my cousin. If she hadn't got the transfer, I was going to go and see Helmut for her, see if I could help straighten things out. He's not too far from Düsseldorf."

Everything fell into place, and I was so happy little champagne bubbles of happiness seemed to be bursting inside me.

WE sat beside each other, drinking, not bubbly but a congratulatory mug of coffee!

An advertisement came on televison for a new range of clothes from America called "Fairy," for size 18 and over.

I stared as I recognised voice and figure. Her blue eyes seemed to twinkle straight into mine as she warbled, "Trust your Fairy Godmother!" and waved a wand which was no longer in three pieces.

I remembered the day we'd met, heard again the tyres screaming as she disappeared after instructing me to "Go for it, kid!" and raised my mug in silent tribute. □

VIKKI cut another slice of christening cake, eased it on to one of her best china tea plates and passed it to her mother-in-law.

"But that's just it," she explained as she handed her a small pink and blue serviette and a pastry fork. "I'm going back to work in a month."

Jean Walker choked on a piece of christening cake.

Calmly, Vikki poured her a fresh cup of tea and urged her to drink it. "There — is that better? It's a little crumbly, I'm afraid."

She raised a napkin to her mouth, pretending to wipe a crumb away but really to hide her grin. It had been easy enough getting her own parents used to the idea that in this family, Dad was going to be Mum — and Mum was going to be the one to earn the bread.

But then, compared to Jim's folk, her parents were positively ultra-modern in outlook.

She smiled encouragingly at her mother-in-law. "It's perfectly sensible when you think about it. I'm earning more money than Jim just now. My career structure is important, whereas Jim can take a few years out without his career suffering.

"They're desperate for science teachers around here. He can find a job whenever he wants it. Once we're organised he can do some night-classes to keep his hand in.

"It's all quite sensible when you consider it," she went on.

She patted the older woman's hand. "I know it takes a bit of getting used to, but honestly, we've thought it all out. Ages ago."

Jean stared at her as if she'd suggested a trip to the moon.

"But twins — you hadn't planned on twins, Victoria!"

Vikki flicked her hair back over her shoulder. They'd known that Jim's parents had humoured them when they'd announced that Vikki wouldn't give up her career as an accountant when the baby came along.

"They think we're crazy. There's no use arguing about it, Jim," Vikki had said. "Once they've seen how well things work out, they'll see we're right."

To have planned your lives around one very small baby was one thing, Vikki admitted to herself. To discover suddenly that you were the parents of twins, and that whatever number you'd first thought of you had to double, had been, well, shattering to say the least.

But they'd cope, they'd told themselves.

Vikki smiled at her mother-in-law reassuringly and then excused

# PARENTS ON TRIAL

herself to attend to her guests. She passed round the family group, pouring tea, exchanging gossip, until Jim came back into the room with a newly-changed and laundered Samantha and William.

It had taken him quite a while, and perhaps Jim was slightly pinker and warmer than the babies themselves, but they did look a picture of perfection, Vikki thought, overcome with a rush of pride that brought a lump to her throat.

THERE was a chorus of oohs and aahs and the focus slipped easily again to the babies. Vikki heaved a sigh of relief and went back into the kitchen for more sandwiches.

She was slicing brown bread when Jim came in.

"Samantha's enjoying every minute of this," he said. "She's busy

**by CAROL GOW**

posing with the family group, staring rather cross-eyed at the camera, whereas William is just a bit bored — like me."

He nibbled a piece of cucumber.

"They want you to go in and pose for a three-generation portrait," he went on. "Uncle William's in charge, so it'll take ages."

Vikki picked up the plate of sandwiches.

"I've told your mum there's been no change in our plans," she said.

Jim raised his eyebrows. "How did she take it?"

Vikki grinned. "Oh, pretty much as we anticipated."

Jim slipped his arm around her. "She'll get used to the idea. And anyway, it's what suits us that counts. I'm going to be really happy staying at home looking after Samantha and William, while you rush off to catch the bus to work."

That night, Vikki and Jim bathed the babies. Samantha was tired out and very cross. The bath soothed her, and, once she was creamed and powdered, Vikki dressed her in her little sleeping suit and walked over to the window with her.

The moon was a pale, paper-thin ghost in the sky. She showed Samantha the clouds, and the roses at the bottom of the garden, then walked back to her crib to wind up the little mobile that waltzed pink giraffes and blue porpoises round the room to a lullaby that made Sam gurgle.

In a few seconds, she was asleep. Vikki was amazed that babies could fall asleep so quickly and so soundly. In fact, everything about the babies amazed her.

She bent her face towards the little bundle, breathing in the baby smell of her, and knowing that despite what she told Jim's mum, it was going to be very hard to make the break.

She waited while Jim changed William's nappy. At the first attempt, it fell off in a little pile round his ankles, but at the second attempt it looked as if it might just stay in place.

She wound up the little clouds mobile over William's crib and watched while Jim tucked him in.

In two weeks, she'd be away for most of the day, she reflected, but she could spend time at night with the twins — moments like these.

It was the right decision, she was sure of it. But that didn't make it any easier. The last couple of weeks with the babies were going to be precious and she was going to make the most of them.

GETTING back to work wasn't as easy as Vikki had anticipated. She hadn't reckoned on how tired she'd feel. So much seemed to have changed since she'd been away.

"But it's just a case of getting into the swing of things again," she confided to her friend, Marie, as they lunched in the corner wine-bar at the end of her first week.

"I think you're tremendously brave, all the same," Marie said, tackling her salad with speed. "I mean — twins! You're so lucky!"

Vikki gulped her orange juice. They could only have half an hour for lunch, so lingering was out of the question.

"I mean, I think if it was me," Marie continued, "I'd go all gooey-eyed and domesticated the minute I found I was pregnant."

Vikki laughed. "Oh, you! You can't even settle for one man, never mind dedicated motherhood!"

Marie shrugged. "You're right. I'm enjoying life too much to settle down to anything at all."

Vikki laughed again. Marie had cheered her up. It was nice to get back into the habit of lunching together once a week to catch up on gossip and news.

They'd been at school together, college together, and though their lives had taken completely different turns, they'd tried to meet regularly and keep in touch.

She stared at Marie across the table. She'd missed all this, she thought, listening to the buzz of the busy wine-bar, feeling the atmosphere that was like a physical tension in the air. In five minutes both of them would be off back to work.

She had missed being a working woman. And yet she missed the babies horribly, too.

Missing them wasn't anything to do with being sensible or silly. It was just a physical sensation like hunger or cold, and not one that she could do very much about.

It was probably a touch of post-natal depression. They'd expected it, she and Jim.

She confided in Jim, and he seemed sympathetic, but it wasn't fair to worry him too much. He was pretty tired these days, a bit preoccupied, too.

Her own parents lived too far away to help, and if she confided in Jim's parents all she'd get were smug looks and "I told you sos."

She came back to the present with a jolt, and picked up the bill. There were a few initial hurdles, she admitted, but all in all, things were going just as planned, weren't they?

THE first crisis came when she arrived home from work one evening to find that the babies had developed a rash. Jim had called the doctor, who'd said it was nothing to worry about.

"But what did he say?" Vikki asked him for the tenth time.

She was hot and sticky. It had been a brilliantly blue day, and the sun had shone relentlessly through the double-glazed window in her office, defying the air-conditioning, so that her head ached with the sun and her feet froze.

On top of everything else that had happened today, she'd missed her bus, had had to stand all the way when she did get one, and was half an hour late.

Jim was vague. "I told you what he said. Doctors never actually say very much. They just hum and haw and try to reassure. He just said not to overdress them, especially in this hot spell."

Vikki gazed down at the twins, who looked perfectly well and happy. They showed no signs of the rash now, but she still wasn't content. She knew what Jim said was right, yet she continued.

"Are you sure they're all right? You just can't be too careful, Jim —"

"I know. Don't you trust me, Vikki? I thought it was a heat rash, but I called Dr West just in case and he popped in on his way to see another patient. It was no big deal, right?"

"You might have phoned me — let me know."

"Vikki, don't be silly. I can't phone the office over every trivial thing that happens —"

"But I worry about how you're getting on with the babies — I want to know, Jim," she persisted.

By the time they sat down to a very late meal of bacon and eggs, they'd had a full-scale argument about nothing very much, due to the way each of them was feeling.

Vikki was tired, hot and nervy. Jim, despite his protestations to the contrary, had been more anxious than he'd admitted.

After they'd eaten in icy silence, Jim hugged her.

Her anger melted. It felt so good to be held close.

She sighed. "I'm sorry. I'm just hot and tired and terribly cross. I shouldn't take it out on you."

"Maybe I should have called," Jim confessed. "I did feel like phoning you. I imagined they had all sorts of things — scarlet fever, measles, anything! I went through the whole range of disorders in the baby books!"

Vikki put her arms round him. "You poor thing! I'm sorry, of course I know you can manage. I'm just being silly."

Silly or not, Vikki found she couldn't help herself. She began to feel shut out from Jim and the babies.

Weekends were just never long enough — her time with Samantha and William flew by. Very often, too, they had visits from doting grandparents at the weekends.

There didn't seem to be anything Vikki could do but grit her teeth and try to get on with things. Things will get better next week, she'd promise herself — but they didn't.

EVERYTHING looked all right on the surface, but the whole fragile structure cracked on the Sunday that Jim's parents came for lunch.

The twins had developed a new wariness. They no longer gurgled or smiled at everyone they met. In fact, they were apprehensive with almost everyone except Jim.

"It's perfectly natural," Jim said. "This phase passes. It doesn't mean they're anti-social or anything like that."

The babies took fright at Jim's parents. Vikki, trying to soothe the babies and reassure the grandparents, discovered that all the babies wanted to do was to go to Jim.

They weren't interested in her at all. In fact, they treated her with almost the same disdain that they treated Jim's parents.

She looked at them, now lying quietly across Jim's chest on the big old sofa. The three of them looked very contented.

"It's just a phase they're going through," she explained to the grandparents. "It's perfectly natural —"

To her horror, her voice broke and she burst into tears. Anxiously, Jim laid the babies down and came to her. At once, they started crying again.

Vikki furiously blew her nose and tried to pull herself together for the sake of Jim's parents, but she couldn't.

In a moment, she found herself sitting in the kitchen drinking a strong cup of coffee with Jean Walker.

Jim and his dad had popped the twins into their pram and had trundled them off down the road, still bawling, but sounding less furious.

"It's just not as easy as we thought," Vikkie admitted, waiting for her mother-in-law's usual lecture.

"It never is, love," the older woman reassured her.

"I suppose you think we're pretty stupid," Vikki said, finishing off her coffee.

"No, of course I don't! I was a bit surprised, I must admit. I hadn't expected Jim to give up his work —" Mrs Walker stopped there, trying her best to be tactful, obviously wanting to avoid dredging up old grievances.

She poured another coffee for each of them. "You've been coping really well, Vikki. Jim's dad thinks it's a wonderful idea. He said he'd have loved to spend more time with Jim and Sarah when they were little. Shared them more, I suppose."

"I like my work, but I miss the babies. And though Jim enjoys caring for them, I think he misses the stimulation of his work," Vikki explained. "He hasn't plucked up enough courage to call in at the young mother's group yet.

"And though he won't admit it, he's pretty tired. I don't think he realised looking after two tiny babies could be quite so much hard work!"

Jean smiled at her. "You've got us, you know. We'd love to help out where we can, provided you don't think we're interfering.

"I know you'd turn to your own mum if she were nearer. I wish you'd let me help."

VIKKI spooned sugar in her coffee, feeling her lower lip tremble at the kindness in Jean's voice. Her mother-in-law would have been pretty much entitled to say, "I told you so."

After all, she and Jim had been pretty cocky about knowing all there was to know about having babies. She'd been trying so hard to prove they were Mr and Mrs Wonderful that she wouldn't allow Jim's parents a look in.

"I thought you disapproved," she began.

Jean smiled. "Of course we did, at first. But then we're a couple of old fuddy-duddies. You don't want to take any notice of us."

Jim's parents stayed late and for the first time, Vikki and Jim were able to talk openly about the trials and tribulations of the twins. It was wonderful, Vikki thought, to have an audience who weren't bored to tears by baby talk multiplied by two.

After they'd waved Mr and Mrs Walker off, she felt more relaxed than she had for weeks.

"Leave the washing-up. Leave everything, darling. Let's just finish the wine while we watch an old film on TV," she said, linking arms with Jim.

Before they settled down, they checked on the twins. They were asleep, their hands flung above their heads in a gesture of surrender.

"Your mum was really kind, Jim," Vikki said. "I expected her to try to talk us out of this, but she didn't. She just said not to expect it to be easy."

"It wouldn't be easy even if you were at home and I were at work, Vikki," Jim mused. "Babies turn your life upside down!"

"Are you happy?"

Jim took both her hands in his. "I love the babies. I love being with them. Sometimes, though, I'd rather be at work. What about you?"

"I love my work. I need the pressure, the challenge. But sometimes I'd rather be home with the babies," she confessed.

They went into the living-room and Jim poured two glasses of wine.

"Swings and roundabouts," he said. "We can work it out. I reckon we're ninety-per cent. of the way there. Don't you?"

Vikki took a deep breath, then she nodded.

She laughed and stretched her arms high above her head. She felt suddenly more confident than she had for weeks. In spite of everything she knew they'd got it right.

Her talk with Jim's mum had helped a lot — not because of anything Jim's mum had said, but because she'd been able to stop pretending it was easy. It wasn't. Parenting was a hazardous business, whether you swapped rôles or not.

It was nice to know that, after all, Jean was on her side and always had been.

BEFORE they went to bed, Vikki and Jim tiptoed through to the twins' room, and gazed down at the two tiny people who had turned their lives upside down.

"I'm sure it gets worse," Jim said with an unmistakable note of pride in his voice.

"I'm sure it does," Vikki agreed seriously.

She tucked in a teddy that had been tossed from William's cot.

"But we'll get better," she assured him. "We may not be perfect parents. We may do things differently from most people. But William and Samantha won't mind."

And by the looks on their faces, it seemed they didn't mind at all. □

by SANDY REID

# "I KNOW THE FACE..."

SADIE JOHNSON was no chicken — she was 60 if she was a day. But her friends in the bowling club were full of praise for her. She was a cheerful character, and if she didn't say a good word about anyone she wouldn't say a bad word.

Dressed up to the nines for a game of bowls, with her grey, flannel skirt and well-pressed, white blouse, she would comfortably have passed for anyone in her 40s.

This day she came back from the bowling-green feeling good. She'd been in great form with every bowl on the jack.

On the way home, she passed the time of day with her neighbour, Mrs Brownlee, and reminded her of her promise to look in later for a cup of tea.

When Sadie reached home, she decided she would change her skirt and blouse and slip on an old dress for the evening. She went upstairs to her bedroom and reached into her wardrobe for her dress.

All of a sudden she felt, well, funny. She had no aches or pains, she just felt queer.

She decided to sit down on the bed, but all of a sudden she slumped flat out on the bed. For the best part of an hour, she lay there, motionless.

THEN Mrs Brownlee walked in at the front door, calling out, "Are you there, Sadie?"

Getting no reply, she tried the living-room, then she poked her head into the kitchen.

Climbing the stairs, Mrs Brownlee tapped at the door of Sadie's bedroom and went in. She was horrified to see Sadie lying on her bed.

"What's wrong, Sadie?" she called, and reached forward to touch Sadie's shoulder.

Although it was a warm summer's evening, Sadie's shoulder was cold, and there was no response from her.

Mrs Brownlee ran as quickly as she could to reach the telephone in Sadie's living-room. She dialled 999, asked for the ambulance and explained her predicament.

"We'll be there in ten minutes," a man's voice said. "Just sit down and keep calm and don't touch anything."

The ambulance men were as good as their word.

"Is she still lying on the bed?" they asked when they arrived in the promised 10 minutes.

Mrs Brownlee assured them Sadie was still lying flat out, and the ambulance men fetched a stretcher.

In two minutes they came down with Sadie lying on the stretcher with a blanket covering her.

"You'd better come along with us," they said. "The doctors will probably want to ask a few questions."

At the hospital, the medical staff asked a few questions, but Mrs Brownlee couldn't help a lot. All she could say was she'd found Sadie lying on her bed, and an hour later she was allowed to go home.

THREE hours after Mrs Brownlee had found her, Sadie woke up. She looked about her and, to her astonishment, she found herself lying in a hospital ward.

Beside her, looking down at her and holding her hand, was a blue-uniformed hospital sister.

"Well!" the sister said. "You've decided to come back to us."

"What am I doing here?" Sadie murmured in bewilderment.

"You can talk perfectly well. That's a good thing," the sister commented. "Now, take hold of my hand."

Sadie gripped tight.

"What's happened to me?" she asked.

"Well, the doctors think you've had a stroke. Thank goodness your speech isn't affected. Can you raise your left arm?"

Sadie raised her left arm.

"Try your right arm," the sister encouraged.

Sadie raised her right arm.

"Now grab my other and squeeze it tight," the sister ordered.

Sadie squeezed it tight.

The sister smiled at her.

"You've got a grip like a blacksmith, and legs like a chorus girl. Try a wee tap dance."

Sadie kicked her legs.

"You're a fraud!" the sister teased her. "When I first saw you I thought you were ill!"

"What happened to me?" Sadie asked.

The sister explained how an old friend had discovered her.

"I don't remember a thing," Sadie said, "until I woke up and found you smiling down at me. When did it happen, anyway?"

"About three hours ago," the sister replied. "I'll send for the doctor to come and have another look at you. He won't believe how well you're looking. You were looking terrible a wee while ago."

"You think I've got a chance, then?" Sadie asked.

"Well, it's up to the doctors," the sister explained. "I'd say you've had a mild stroke — a kind of a spasm."

Sadie felt very comfortable lying in bed with the smiling face of the sister above her.

"Don't be frightened to move around," the sister said.

"How long do you think I'll be in here?" Sadie asked.

"Hard to say," the sister replied. "That's up to the doctors — and you, of course."

By this time Sadie felt able to have a longer look at the smiling sister who was sitting beside her bed. She saw a smart-looking, middle-aged woman with a pleasant smile, and a hair-do that looked as if it had just come out of the hairdresser.

"What's your name?" she asked.

"I'm Sister MacPherson and I'm the night sister in your ward."

"I'm very grateful to you," Sadie said. "It was nice to have someone holding my hand and talking to me."

"Well," Sister Mac explained, "I don't think I can sit much longer with you, because I must have a look at the other patients. But I'll be back later to check on you."

SADIE closed her eyes and fell sound asleep, but woke to find the smiling face of Sister Mac gazing down at her.

"Are you sure I'm going to be all right?" Sadie asked.

"You're lucky," Sister Mac said. "Your speech is all right, and you've got strength in both hands and legs. Of course, we've still got a lot of tests to do on you before we'll let you go."

"You think I'll be as good as new?"

"No reason why not," Sister Mac reassured her.

"Will I be able to play bowls again?"

"Oh, are you a bowler?" Sister Mac asked with added interest. "I'm a bowler, too. It's great fun."

"It certainly is," Sadie said, "but I didn't think you'd have a lot of time to play bowls — not in your job."

"Oh, mostly I'm on night shift, but I get an occasional day off as well. It's nice to get out of my uniform and get dressed for bowling."

"We must have a get-together once I'm on my feet again," Sadie suggested.

"Oh, you'll recover all right," Sister Mac said. "Given time you'll be as good as new."

Weeks passed and Sadie slowly recovered. Most nights Sister Mac visited her, and in the silence of the night they gossiped quietly to each other like old friends.

CAME the day, a month later, when Sadie was allowed to leave the hospital.

She said a cheerful goodbye to all the nurses, and the night before she left she shook hands with Sister Mac.

"Remember, Sister," she said. "We'll have a get-together one of these days."

At home, Sadie discovered that her legs were not as strong as she thought, but she was grateful to be back in her own kitchen again.

Some days she would wander down to her own bowling-green, which wasn't far away, and watch her old friends playing. Gradually, she got into the swing of things and threw a few bowls herself.

A year passed and by the end of that season, Sadie got a chance to play for her club in a match against a neighbouring green.

On the day of the match, Sadie found she had been drawn to play against a neatly-turned-out, middle-aged woman who looked as if she had just come from the hairdresser — and a very good player she was.

Sadie enjoyed her game. During the match, she kept looking at her opponent as they chatted to each other.

"It's a funny thing," Sadie said, "but I'm sure I've seen you before."

"I've been thinking the same thing," Miss MacPherson admitted, "but I can't place you. Are you a member of the Church Women's Guild?"

"No, I seldom go to church these days, but it'll come back."

As they stood beside each other to throw their last bowls, Sadie suddenly said, "I've got you, I'm sure. It was the lack of the uniform that kept beating me.

"But I'll never forget your smiling face and how nice it was of you to keep holding my hand. You're Sister Mac!"

"I am, indeed," Miss MacPherson replied. "Weren't you a patient at the hospital at some time?"

"Well, yes, I was," Sadie said. "But you can't remember me."

"Of course I remember you! It just came back to me. What fooled me was your being introduced as Mrs Johnson. I really only knew you as the cheerful patient called Sadie."

"It's almost eighteen months since I was in hospital," Sadie recalled. "Fancy you remembering me!"

"I remember you telling me you were a bowler," Sister Mac said, "and you asked me if you'd ever be able to play bowls again."

"And you said I'd be as good as new," Sadie added. "But you didn't tell me you were so good yourself."

Sister Mac smiled. "I didn't tell you you'd be a better player — just as good as."

"It's marvellous to see you again," Sadie said. "I remember one thing you've forgotten."

"What's that?"

"We said we'd have a get-together," Sadie reminded Miss MacPherson. "And there's the clubhouse. What's keeping us . . . ?" □

# Bright New World

**by OLWEN RICHARDS**

WHEN the present seems unbearable and the future non-existent, the only place to go to is the past. That was where Alison knew *she* had to go the day that her divorce came through — somewhere far away in time, long, long before she'd met and married Frank. Somewhere before the love, the pain, the heartache and the disillusionment. Somewhere even before Kate, the precious little girl who looked so like her father.

She rang her mother and arranged to go to tea. There'd be a glorious spread of sandwiches and cakes, of course. There always was. Mrs Simmonds took delight in pampering her family.

Alison knew she meant well, but for a long time now she'd come to dread those cosy afternoons. They'd made her painfully aware there was an empty chair beside her — Frank's chair, the one she'd been too eager he should have all of seven years ago, when she fell far too swiftly and deeply in love to hear her parents' warnings.

Today she had no appetite at all. The very thought of food appalled her. Even so, it was the only way.

SHE held her teacup in her hands, felt the warmth which didn't comfort, and wondered how to start.

Her mother, fussing over Kate, brushing crumbs of cake away and wiping sticky fingers, didn't notice Alison's discomfiture.

When Alison spoke, however, it was impossible to hide the quiver in her voice.

"I've got to get away, Mum, just for a little while."

Mrs Simmonds nodded.

"You've been through so much recently," she said. "A break would do you both good."

"But that's the trouble, Mum. I want to be alone to think things out. I hoped you might take Kate . . ."

Mrs Simmonds pursed her lips.

"*She* needs a holiday, too. It can't have been much fun for her. The separation must have hurt and now the house is up for sale . . ."

"You know I can't afford to keep it on, Mum," Alison said defensively.

"I know you wouldn't want to, even if you could. It's got too many memories. But lots of them were happy ones for Kate," the older woman pointed out.

"Yes. But if I don't have a chance to find myself, I'll be no use to her. I really have to go."

Mrs Simmonds gazed at Alison's welling tears.

"Its no good trying to run away," she said, with sorrow in her voice. "It may just make it harder to come back.

"But," she added as the tears spilled, "if you're determined . . . Where will you go?"

"I've no idea. Somewhere cheap, of course. There's precious little of our savings left. Frank saw to that. Still, I've got a job lined up next month and I can soon pay back whatever this trip costs," Alison assured her mother. "It won't be much. A long weekend, that's all."

"Well, if you must, you must." Mrs Simmonds forced a smile as she went on, "Anyway, I ought to get myself in training.

"I'm going to be with Kate all day once you've started work, and it's a long time since I did anything more strenuous than half an hour's play. Still, I suppose it's something that you don't forget."

Like broken marriages. You don't forget those either, Alison told herself inside the silence of her mind.

ALISON knew exactly where she'd go. It came to her that night, as she lay wide-awake and staring at the darkness, came like a flash of lightning.

She had a sudden vision of the tiny town she'd been to as a

teenager. She'd just left school and, with a whole two weeks of freedom before starting work, she'd spread her wings and flown the family nest.

It had been wonderful to feel grown-up, to holiday without her parents. The days had been all blue and gold, all sea and sun.

If the local boys had made her heart beat faster now and then, they hadn't wounded it, for she had been in love with freedom and with simply being young.

Early next morning she packed Kate's clothes and toys into a suitcase, bundling just the bare essentials into another for herself. She wouldn't need a lot.

She didn't, she thought sadly, have a lot. Frank had always kept the household short of cash, although he'd spent lavishly on himself. Still, once she was earning, things would be different.

Her old employer had been only too delighted when she'd asked if he could take her back. She'd been a good PA and, despite a few years' absence, she hadn't lost her skills.

He'd offered her a salary considerably better than she'd earned before. Even with inflation, it was still a rise, and quite enough to keep herself and Kate, provided she sold the house.

She turned and glanced at it, as she and Kate were hurrying for the bus. She'd rung the agent. When she returned on Tuesday the "For Sale" sign would be in the garden.

Life would be starting over and she must be ready for it . . .

★ ★ ★ ★

At six that evening, Alison dumped her bag beside a bar stool in a little pub and ordered lime juice with soda. The cheery woman behind the bar filled the glass to overflowing.

It was a welcome sight. Alison had no idea what thirsty work it was just trying to find a bed in mid-July. Like most things she'd done recently, the seaside break was hastily conceived and far from adequately planned.

The woman nodded at her case.

"On holiday?"

"I meant to be. I simply never realised how full the town would be. There's not a single guest-house with a vacancy. I think," Alison added ruefully, "that I'll be forced to head for home tonight."

She sipped the remnants of her drink.

"I don't suppose," she said, "that *you* do bed and breakfast?"

" 'Fraid not, dear."

Alison sighed.

The woman gazed at her and saw the drawn face, pale and tired, darkened underneath her eyes from lack of sleep. Too young and far too pretty to be looking so distraught, she thought.

"On the other hand," she said, refilling Alison's glass, "we've got a boxroom that we never use. I'm sure Mr Wilcox, that's my husband, wouldn't mind . . ."

"Oh, that would be marvellous!"

Mrs Wilcox laughed. "It's nothing special. No hot and cold, no phone or TV. Absolutely nothing but a bed and wardrobe."

"That's all I need," Alison assured her.

"Maybe it is. The visitors we get in here are always saying how the sea air makes them sleepy."

"I'm not one for late nights at the best of times," Alison said. "And this weekend I hope to have a rest. The room would be ideal."

"I wouldn't charge you for it. But if you wanted meals — "

A tall young man, who had been busy serving, put the last pint down and moved towards them, smiling broadly.

"If I were you," he advised, "I'd not say no. My mother's just about the best cook I've ever met."

Mrs Wilcox blushed with pleasure.

"This is Mark," she said.

He held his hand out solemnly to Alison.

"I'm just a temporary barman. Mum and Dad think I do it for the money, but in reality I'm only here because I need a decent meal! See you over supper!"

He hurried off to serve a customer, and Mrs Wilcox leaned across the bar to Alison.

"He's actually an accountant," she said proudly. "Very clever. Got his own house now. But in the summer when the town is packed and we're really pressed, he comes in of an evening to help out.

"Since we close so late, it's hardly worth his going home. Works out very well for everyone. He lets his house to visitors, which pays a bit more off the mortgage, and I get my son back for a while."

"It sounds ideal."

"It is. You've no idea how hard it is to let your children go."

Alison stared into her glass. She would have to do that one day, she reflected, and besides, she was already missing Kate.

"Anyway, as I was saying, if you wanted meals, we don't do anything except the usual bar snacks in here," Mrs Wilcox explained. "But you'd be more than welcome to eat with us. It wouldn't be exactly posh. We have to grab a bit of supper in the kitchen out the back. That's usually round eight o'clock when we've got extra staff."

Alison smiled. "From what your son says, I'd be a fool to turn that offer down!"

THE smell of steak and kidney pie pervaded every corner of the kitchen that evening, and Alison was surprised to find her appetite was suddenly so keen.

Mark watched her with amusement as she let herself be talked into a second helping.

"Told you Mum was good!" He grinned.

"Nonsense," Mrs Wilcox said, "it's all the fresh air that does it."

"But she's only just arrived," he argued. "Look out tomorrow when she's had a whole day sightseeing! We'll need to roast an ox!"

Everybody laughed and Mr Wilcox poured some wine.

"To happy holidays," he said.

"To holidays," was all that Alison managed.

Mark eyed her curiously for a moment, then he handed her a sheet of paper.

"It's a map. I'd hate you to get lost."

"Thanks, but I've been here before. It was some years ago, admittedly, but I think I know my way," Alison said.

"Well, take it anyway. It's quite surprising how a town can change."

Mark was right, of course, as Alison found next day. Some of the tiny streets she thought that she remembered were no longer there, but in their stead were several blocks of high-rise flats and one great, multi-storey car park.

It was surprising how the town had changed, but not the town alone, if she was honest.

The sea-front shops were smaller, their glitter less appealing. The promenade seemed shorter, somehow, and the beach less golden. The donkeys giving rides were now a sad and shaggy trail, the candy floss was a synthetic pink, which didn't tempt her as it used to.

"Well?" Mark asked her over a fragrant casserole at supper that night.

"It's different," she admitted. "But, then," she added slowly, "so

▶ *over*

The Wonder of Water...

**BONNINGTON LINN, THE FALLS OF CLYDE**

*This is the upper of the falls and originally had a leap of 30 feet. In 1924-26, the Clyde Valley Company built here the first Scottish hydro-electric development for public supply. At nearby New Lanark, only 20 minutes' walk away, there is a visitor centre with an audio-visual presentation, and a display featuring the wildlife and flowers of the area.*

am I. I was eighteen last time I came, and when you're eighteen all the world is rainbows."

Mark smiled. "I can't remember that far back. Sometimes I think I never was eighteen."

"You must have missed a lot," Alison murmured wistfully.

"I could make up for it!" He laughed. "It's not too late. There's going to be a carnival tomorrow. I could show you round and you could find the rainbows."

"Sounds like a good idea," Mrs Wilcox said. "And in the evening there's a barbecue down on the beach."

"But Mark — " Alison began.

The Wilcoxes exchanged a knowing glance.

"I think he deserves a night off now and then. Besides, I'll have a rest myself, not having to feed him!" Mrs Wilcox declared.

"It'll be good for him," Mark's father murmured later as he helped his wife wash up. "I haven't seen him look so happy since — "

"It will be good for both of them," she put in hurriedly. "There's too much sadness in *her* eyes, too, for a girl of that age."

MARK hired a giant sun umbrella, and he and Alison spent the morning in its shadow, watching as the beach grew busy.

Overnight, it seemed to Alison, the donkeys had grown sleeker and more lively, and, when Mark bought sticks of candy floss, it tasted every bit as sweet as in her memory. She was reflecting on this when he spoke.

"You know, I wouldn't have believed how good this stuff could be! It must be that hidden additive."

Alison glanced at him, puzzled.

"The company." He grinned. "It changes everything."

There was a sudden commotion as children ran from all sides, screaming with delight, as the little canvas cubicle for Punch and Judy opened up. Alison shivered slightly then looked away.

"You don't like Punch and Judy?" Mark asked.

She shook her head. "There's too much sorrow in the world already. I hate the sight of more."

"It's only make-believe, you silly!"

"Maybe that makes it worse," she said.

Mark's face clouded momentarily.

"Maybe it does," he answered slowly. "Come on, let's find some lunch and then go to the carnival.

"I promise," he said, cheering up, "there won't be anything but absolute escapism this afternoon."

They applauded the Rose Queen and her fairies dressed in bright crêpe paper, guessed the weight of cakes and wandered round the side-shows.

Mark tried his hand at hoop-la, and was rewarded with a big, blue, cuddly rabbit, which he handed to Alison.

"Kate will love this," she said, as she stroked the floppy ears.

"Your sister?"

"My little girl," she explained.
She saw him glancing at her left hand.
"I'm divorced," she murmured.
"Sorry," he said gently.
"Don't be. I was extremely silly at nineteen — headstrong, plunging into things without a second thought. I've got more sense now and I've changed. That's why I came away, to find myself before I start again."
"You want to talk about it?"
"Sometime. Not yet, though. It would spoil the evening, and I'm looking forward to the barbecue so much."
"Perhaps tomorrow?"
"Thanks," she said, and, for the first time, when she smiled, Mark thought he caught a hint of something deeper than politeness.

THEY took a picnic on to the cliffs next day, and Alison spilled out her troubles.
Mark lay beside her, chewing clover, listening.
"It must have been a bad time," he said when she finished.
"Yes, but it's over. And," she added, "I feel better for talking to you. I thought I could just come here and escape. You've made me accept I have to face reality."
She paused. "You've been so kind, as if you understood exactly what it's like."
Mark reddened slightly.
"You must think," he said slowly, gazing at the remnants of the food which Mrs Wilcox had provided, "that I'm a real mother's boy — thirty-one and still at home for half the year."
Alison shook her head. "I'm pretty close to home myself these days."
"The truth is," Mark continued, "I was engaged myself once. That's why I bought the house. But, well, she wanted brighter lights and bigger things. If only she had told me — "
"She didn't?"
"No. She simply upped and left three weeks before the wedding. Left a note . . ."
"That's awful. I'm so sorry."
"As you said about your own split yesterday, please don't be," he assured her. "It would have been disaster if we'd gone ahead. I reckon I've been happier on my own."
He sighed.
"But not entirely happy?" Alison ventured.
"No. I always hoped I'd have a wife and family. I'm not a loner, though I must admit I've had no heart for anything but work since all that happened. Once bitten, twice shy, I suppose."
"It might work out a second time," she pointed out. "You have to try."
"And you," he asked, "are *you* so keen to try again?"
"I wasn't," Alison said. "Until . . ."

Mark glanced up hopefully.
"Until . . . ?" he prompted.
She shrugged. "Until today."
He smiled. "I'd like to think I've played a part in that."
She blushed and looked away.
"I have to work tomorrow," he went on gently, "but could we meet again?"
"I'm going back."
"I could visit you, and meet your daughter."
Mark put his hand on hers, and Alison smiled.

MRS SIMMONDS watched with unfeigned pleasure as her daughter cut herself a second slice of chocolate cake.
"Well? How was it?" she inquired.
"Different from what I remembered," Alison told her.
"That's why they say you never should go back, dear. Places change."
"And so do people, Mum."
"You didn't find yourself then, after all?"
Alison sat in silence for a moment, gazing at a small, excited Kate as she sat playing with her giant fluffy rabbit.
"I certainly found something. It's too early yet to be quite sure what. But I think I'll be returning soon. Once the house is off my hands, I might," she added, "even move to that area."
"Your job — " her mother started to protest.
"There will be others. I mean," Alison added dreamily, "there was this little pub I stayed in.
"When I left, they mentioned they were short of staff. The son was helping out behind the bar, but he was useless in the kitchen, and they were thinking seriously of building on a dining-room if they could get a second cook."
Mrs Simmonds made a mental note of that word "son," and gave herself a very private smile. There was a whole new world out there, just waiting for her daughter to discover it, and this time she'd be wise enough to take it slowly, step by step. □

## CITY OF GLASGOW CATHEDRAL

The City of Glasgow Cathedral has its origins in the mists of time. In the 6th century, St Mungo established a church from which the present cathedral grew, on a site that had already been consecrated by St Ninian in the 4th century. The town that developed around the church was called Glas Can — The Dear Green Place, in Gaelic. The city was the Culture Capital of Europe in 1990, which demonstrates how its townsfolk have shaken off the reputation of the terrible Depression of the 1930s.

GLASGOW CATHEDRAL : J CAMPBELL KERR

# Recipe for Happiness

IT'S spring again, and the dogwood violets flower in the woods. I'll take a walk that way, and I'll stand under the embrace of the trees and I'll remember. And I'll smile a little and I'll cry a little.

It's the same pattern every year. I'll look back and see myself as I was all those years ago, when I was young and full of hopes and dreams, when all my life was before me.

All those years, each threaded with vivid memories . . .

I WAS brought up in a small, mining village which was set in the green heart of West Yorkshire. It consisted of row upon row of neat terraced houses, a few straggling shops and Hawkley Colliery, to which the village owed its livelihood.

Hawkley pithead sat arrogantly upon the hump of the hill as though dominating the landscape. It had a strange beauty, its twin wheels never failing to remind me — a fanciful child — of two great, staring eyes watching over us all.

All the houses were identical and no-one possessed anything that anyone else didn't have, including a measure of poverty. But the two up, two down little houses with a scullery and wash-house attached were homely and as clean as hard work and carbolic soap could make them.

Solidly built in stone, they were set with sash windows and stout wood doors. The back yards were unevenly paved and housed the outhouse.

As a child I'd had an unreasoning fear of the outhouse. It was bad enough during the day, when I'd find myself shrinking away from the flaking, white-washed walls, averting my eyes from the huge spiders that festooned the ceiling no matter how many times Mother took a stiff brush to it.

But at night, the short walk from the back door down to the bottom of the yard became a journey of a thousand miles. I'd run both ways, my heart hammering against my ribs, my flashlight creating a crazed, bobbing light.

I was 11 before we had a bathroom installed, but by then it was too late. I never lost my fear of confined spaces any more than I lost my fear of the dark.

After that, there seemed to be a flurry of modernisation going on around us. Doors and windows were painted, bathroom extensions grew like mushrooms, window-boxes clung to sills.

The end result conjured up in me the image of a long row of old ladies, all dressed up in party frocks, their ankles neatly crossed.

When I said so to Mother, she shook her head and cried, amused,

"You and your imagination! I don't know where you get it from, I really don't."

MY mother had been a fine woman, somewhat faded, true, but with enough prettiness left in her to remind one of the vivacious girl she had once been.

If she ever hankered for better things, then she never betrayed the fact, for her heart was firmly entrenched in her home and with those who dwelled within its walls.

I was 15 when my father died. Congestion of the lungs, Dr Price called it, something that stalked all miners. What is taken out of the earth is paid for — and in full, at that.

My father had been ill for a long time, and we'd grown used to his coughing, to the breathlessness that overcame him at the slightest exertion. It never occurred to me that he might die.

It was my mother who told me.

We were standing in the wash-house. Hot steam clouded the air and brought a sweaty flush to our faces. She was feeding a sheet through the iron mangle and I stood ready to catch it.

She suddenly fastened stricken eyes upon me and said bluntly, "Your da's dying."

Her voice was hollow and flooded with disbelief, as though she herself couldn't come to terms with the fact.

I stood there, rooted with shock, my throat closing with fear. I was too young then to hear her cry for help, her need for solace. It is only now, many years too late, that I finally understand.

Then she began to cry. The sound frightened me, for I had

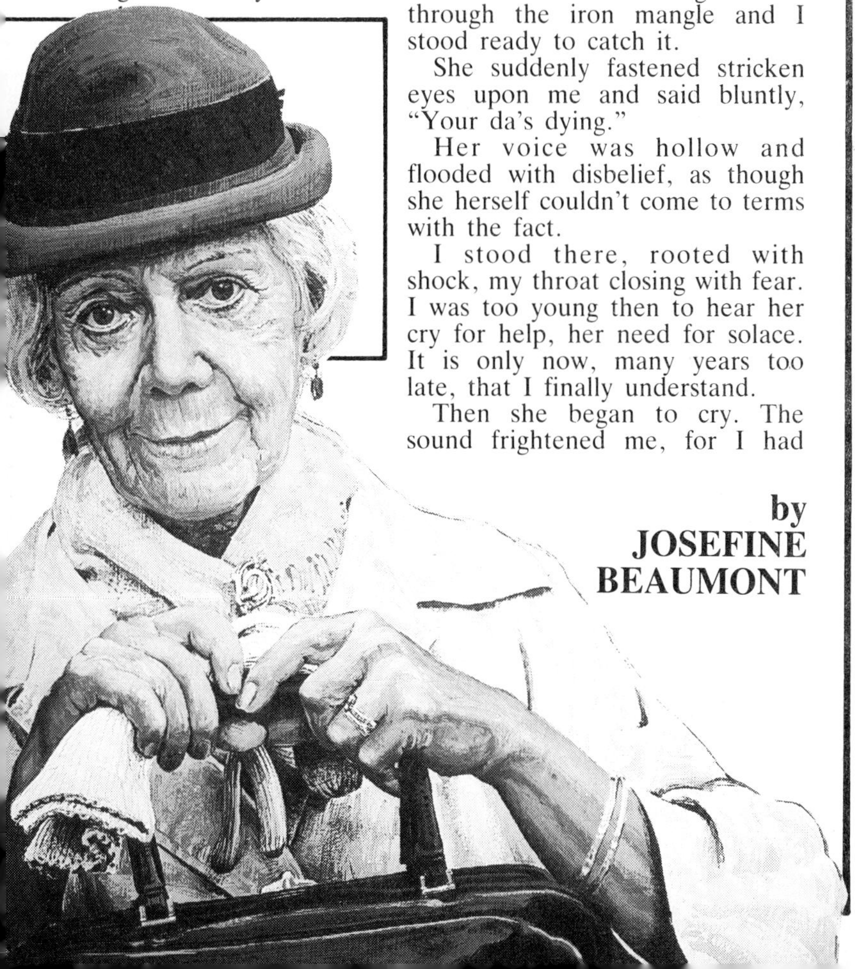

**by**
**JOSEFINE BEAUMONT**

LOCH BROOM, ROSS-SHIRE, from BRAEMORE : J CAMPBELL KERR

never heard her cry before. Laugh, yes, but never cry, and because of it, I wrenched myself around and I ran and ran and ran.

It was David who found me.

I cannot in truth recall a time when I hadn't loved David Harper. He'd always been there in my life. He was a big, shy, handsome boy, and I'm afraid to say I trailed after him shamelessly.

He never seemed to mind. His love for me was as great as mine for him. That's the way it was all through our lives together.

"So now you know," he said, sitting on his hunkers and staring out at the stretch of fields. "I'm sorry, hinny."

Tears sprang to my eyes at the term of endearment. He'd just come off shift and his face was coal-blackened, but nothing could dim the brilliant green of his eyes.

I laid my head on his coal-dusted shoulder. I think we both knew then that my mother's words heralded the end of my childhood.

He was only 17 then, a boy, really, but the pit has a way of turning boys into men overnight, and he was as old then as he was ever going to be.

"We'll get married next year," he assured me.

I knew then that everything was going to be all right.

And that's the way it was. Four months after my 16th birthday, Reverend Mr Braithwaite, who had married both sets of parents and who had christened every single child in the village, officiated at our wedding.

When I walked down the aisle, it was alone, for in my heart no-one could take my father's place. The whole village turned out, and no girl could have asked for a lovelier wedding.

I LOOK back on my life and see it as a happy one. There was no desire in me to move away, maybe to try for a better life — because to my mind there was none.

Davie and I never had much money, but that didn't matter, for we had love and mutual respect, and that was all that mattered.

## LOCH BROOM

A broad, fertile valley leads from Braemore Junction to the head of Loch Broom in Wester Ross, with the road running through dramatic forests for several miles. The loch itself has become a favourite for the factory boats of Eastern Bloc fishing fleets, leading to a cosmopolitan atmosphere in the attractive little town of Ullapool. This whole area is first-class for fishing, walking and pony-trekking, and Ullapool is a jumping-off place for the Outer Hebrides.

There was a kindness in Davie, a gentleness that carried us through any hard times that faced us. I treasured his qualities in my heart, and the memory of them was to comfort me when he was gone and I was left all alone.

I was almost 30 before we had a child. We'd been afraid we might be childless.

All our friends had families, then just when we'd reconciled ourselves I found myself pregnant.

It was a long, hard birth with complications.

When it was over, Dr Price said firmly, "No more babies for you, Connie. I don't want you to risk another pregnancy."

His words fell upon me like blows. I had envisioned a whole house full of children. But still, we had our son.

We named him Donald, after my father, and he became the apple of our eyes, our pride and joy. He was a funny lad, though, very quiet and studious, and he always had his nose stuck in some book or other.

Deep inside me, I longed for him to break out and go mad, maybe come home with a cut lip or a great hole in his pants like the other lads. He never did, though. It made me feel a bit sad, if I tell the truth.

"He was born old, that lad," Davie once said to me.

I couldn't help but agree.

WHEN Don won a scholarship to grammar school, we were fit to burst with pride, although in a secret corner of my heart I feared he'd grow away from us.

"Well, there's one lad who won't be following his da into the pit, thank goodness," Davie said to me. "Though I don't know where he gets his brains from — certainly not from me."

"Me neither!" I said with feeling.

Our eyes met and we grinned at each other. I'd been hopeless at school.

"You were as thick as two short planks!" David commented, eyes twinkling.

"Three more like!" I sighed. "Don't remind me."

"Daft as a brush," he agreed.

I stared at him, wounded.

"I wonder what you saw in me, then!" I cried.

"Ah, but you had attractions no other lass in the village had," he told me.

Slightly mollified, I raised my eyebrows. "Oh, really!"

He pulled me on to his knee. "It was your loving heart I liked."

I sighed and laid my head on the comforting pillow of his shoulder.

"I should get the supper ready," I reminded him.

"Blow the supper," he said. "It's nice sitting here."

For a brief moment he stared at the flickering coals of the fire. A log fell, showering the hearth in reddish-grey ash, as he murmured softly, "Are you happy, lass?"

I could only nod. Tears of gratitude filmed my eyes. He was always asking that — "Are you happy, lass?"

I was a lucky woman.

I don't think we were surprised when Don went on to university, but it was a big blow when he moved into a flat in the city after he graduated.

By the time he was 25, he was running his own business in a shared partnership with another young man he had met at university.

SIX months later he brought Madeline home to meet us.

I remember my nervousness as she climbed out of the car.

She was one of those smart, city girls. I felt frumpy in my cotton frock, and when I saw her black, needle-thin-heeled, patent shoes my toes curled in my sandals.

Davie's hand found mine. I stole a glance at him. It was worse for him, for at best he was a shy man even with those he had known all his life.

We needn't have worried. She was a wonderful girl, as bright and as gay and as lovely as a butterfly. She took to the village like a duck to water.

After supper, she insisted upon helping me with the washing-up. Looking at her long, thin, white hands and the slim, red nails I said, "You dry."

"It's so beautiful here!" she exclaimed, staring out of the window at the stretch of green fields. "Do you think we could go for a walk later?"

"If you like," I said shyly, warming to her.

"I'd love it!" Her eyes shone. "I bought a pair of wellies just for today."

So we tramped over the hills, leaving the men to forge ahead of us. Madeline looked faintly ridiculous in her smart suit and the shiny new wellies, but I loved her for not minding.

We paused, breathless, and she turned to me and announced, "I love your son."

"I'm glad," I said simply.

▶ *over*

## THE JAPANESE GARDEN, COMPTON ACRES

The beautiful gardens at Compton Acres look across Poole Harbour in Dorset. Open every day from 1st April to the end of October, the gardens are sub-divided into specialised areas, one of which is the Japanese Garden. All the stones and ornaments in it were brought to England by a Japanese architect and erected by Japanese workmen. This Japanese Garden is reputed to be the only completely genuine one in Europe.

JAPANESE GARDEN, COMPTON ACRES, DORSET : J CAMPBELL KERR

Don and Madeline were married three months later. They were happy at first. You'd have had to be blind not to see it.

I don't know when it all began to go wrong. I only know that I noticed Madeline's vivacity begin to fade away like a slow-burning candle.

But I had troubles of my own. Davie became ill.

In those early weeks, we played a make-believe game that everything was all right, but you cannot hide from the truth for ever, and in the end it met us face to face.

We lived very quietly together those last few months.

"I feel like having a tramp over the hills, lass," Davie said to me one day.

He was staring out of the window and I felt my heart wrench painfully. He looked so tired!

I wanted to ask him if he was up to it, but the words died on my lips. Silently, I fetched my coat, and hand in hand we left the house together.

As we paced steadily through the woods, he smiled down at me and asked, "Are you happy, lass?"

Lifting my face to his I nodded, unable to speak. My throat was too full.

When we finally stood on the hill, staring down at the fan shape of the village, he suddenly said, oh, so gently, "I'm sorry, lass."

It was my undoing.

"Don't!" I cried brokenly.

Davie pulled me into his arms and murmured gently, "Oh, Connie, lass! Don't cry. I've always hated to see you cry."

"I'm not crying," I lied, thrusting back the tears.

"Ah, hinny!" His hand cupped my chin. "You're a bonnie lass. Did I ever tell you that?"

"No, you never did." Tremulously, I smiled up at him.

"Well, I'm telling you now."

"Better late then never, I suppose." I sniffed and Davie grinned.

"We've been lucky, bonnie lass," he said.

I clung to him and breathed softly, "Yes, we have."

To this day I can still see us, the wind blowing into our faces, a gentle sun caressing us.

We were afraid, clinging to each other and thinking, why us?

If there is a time for all things, then that was when, without words — for we needed none — we said goodbye.

DONALD was very good to me in the early days after his father died. He set aside his own pain, made arrangements, fussed over me in that practical way of his.

I bore it all with stoicism, when all I wanted to do was to crawl into a dark corner and close my eyes and never open them again.

But I was stung to a fury that surprised us both, when he suggested I move into one of the smart flats near where he and Maddie lived.

"I only want what's best for you, Mother," he explained. "And there's nothing left for you here now."

"If you really believe that, then I feel sorry for you, Donald," I said quietly.

He didn't understand, for a baffled look came over his face.

Life went on. I'd never thought of myself as the crying kind, but many a dark night I'd lie in my lonely bed and let the tears fall.

Then one Friday evening, Donald came to see me. I took one look at his face and I knew something was wrong.

"You'd better sit down before you fall down," I told him. "And tell me what's the matter"

As he dropped into a chair, I poured two drinks and thrust one in his hand.

He took a gulp, then said accusingly, "Mother! This is whisky!"

"I'm a big girl now, dear," I said mildly. "I am allowed an occasional drink."

I noticed a disapproving look settle upon his face, and I sighed inwardly. Love him as I did, he could be a real stick-in-the-mud at times.

"What's the matter?" I asked quickly.

"I've — I've left Madeline," he said dully.

"Left Maddie?" I echoed. "What on earth for?"

"We had a row," he told me, looking pompous, "over a pair of slippers.

"Oh, I know," he said, catching sight of my face. "I know that sounds ridiculous. But so was her behaviour."

"What did she do?" I stared at him.

He hesitated then confessed, red-faced, "She threw them at me! Can you believe that? Talk about ingratitude!

"When I think of all the things I've given her — that house, for a start, and the car. Last Christmas, I bought her a lovely pearl necklace and she hardly thanked me.

"She needed new slippers, Mother. Her others had holes in them. You'd think she'd be glad I noticed things like that," he continued, warming to his self-pity. "Most men wouldn't. You'd think she'd be grateful."

"Don't be such an ass!" I said shortly and he flushed. "What do you want her to do? Go down on her knees?

"It's your home too, Donald. You get as much pleasure from it as she does, and anyway, it's easy to buy things when you have money."

MOTHER!" He looked aghast.

"Your grandad had a saying," I told him. "He called it his recipe for happiness. All you had to do was to look at what you had in life, and not at what you didn't have. Do you understand what I'm trying to tell you?"

"No," he answered sulkily, looking about 12 years old.

"I know you mean well, dear," I said gently, "but a little thought and a little caring goes a long way — further than money ever stretches, anyway."

"I just wanted her to have a good life!" he protested. "What's so wrong with that?"

"Nothing," I snapped, "if it's given freely. Your father and I never had much money, I know, but still we had a wonderful life together. That's why I couldn't ever leave this village.

"This is my home, Donald, the one I shared with your dad. I find a comfort in these four walls, in this way of life. Your dad gave me more important things than money — the ones money can't buy."

Going to the bureau, I took out the small prayer book I had carried at my wedding. Opening it, I handed it to Donald, who stared at the pressed flowers which clung to its pages.

"Dogwood violets," I explained gently. "They grow wild in the woods. Many a time, on his way home from a shift, no matter how tired he was, your father would walk all that way and pick me some. Now do you understand, Donald?"

"Oh, Mum!" He buried his face in his hands.

Reaching out, I stroked his hair as I used to do when he was a small boy.

"I'll make up your bed for tonight, but in the morning I want you to go back to Maddie and tell her that you love her. Believe me, Donald, where your heart is, then that's your home," I promised my son.

It must have been about seven in the morning when I heard Donald moving about, but it wasn't until I heard the back door click that I jumped out of bed and ran over to the window.

What I saw made me smile. He was stalking across the fields with fierce determination, and my heart swelled because from the back he looked just like Davie.

He was gone for a long time and I stood there, heart in mouth. Then I saw him, looking every inch his father's son, with a bunch of wild primroses clenched in his hand.

It was going to be all right . . .

SOME of my happiest times are when my four grandchildren spend the weekend with me. I shouldn't say it, I know, but of all of them, little Davie holds a special place in my heart.

I like to see them swarming all over the house. My heart lifts to hear the happy babble of their voices. How Davie would have loved them so!

Sometimes we all tramp over the hills. Little hands cling to mine, surely one of the best feelings in the whole world! Little legs valiantly attempt to match my stride.

On the hump of the hill I never fail to pause, to feel the sun on my face, to breathe in the clean air, to savour the feeling that I am very close to Davie.

Though it is fanciful of me, I believe I hear his voice, warm and loving and carried by the gentle breeze that tugs my hair. It says to me and to me alone, "Are you happy, lass?"

And my heart replies, "Yes." □

AT first, Greg had been tolerantly amused at Madge's new bout of nervous anticipation. It had started from the day they got the invitation.

But after he'd been driving for two hours and was now trying to find his way in a strange town, his wife's restless fidgeting was an increasing distraction. How could he follow Jeff's directions — in failing light — when Madge kept breaking into his concentration?

How often did he have to assure her that she looked fine? The perm was still OK. No, she hadn't put on too much lipstick. Most of all, how could *he* tell whether Jeff's parents would like them or not?

"Better start looking out for Malborough Avenue, Madge."

Greg decided to enlist her help in the hope of taking her mind off such trivialities. He was wrong.

"We're almost there!" The high pitch in her voice told Greg it was not a question, but rather an exclamation of mixed panic and alarm.

He sighed patiently and tried humour.

"We're not visiting royalty, love," he teased. "Relax. I'm sure the Hartwells are quite human."

"How funny," Madge said icily. "Any more witty comments?"

Greg smarted under the rebuke and tried to hit back. "If you're like this now, goodness knows what you'll be like at the wedding."

"Typical male thinking," Madge retorted in her old parade-ground voice. "Should have realised you just can't understand these things. Of course I'm excited about Carol's wedding. What mother isn't? But this is different."

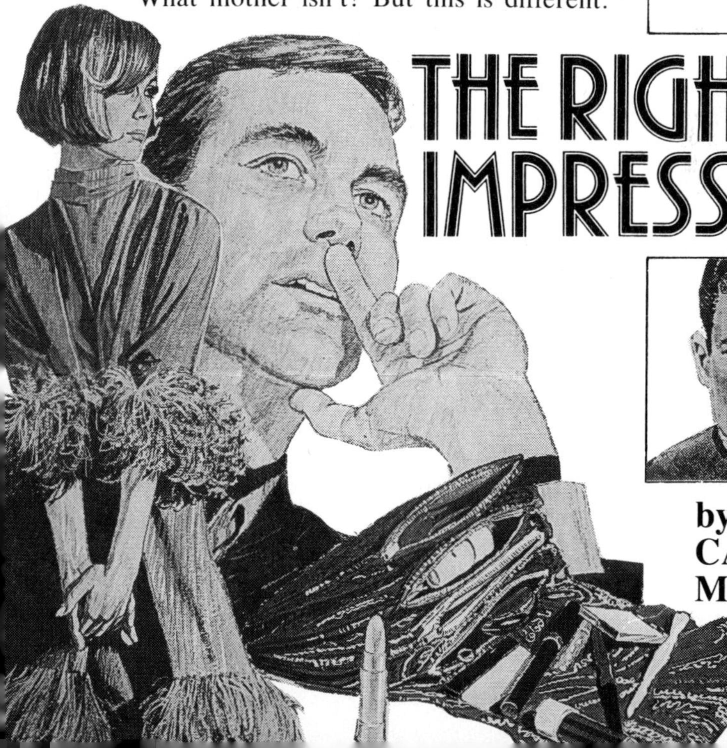

# THE RIGHT IMPRESSION

by
CATHIE
MITCHELL

It was a logic Greg couldn't follow.

"Why worry about what Jeff's parents might think of us? He's marrying our daughter — not us!"

Even without looking round, he knew Madge's big, brown eyes were boring into him.

"That's not the point," she said into his left ear which twitched and turned red. "We want to create a good impression for Carol's sake. Don't want to embarrass your daughter, do you?"

"Of course not," Greg mumbled, keeping his eyes fixed on the road ahead, afraid that if he glanced at Madge she would read the truth in his eyes. She was rather good at that after 30 years!

OK, so he was a bit nervous. No, that was too strong a word. Unsure would be more accurate. But he wasn't going over the top about it!

If the two lots of parents didn't hit it off, what was the big tragedy? The only important thing was how Carol and Jeff felt about each other.

"Can't imagine what I'll find to talk about with Mrs Hartwell." Madge was back to speaking her thoughts, as if she had given up asking Greg.

But he, rashly, still plunged in to help. "Hasn't stopped you in the past. Just be yourself and you'll be fine."

"She's a college lecturer! What was it Jeff said? Doctor of Biology? I've been a housewife for the last thirty years. What on earth can I talk to her about that would be of even the slightest interest?"

"I'm sure Mrs Hartwell isn't that different from the rest of us lesser mortals!" Greg snorted. "She probably enjoys a good gossip as much as any woman."

Madge spoke again into his left ear. "You being the expert on women, of course! And what about her husband? You talk to professors every day at the gas works, I suppose."

Greg dismissed the sting with a shrug. "Have to take me as he finds me. I've read quite a bit. Plenty I can talk about."

"Like what?"

"I don't know! Let's just see how things go —"

"She'll want to know how the wedding arrangements are coming along. Said she was looking forward to that. Must admit, she sounded very pleasant on the phone," Madge conceded.

"Didn't Carol tell you she's very nice? Look how well she seems to get along with both Jeff's parents, and that's the important thing."

Greg drew a deep breath, and his face softened as he took a hand from the steering wheel and patted Madge's. "Everything will go fine, dear. Tell you one thing, if Mrs Hartwell doesn't take to you, then she'll be the first."

Madge sighed. "Oh well, the weekend can't be any worse than I imagine," she declared with an unconvincing laugh.

They drove in silence for a bit, with Greg concentrating on the unfamiliar roads.

"Can't be far now," he said. "There's Marlborough Avenue."

It was like a torch to dry tinder. Madge was erect in her seat, leaning forward to wipe the windscreen with a gloved hand and peer out.

"Aren't they all such big houses!"

"Should be a turn-off to the right — there it is!" Greg said with satisfaction.

THEY were into a narrow road lined on both sides with dark trees.

"We seem to be going into the country!" Madge exclaimed.

"The house *is* in the country. On its own, Jeff said." He shot her a quick, hopeful look. "I've just remembered something. Didn't Jeff say his mother was in the WRAC?"

"Might have done . . ."

"Of course she did."

"What of it?"

"So were you!" Greg's eyes were shining now. "You can always talk about that. Should be plenty of yarns you could swap about the old days. Bet she'd enjoy that."

Madge looked horrified. "Never!"

"Why not?"

"For goodness' sake, she has degrees and everything. She mst have been an officer. I was just a sergeant."

"What's wrong with that? I think it was jolly good. I never even made lance-corporal!"

But Madge had long since determined that this was one topic to avoid. It would serve only to underline the difference between both women.

"Don't you dare mention the WRAC," she warned.

Greg gave up. It was obvious that no matter what he said, Madge was determined to remain on edge at least until they reached the house.

"Here we are."

He swung the car on to a gravel driveway and stopped in front of a very large house.

Madge hesitated as she got out of the car. "You're sure this is it?"

"It's exactly as Jeff described it."

As they approached, the front door swung open and a beam of bright light flooded on to them.

Mrs Hartwell stood framed in the light, a large figure, and not too slim, thought Madge, with some satisfaction. It was obvious that she had been watching for their arrival.

"You found us all right," their hostess called.

Advancing up the few steps, Madge began to make out the face. It was split with a wide, welcoming smile which eased Madge's tension almost immediately. The handshake was firm and warm.

"No problems," Greg declared. "Thanks to your son's directions."

Moving into the light of the hallway, Greg threw a quick glance at Madge, looking for her reaction. The look on her face puzzled him.

"I seem to know you," Madge said quietly. "But I don't see how —"

Mrs Hartwell was staring back. "You look familiar, too. Carol said you were in the WRAC. A sergeant, I believe."

GREG tensed. Another glance revealed the expected astonished look on Madge. They had not even thought of their daughter letting this particular cat out of the bag.

Now her poor mum had to begin conversation with the one subject she had hoped to avoid.

But he felt a quiet sense of pride at how quickly Madge regained her composure. Well, she hadn't been made a sergeant for nothing.

"Yes." She spoke with controlled calm. "A long time ago, of course."

"I seem to know your face," Mrs Hartwell persisted. "Were you stationed at Mill Hill, by any chance?"

"As a matter of fact, I was." Greg was sure that he was the only one who could have spotted the tightness in Madge's voice.

"Sergeant Bellow!" Mrs Hartwell almost shouted the name and that brought a puzzled-looking Professor Hartwell out into the hallway. "That's what we used to call you! Oh, I'm sorry. But it was your voice, you see."

"You're quite right," Madge murmured, squaring her shoulders. All right, so it was out.

"The girls did give me that nickname." She hesitated, looking harder at the other's face. "I didn't really know any of the officers . . ."

"Officer!" Mrs Hartwell almost exploded with laughter. "Good gracious, I was a cook!"

Madge blinked. "Cook," she repeated numbly.

Then suddenly, as sometimes happens, the past was clear in her mind. "Not — Porky!"

"The same. And of course you remember why they called me that?" She giggled. "As you can see, I haven't changed all that much!"

PROFESSOR HARTWELL called out to his wife, "Aren't you inviting our guests in, dear?"

She didn't hear him. The two women had forgotten both men as they almost locked arms, laughing and clearly trying to out-talk each other.

Greg looked past them to Professor Hartwell. Both men shrugged their shoulders, moved to shake hands and went inside.

"I think we'll go into the living-room and close the door." Professor Hartwell smiled. "No telling how long those two will be at that door."

Settled with a drink on a comfortable easy chair, Greg smiled, too, as even through the closed door he could hear the loud shrieks of laughter. □

EMMA'S finger idly traced a pattern on the window-pane as she watched Max walk away from the house and down to the sea.

He might have been a total stranger, she thought sadly.

He wasn't, of course.

Emma had been 13 years old when her mother, a widow for nine years, had remarried. She could still recall her excitement on the first morning she had woken in her new home to see, not the familiar mass of the tall buildings that was the Midlands, but the beautiful, rugged coastline of North Scotland.

Her stepfather, Josh, soon became as dear to her as any father could be, and then there was Max, her new stepbrother and soon her

by SHIRLEY WORRALL

# MOMENT OF TRUTH

closest friend in this wonderful, new world.

Max had been 20 at the time, but despite the difference in their ages, which to Emma had seemed immense, they had grown closer than many brothers and sisters.

So what had gone wrong, Emma asked herself again?

From her window, she saw Max stop at the water's edge and gaze out into the distance. Seemingly oblivious to the biting cold, he wore only a thick sweater and jeans.

For the last 14 years, they had been such good friends. Now Emma felt as if she'd never known him at all. Somewhere along the way, something very precious had been lost.

In three days, Max would be leaving to start his new life in America. In fact, if Emma hadn't managed to swap duties at the hospital where she worked as a radiographer, and so grab a four-day holiday at her old home, she wouldn't even have seen Max before he left.

It was such an unexpected decision. Emma still wasn't sure which hurt the most — the fact that he was leaving, or the fact that he hadn't bothered to tell her himself.

She had been stunned when her mother had told her the news.

She could appreciate his working over there, but there was a world of difference between spending a couple of months there and making it his home. But like it or not, Emma didn't know when she'd see him again, after his plane left on Thursday.

Emma had arrived yesterday, but Max had barely mentioned the move to her. They seemed to have lost the ability to confide in each other.

WITH this thought uppermost, Emma left her bedroom, ran down the stairs, picked up her coat and left the house. The salty air was bitterly cold but invigorating, and she pulled on her warm, padded coat as she walked.

Max hadn't moved. The stiff breeze whipped at his already wayward, brown hair as he gazed across the water to where the cliffs of Hoy rose majestically from the sea.

He looked happy in his solitude, making Emma think he might resent her intrusion, but when she reached his side, he turned briefly and smiled.

"It looks as if we could be in for a storm," he commented.

Emma gazed up at the threatening grey clouds. "Yes."

Without speaking more they began walking. How many times had she walked this stretch of beach with Max, Emma wondered? Countless times.

"You'll miss all this," she said lightly. "You'll have to learn to cope with subways and freeways and whatever else they have in New York."

"I'll be back to visit." Max thrust his hands into the pockets of his jeans, and gave her a teasing smile. "In any case, you're a fine one to talk. It didn't take you long to seek out the bright lights."

It hadn't. At the first opportunity, Emma had applied for a post at a London hospital. It was a decision she had never regretted — until now, perhaps.

Although she loved her work at the hospital and the many friends she had there, this was still her home, and a place she neeeded to visit every now and again. It wouldn't be the same without Max, though.

"I'll miss you," she told him.

Max laughed softly. "You never see me. The last time I saw you was when you and Gary spent the weekend here. How is he, by the way?"

He hadn't said he'd miss her, Emma noticed. "Gary? Oh, he's fine."

That weekend with Gary was something Emma preferred to forget.

Gary was a doctor at St Luke's, and Emma had been going out with him for six months. It had taken almost that long to find enough time to leave their busy schedules and visit Scotland together.

Fiercely proud of her home, Emma had longed to show it off to Gary. All in all, it had been a strange weekend. Her time had been taken up with Gary, so that she hadn't found time for her usual chat with Max.

She had missed that, and she'd also had the feeling that Max was keeping his distance.

Not that she had worried about it at the time. There had been too many other things to worry about, like Gary's ideas about the future.

As far as Emma was concerned they were just good friends, so she was more than a little surprised when Gary made it quite clear to anyone with more than a passing interest, that he was thinking of marriage.

She was fond of Gary, naturally, but she wasn't sure she loved him enough for marriage. In fact, the more Emma thought about it, the more convinced she became that she didn't.

"I know we haven't discussed it," Gary had said on the journey back to London when she questioned him. "But we've been together for quite a while. It seems the obvious step."

"But the way you were talking," Emma insisted, "everyone must have assumed that it was as good as settled. We haven't even thought about it."

"*I've* thought about it," he pointed out.

"I haven't."

It had been the beginning of the end. The last thing Emma wanted was to encourage Gary then see him eventually hurt, so she had quietly brought their relationship to an end.

MAX bent down, picked up a flat pebble and skimmed it across the water. "Have you named the day yet?"

Emma felt a tide of colour invade her cheeks. "No. Actually, we don't see each other any more, except at work of course. Gary was —"

"Rushing you to the altar?" Max suggested drily, as perceptive as ever.

"Something like that." It had been exactly like that and that was what she hadn't liked.

Emma didn't think she had to explain any of this to Max — he'd always understood her so well. She had always imagined she knew him well, too, but perhaps she'd been wrong.

With an inner smile, she remembered the day that his first play had been shown on television. Brimming with pride and excitement, she had bored her friends rigid, making them promise to watch it.

When it had finally been shown, Emma hadn't understood a single word. She had been expecting a comedy, in keeping with Max's sense of humour, but the play had been very serious. None of her young friends had been in the least impressed.

## A Dream Of Love

If dreams came true then mine would be,
To be with you eternally,
To walk together hand in hand,
Obeying only love's command.

If dreams came true all hearts would know,
Mysterious warmth of inner glow.
None then would ever lonely be,
For like the branches of a tree,
Embracing arms would reach and hold
The gift of love, worth more than gold.

— *Georgina Hall.*

The play must have appealed to a more mature audience, though, because it had been the start of his success as a playwright. His work had taken him to America, and now it was taking him there again, for good this time.

His plays had changed over the years, becoming more light hearted — or perhaps Emma was old enough to understand them these days.

"There's a seal." Max pointed to the unmistakable dark shape in the water.

They stopped walking to watch the seal. The seal, equally curious, stared back at them with enormous, soulful eyes.

"Do you remember the first one I saw, Max?"

"How could I forget?" Max grinned. "You came hurtling up the beach, pigtails flying in all directions, to tell me we were about to be invaded by sharks."

Emma laughed at the memory. "You don't see many seals in the Midlands."

She huddled deeper inside her coat against the cold. "It was such a different life coming here. You don't miss what you don't have, but when I came here I had a stepfather who doted on me and —"

"He still does."

He did. Dear Josh. "And I had a ready-made brother who spoilt me, too. All my friends fought like cat and dog with their horrid brothers.

"They all envied me. They all had crushes on you, too." Emma laughed. "Do you remember?"

Max nodded, his lips curving into a smile. "I used to come home from university to find a queue of adoring fourteen-year-olds waiting for me."

Emma had been right at the front of the queue, she remembered. She'd forgotten until that moment, but at the time, she had suffered a strong case of hero-worship.

"It all seems a long time ago," she said quietly, stifling a sigh.

"It's just as well!" Max retorted. "Believe me, there's nothing more wearing than an adoring fourteen-year-old!"

Emma laughed, but that overwhelming sense of sadness was still with her. There was nothing she could put her finger on, but in some way, her friendship with Max had changed.

THIS was the parting of the ways, Emma realised, when the "do you remembers" come thick and fast, as if you have to dust off the memories before clinging to them for ever.

"Max, why didn't you tell me you were going to America?" she asked at last.

Max looked surprised by the question. "I planned to, the next time I spoke to you. I didn't think it was important. You have your life, I have mine." He frowned. "Does it bother you?"

It not only bothered her, it hurt, yet she couldn't understand why it should. Perhaps she was just being fanciful. She was certainly being a little arrogant to assume that Max should consult her on his every move.

"Of course not," she said briskly. "It was — a surprise, that's all."

They had no claims on each other. Their only link was the fact that her mother happened to be married to his father.

This thought did nothing to lighten Emma's mood. What did the future hold? Presumably they would keep in touch, on birthdays and at Christmas, but what about the rest of the time?

She'd been living in London for six years, only visiting occasionally, so why did she feel this acute sense of loss? Because for 14 years, she had taken Max for granted, she supposed.

In the distance, the Atlantic waves crashed fiercely against the cliffs. This time next week, Max would be on the other side of that vast ocean.

"You will send me the occasional postcard?" For some absurd reason, Emma felt close to tears.

"I expect I'll manage that!" Max smiled, adding a teasing, "And you'll send me an invitation to the wedding?"

Emma was forced to laugh. "I told you, there isn't going to be a wedding."

"There will be," Max said quietly. "You've been getting through boyfriends as if they're going out of fashion. One of these days, one of them will be around long enough to get you to the altar."

"You've a start of seven years on me," she pointed out with a poor smile. "You ought to get there first."

"Mmm," Max said doubtfully. "I think all those fourteen-year-olds you lined up have put me off for life."

They both laughed, but seconds later the laughter died, leaving a cold and empty silence stretching in front of them.

ONE day, Emma supposed they would both be married. Max was a very attractive man, never short of female companionship, and, as he'd pointed out, she'd had several boyfriends.

None of them had ever meant anything though, she thought desperately. In fact, as she picked her way carefully along the pebbles, she couldn't imagine any man making up for the fact that Max was about to walk out of her life.

She began to wonder if she had ever recovered from that case of hero-worship.

"Sometimes I wish I was still thirteen years old." Emma sighed.

Max stopped walking and looked at her curiously, his eyes tender and concerned. "Why?"

"I don't want you to go." The words hovered on her lips but they seemed far too absurd and childish to utter.

"I don't know," she murmured.

The first spots of rain fell and, welcoming the distraction, Emma said brightly, "I don't know about you, but I have no intention of getting soaked."

As they hurried back to the house, Emma was conscious of something acutely close to shyness. She'd looked up to Max as a big brother, then a friend, yet she still felt shy.

They reached the house. Max opened the door and stood back to let her pass.

"There are some phone calls I have to make." He strode across the hall, saying over his shoulder, "I'll see you later, Emma."

Watching him walk away, Emma experienced a sharp sense of betrayal. Perhaps that was what this was all about. She felt betrayed by Max.

He'd picked her up and dusted her down time and time again, but now that was over. He was walking out of her life — and he didn't care.

The phone calls seemed to take most of the day. Max missed lunch, then he went out for a couple of hours in the evening.

Emma opted for an early night, going to her bedroom just after ten-thirty. She crossed the room to draw her curtains, and the breath caught in her throat at the sight of the Northern Lights.

Without pausing for breath, she ran outside to stand beneath that great, colourful sky. Many times she'd seen the Northern Lights, the aurora borealis, flickering across the night sky. Never before had she been so struck by their almost frightening majesty.

The sky was filled with lights, from red to blue, purple to green. The entire northern sky was a vivid red, and to the west it was a shimmering green.

She folded her arms, feeling very small and insignificant beneath the awesome spectacle. Her problems seemed meaningless.

Future generations would stand as she did and wonder at the sight. Years from now, her children would stand beneath the canopy of light, and her children's children.

In her mind's eyes, Emma could see those children with Max's hair and eyes.

Beneath that splendid sky, everything became clear. She wanted Max, and she wanted his children to be their children. She wanted him with her always, not as a brother but —

I'VE brought your coat, Emma."

The sound of Max's voice made Emma jump and she spun round, wondering how long he had been standing there.

Everything about him was so achingly familiar, and the thought of his leaving brought a lump to her throat.

"Isn't it amazing?" she said, turning eyes that were filled with tears, from Max and to the sky.

"Magical," he murmured.

Yes, magical. They could be the only two people left on earth, and Emma fiercely wished they were.

Standing behind her, Max placed his hands on her shoulders and that one act was her undoing.

She turned in his arms.

"Max, I wish you weren't going to America," she blurted out.

He held her tightly and for the first time in weeks, Emma felt warm and safe. She wished she could have stayed for ever in that haven beneath the night sky.

"Do you?" Max asked softly.

Emma nodded, and the small movement caused a stray tear to roll down her cheek.

Max lifted her face and, with a small smile, brushed the tear away. "Then I'll have to come back, won't I?"

Emma's eyes widened. Would he really come back, just because she wanted him to?

There was so much she wanted to explain. She longed to tell him how she felt, but loving Max was so fresh and new that she couldn't find the words.

His eyes blazed into a sudden brilliance, and Emma knew that, as always, she didn't need to speak. Her expression said everything for her, and Max knew her so well.

Max lifted a gentle hand to her face and she reached out to hold it against her skin.

"Don't you know, Emma, that I was only running away?" he confessed. "If it wasn't to be Gary, I knew the time would soon come when you'd give your love to someone."

Emma shook her head. "Only to you, Max."

"I've loved you, Emma," Max murmured, "for ever, it seems."

As he lowered his head to kiss her, the Northern Lights, silently and unnoticed, faded from the night sky . . . □

# WHEN LUCK RAN OUT

**by CAROL WALLACE**

RICHARD considered himself a lucky man, the kind of man wh could buy the last raffle ticket in the book and win the sta prize. He never bumped into the boss when he was late goin into the office, but he could be guaranteed to share the lift with hir when he was late leaving.

He'd grown up with an adoring mother and four adoring elde sisters, who'd treated him somewhere between a cosseted pet and th nearest thing to competition Tom Cruise had ever had.

That was why he was unprepared for disaster to enter his life in th form of Louise Goode. He reached the door of the Accoun Department fractionally ahead of her and held it open gallantly.

She seemed to hesitate, checking a slip of paper before walking i purposefully.

"May I help?" he suggested, taking her elbow and guiding he firmly towards his desk.

She really was cute, he thought, staring at her freckles, the curl and the wide, full mouth that made her seem friendly and fun despit the severe, dark-blue business suit.

"Mr —?"

Richard held out his hand.

"Richard Smith," he offered, wishing for the millionth time that h had a more interesting and intriguing surname.

She smiled.

"Goode," she said. "Louise."

"Hello, Louise!" He beamed at her, and sat down on his desk.

It occurred to him that his departmental head had mentione something about a new secretary — and very nice, too.

"Goode," she repeated as if she suspected he was slightly hard c hearing. For good measure she added, "Ms."

Richard nodded, amazed at her ability to imitate a bumble bee. H allowed his head to continue to nod up and down because it gave hir time to think.

"Goode by name and Goode by nature, eh?" he ended up sayin weakly.

Louise Goode's deep blue eyes watched him frostily, and Richar tried hastily to make amends.

"You'll like it here, Louise, I'm sure. Paul — Mr David to you — is a bit of a stickler for routine, but I'm sure you'll be able to handle him all right.

"Listen —" He slid off the desk and put his arm round her "— you're bound to be a bit lost, the first week and so on. Why don't I take you out to lunch? I know all the best places . . ."

"Ah, Ms Goode. I'm so pleased you've arrived. I see you've met Richard." Mr David frowned at him. "Ms Goode is our new assistant head of department, Richard."

He turned to Louise, and the frown was replaced by a smile. "Richard is one of four staff who'll be working directly for you, Ms Goode."

RICHARD stared morosely into his ten o'clock cup of coffee. So he'd got off on the wrong foot with Louise — Ms Goode, he reminded himself. Things would improve, though. He'd had lots of girlfriends and had stayed friends with all of them.

He gazed across the floor to where Louise stood at a filing cabinet, flicking through files and occasionally jotting down notes. He sighed, staring at the mane of red hair, the jaunty way she stuck her pencil behind her ear.

If love was this sick feeling in his stomach, the trembling in his hands and the sudden loss of the confidence in himself that had taken all of his 27 years to build up, then he was in love with Ms Goode, and he'd got it bad.

By mid-morning, he'd talked some sense into himself. She was just a girl — goodness, weren't half of the population female? There was nothing special about her.

He piled a bundle of six files together and stood up.

"Richard?"

He turned and bumped into Louise Goode, sending the files slithering to the floor. He rushed to rescue them, grabbing at them and only succeeding in making them spill their contents.

"I'm sorry — I'm not usually so clumsy!"

The self-controlled, suave side of him told him not to gabble, to leave the files and talk to her, but he couldn't. He gabbled and grabbed and worse — oh, much worse — he felt himself blushing from the tip of his toes to his hair-line.

I haven't blushed since I was 14, he wailed to himself in a silent voice.

"Richard —" Her voice was calm and deliberate, as if she was soothing a flustered child "— I'm going for lunch now. Will you join me?"

Richard gulped, regaining his composure. Well, there you were, he told himself. He just had this knack of making the right impression. So maybe he'd got off on the wrong foot, but that was in the past.

He straightened his tie, his mind racing ahead, choosing just the right kind of restaurant. He pictured the two of them at a small corner table, deep in conversation, finding out how much they shared . . .

He nodded, and opened his mouth to tell her all about his plans, but Louise placed the last file neatly on top of the pile he clutched in his arms and forestalled him.

"Right. We'll eat in the canteen. It'll give us a chance to go over these reports you've written. I'd like to suggest one or two ways in which we can improve —"

The rest of her sentence faded as she swept out of the department.

Ms Goode, Richard thought, I love you. He strode after her.

LUNCH, Richard had to admit later, had been a disaster. Not only wasn't it the cosy tête-á-tête he'd dreamed about, but he'd managed to convince her that he was clumsy, stupid and thick.

First he'd got caught in the revolving doors, next he'd tried to help them both to coffee and succeeded in jamming the lever so that coffee not only filled the paper cups, but the tray, the inside of his left shoe and a considerable area of the tiled floor.

On his first bite into his wholemeal cheese roll, he'd loosened the cap on his left eye-tooth, and was afraid to finish his roll, smile, or talk.

After 10 minutes, during which she'd eaten her salad, drunk her coffee, and demolished his reports, all with an efficiency that amazed him, Louise Goode smiled.

"Well, that takes care of that!"

He grinned at her, feeling his heart soar and his tooth wobble. Right, he thought to himself, now for a chance to impress.

He leaned forward on the table, only vaguely aware that his right sleeve was steadily absorbing a wayward pool of coffee.

Louise was already on her feet, shuffling her papers and grabbing her brief-case.

"Back to work, then," she said. "Oh, don't get up. Stay there and finish your coffee," she added.

Richard stared straight ahead. His left foot was filled with cold coffee. His right elbow felt spongy and damp. Clutched in his left hand was the cap from his tooth.

Worse than that, those 10 minutes with Louise had convinced him his condition was fatal. He was in love with Louise Goode.

He had to find ways of impressing her, to change the wimpish impression he'd created, he thought.

Richard sat at his desk all that afternoon, doodling. If she had a fluffy, white, Persian kitten who needed rescued from a tree . . .

He drew himself in a Superman outfit clambering up a leafy, green tower, plucking the animal to safety and depositing it in her arms.

He drew a presentable likeness of Louise clasping the kitten, a large balloon coming out of her Cupid's bow mouth, and carefully printed inside, "Oh, Richard! You're so brave!"

He frowned. She just wasn't the type who'd possess a fluffy, white kitten, he decided honestly. If she did, and it got stuck in a tree, she'd probably rescue it herself.

He glanced sideways at the piles of reports which menaced him from the corner of his desk. Reluctantly, he peeled off the top bundle and began work.

BY the end of the second month, Richard had been forced to admit to himself that the situation was hopeless. He confessed as much to Linda, his sister, when he called to take his one and only nephew to the zoo.

"I'm crazy about her," he admitted. "You should see her, Linda. All red curls, and the bluest eyes you've seen in your life."

"It sounds to me," said Linda shrewdly, strapping Kevin into his buggy, "that it's not so much a case of love at first sight —"

She hesitated maddeningly as she struggled to fasten the zip on Kevin's little, red anorak, while Kevin took a sudden fancy to her nose and decided to find out if it really was attached firmly to her face.

Richard knelt down and distracted him with a yellow toy rabbit.

"As what?" he prompted.

Linda stood up and swept her hair back off her face.

"As what?" she repeated blankly, her hands on her hips.

"Not so much love at first sight as —"

"Oh — well, a challenge. You must admit, Richard, you've played the field a bit. You're not used to being given the cold shoulder."

"That's not true, Linda." Stung, Richard searched his memory. "There was Jennifer . . ."

Jennifer had told him he was the most boring person she'd ever met. He had been only 12 at the time, certainly.

"Let's face it, Richard," his sister went on. "You just can't bear the thought that this Louise just doesn't fancy you. It's a game and you've got to win."

Linda was teasing him, but her comments stayed with him as he drove off with Kevin singing his favourite advertising jingle in the back of the car with the fervour of a chap who didn't have a single care in the world.

"Just you wait, Kevin," Richard said, eyeing him in the mirror as he stopped at the traffic lights. "Life isn't all fun and fish fingers. Wait till you fall for a woman who doesn't seem to notice you exist."

Sundays at the zoo with Kevin had become a habit. Two gentlemen on their day out, they had evolved a regular routine, and woe betide Richard if any part of it were omitted.

The first stop was to buy two packets of peanuts for the animals and two large pink and white ice-creams for themselves. Then they ambled slowly towards the monkey house.

Kevin's pace quickened as he neared the enclosure. He know all the monkeys by name, and was always scrupulously careful about sharing the peanuts.

Richard, on the other hand, got slower, for standing by the wire netting of the enclosure he could see Louise Goode. He decided to jettison his pink and white ice-cream but just as he spotted a suitable litter bin, Louise Goode turned round.

She didn't, he had to admit, look all that pleased to see him.

Richard smiled bravely, a slightly dishevelled toddler hanging on to one hand, and a fast-melting ice-cream in the other.

They said hello and passed the kind of remarks people do when they're preparing to smile, say goodbye and go off in different directions. Richard knew that, and Louise knew that. But thank goodness, Richard thought, that Kevin didn't know anything about signals, sighs or body language.

He glanced up at the two of them, assumed that Louise was a friend and took a hand of each of them firmly.

"Penguins," he announced, and led them off.

BY the time they'd toured the zoo and stopped off at the café for a cup of coffee, Richard had begun to relax. He hadn't spilled coffee on Louise, he hadn't tripped over his own feet. In fact, he'd managed to act like a completely normal person.

While Kevin peered perilously into the ornamental goldfish pool by their table, he explained that he took the toddler out every Sunday.

"It gives Linda — my sister — a chance to get on with some painting. She's good. In fact, she's preparing for her first exhibition."

He smiled, embarrassed slightly at the pride in his voice. "Colin, her husband, died a year ago, very suddenly." He hesitated. "Since then she's put everything into her work — and Kevin."

He didn't know why he was telling Louise all this and he wished he could stop. He cleared his throat. "We're a close family, you know, and I try to help as much as I can."

Louise nodded, and for the first time she seemed to enjoy his company.

"You're lucky, having a family, being close." She sighed. "Me, I'm the independent type, always have been. It means it's easy to move around with the firm, go after promotion. No roots," she added.

▶ *over*

## The Wonder of Water...

### THE REEKIE LINN

*Situated just off the A926 road between Blairgowrie and Kirriemuir, this waterfall is formed by the River Isla pouring through a deep cleft. The path through the woods leads to a viewpoint level with the top of the falls. The Isla flows onward to the Den of Airlie, where it joins the River Melgum. Curiously, a spot here near Airlie Castle has a strong reputation for being haunted. The late Princess Mary and the late Mabell, Lady Airlie, were among those who experienced an overwhelming sense of terror.*

He nodded, glad they were talking on a personal level.

"I'm glad I met you and Kevin, today, though," she said suddenly. "Zoos can feel pretty lonely places on a cold Sunday."

The small, cosy café suddenly seemed the most intimate place in the world to Richard.

Louise seemed to think so, too, because she shrugged, as if trying to shrug off the remark, laughing now, pulling back from him.

"Well, I'd better be going," she said. "I want to write up some reports this evening."

"Let me give you a lift," Richard suggested. "We can drop Kevin off, and then perhaps we can go to a film. I know a nice place where we could have Sunday lunch."

Linda wouldn't mind if he changed his plans . . .

"I have my own car, thank you. And I'm sorry, I do have work to do," she said firmly.

Louise stood up. She turned to go, then hesitated. "Why do you have to spoil things, Richard? Why do you have to see yourself as —" she seemed at a loss for words "— the lead in a bad romantic movie?

"Today I thought I saw a different side of you, but all you've got to offer is a line in chat. Do you see every girl as simply a challenge?"

She rummaged in her bag.

"I've been meaning to return this," she said frostily. "I'm sure it wasn't supposed to be attached to the Patterson report."

She placed a sheet of paper on the table, then she was gone.

Richard sat Kevin firmly in the chair opposite him and watched him finish his chocolate milk.

"Just when you think you're getting along together, off she goes." He sighed.

"Off she goes!" Kevin repeated, giggling as if it were the best joke he'd heard in a long, long while.

Richard stared at the sheet of paper in front of him and groaned. It was the drawing he'd done of Louise, the white kitten and himself in his Superman cloak.

He had Sunday lunch with Linda and Kevin as usual. When Kevin went for a nap, he helped Linda wash up, then poured them each a glass of wine.

THEY flopped down on the two big armchairs in front of the fire, and Linda sighed. "I'm going to miss these Sundays. You've been so good, Richard."

Richard had the distinct impression he was being given the cold-shoulder treatment for the second time that day.

"Am I going away?" he asked with studied politeness.

Linda laughed. "I hope not. I hope you'll still take Kevin to the zoo on Sundays — I hope you'll always be around, but . . ."

She sprang up and refilled his glass. "This Louise Goode. You're serious about her, aren't you?"

Richard looked at her closely. "How did you guess?"

"Good, it's time you got on with your own life, and it's time I stopped leaning on you so much. You know how much it's meant to me, your being there when I needed you. I didn't know how I was going to go on . . ."

Perhaps it was at that moment, Richard thought, that he realised he'd never been in love before, not the way that Linda had loved Colin.

He stared into his wine. Oh, he'd had plenty of romances, with candlelit dinners, walks in the park, cosy evenings in front of a log fire.

He remembered Joanna, with the long dark hair and fiery temper; Gina, part Italian, part Swiss, who cooked him pasta and beat him at chess.

Then there was Vicky. He couldn't pass a bookshop without remembering how they'd met, each reaching for the same copy of "The Complete Poems Of T.S. Eliot." He'd never admitted to her that he'd actually been trying to reach the latest Jeffrey Archer as a birthday present for his mother.

Louise Goode was right. He was always playing a part, being what he thought the women in his life wanted him to be.

Why couldn't he be himself, the way he was now, with Linda?

"You like her a lot, don't you?" Linda said, breaking into his thoughts.

He nodded. "Yes. But I don't think I'm part of Louise's plans," he said simply.

RICHARD did a lot of thinking that night, and on Monday morning he arrived early at the office. He stood by the lift till Louise appeared.

"Louise — can I talk to you?"

"I want to talk to you, too, Richard," she said, but this time her voice was softer. "I was a bit harsh at the park. I was — well, rude. I'm sorry. I'd like to explain."

"I'd like to explain, too," he answered, feeling shy.

They arranged to have lunch together.

"You choose," they both said together, then laughed.

Louise was called to the telephone, and Richard returned to his desk and stared at the pile of work in front of him.

He wasn't in love with Louise Goode. That was silly — he didn't know her. He liked her. He wanted to get to know her better, but that wasn't being in love.

He thought about Linda and her sadness. Sometimes love hurt. It was safer to go on playing the romantic lead in a bad movie, he told himself.

But Louise wouldn't accept that, and neither would he. He sat, hardly daring to breathe, feeling that somehow the whole world around him was as fragile as eggshell.

It was just the very beginning . . . □

GLENDA examined her reflection in the mirror, turning her face to the left and right and peering critically at the lines around her eyes and mouth.

She turned to Nan, uttering a huge sigh.

She said, "I'm fifty-eight years old, and I look every day of it. Don't deny it."

"I'm not denying it," Nan replied.

"You mean, I really look fifty-eight?" Glenda was mortified. "Honestly?"

"Sometimes more," Nan said firmly. "When that ankle of yours plays up and you come hobbling down the street wincing at every step, you look older than I do — and I shall never see sixty again."

Glenda sat down in the armchair and frowned as she sipped her tea.

"You're a good friend, Nan," she admitted, "and I couldn't have got through the years without you, but I wish you wouldn't be so honest all the time. Flattery is what I need at the moment."

"I can give you plenty of that!" Nan retorted. "Glenda, my dear, you're slim as a willow, lovely to look at, and as glamorous as a film star."

Glenda exploded into the bubbling laughter which was always close to the surface, waiting for a chance to erupt.

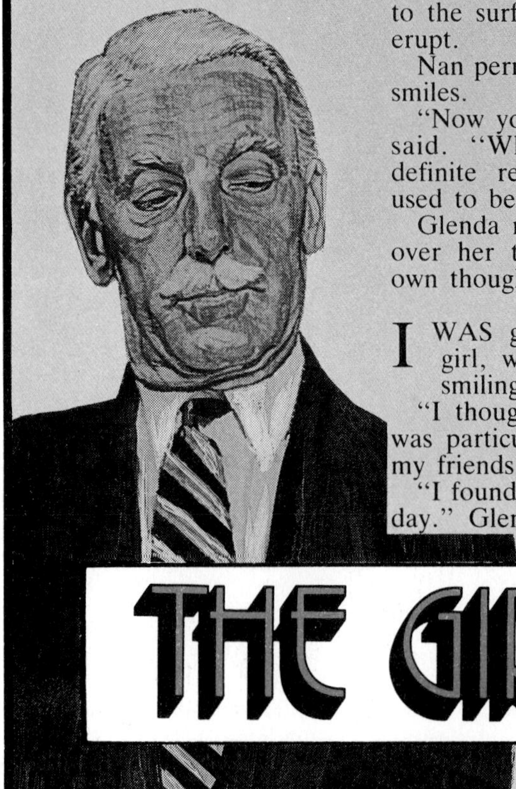

Nan permitted herself one of her rare smiles.

"Now you *are* looking younger," she said. "When you laugh, there's a definite resemblance to the girl you used to be."

Glenda nodded and dipped her head over her teacup, going deep into her own thoughts.

"I WAS good looking when I was a girl, wasn't I?" she asked at last, smiling reflectively.

"I thought so," Nan agreed. "But I was particularly plain, so I thought all my friends were beautiful."

"I found an old photograph the other day." Glenda got up and went to the

# THE GIRL OF

by
HEATHER
STEVENS

# YESTERYEAR

bureau, returning with a dog-eared snap which she held in front of Nan. "That's me — the happy brunette in the front."

"So it is." Nan squinted at it, and added, "And the miserable little mouse at the back is me.

"Now, you must admit, I haven't changed all that much. I wasn't much to look at then, and I'm not now, but you can tell it's me all right."

"I've changed out of recognition." Glenda went to the mirror again, staring hard at her reflection. "If only I could get rid of these lines," she mourned.

"You've paid for those lines with a lot of hard work and worry," Nan said firmly. "They tell the story of your life, my dear. So why bother to get rid of them?"

Glenda prodded the furrow on her brow with a fingertip. She murmured, "I should have looked after myself a bit more when I was younger. I could have taken a bit more care.

"Look at Chrissie Lennox," she added. "She's exactly my age, give or take a few months, and she looks years younger."

"Of course she does," Nan retorted. "Chrissie gave up work at twenty when she married a man with a bit of money. As far as I can tell, she's done little since, except paint her face and tour the shops.

"You, my dear, were widowed in your thirties and had to work non-stop for years to keep your children clothed and properly fed.

"You can't expect to look like Chrissie Lennox, and I'm sure I

don't know why you should wish to. There's nothing sillier than a woman close to sixty who tries to pretend she's forty-five."

Glenda pulled out a curl of her neat, grey hair and scowled at it. She muttered, "I wonder if my hair would take a colour rinse? Pale blue might look quite nice."

Nan put her cup down in its saucer with a sharp "clink."

"I don't know anything about colour rinses," she said, "but I left a pile of ironing because you said you had something urgent to discuss with me. Since I've arrived you've done nothing but simper in the mirror and ask a lot of silly questions.

"If you've got anything important to tell me you'd better do it now, because my Dan will soon be home expecting his tea, and it's not going to make itself."

"I'm sorry." Glenda went back to the armchair and sat down, biting her lip apprehensively. "There is something I want to say, Nan, but I don't know if you'll approve."

"Probably not," Nan replied shortly. "but you might as well tell me."

GLENDA paused for a moment, staring again at the old snapshot, then she handed it over to Nan.

"Do you remember the fellow standing behind me, with his hands on my shoulders?" she asked.

▶ over

## Night Song

THE harvest safely gathered in,
 the farmer wends his way,
A weary and contented man at
 close of busy day.
The fields he tends with loving care
 bathed in the sunset's light,
And slowly, all embracing, falls the
 curtain of the night.

The barn owl opens sleepy eye, wild
 creatures hide from sight,
Small mouse within his hidey hole lies
 quivering with fright.
The night wind stirs the rustling trees,
 the stars shine diamond bright,
And o'er the sleeping countryside,
 whispers goodnight, goodnight,
 goodnight.

— *Georgina Hall.*

"Alec Wilson," Nan said, her voice softening. "Oh, yes, I couldn't forget him. All the girls were after him, although he never looked at anyone but you, Glenda.

"We were all green with envy when the two of you got engaged. I never did understand why you let him slip away."

"We had an argument," Glenda confessed.

"I know that, but you never would tell me what it was about."

"I was weak and silly." Glenda sighed deeply at the memory. "Shortly after he put the ring on my finger, Alec told me about his plans to emigrate to Australia. He thought I'd be as thrilled and excited as he was.

"But I wasn't, Nan. The thought of going to the other end of the world terrified me. If anything had gone wrong, we wouldn't have had the money to turn round and come home again.

"I couldn't cope with the idea of leaving my family and friends, and perhaps never seeing them again.

"Alec was older than I was," she went on. "He'd travelled, seen the world. I was only nineteen — I'd barely stepped foot out of my own home town.

"I said that if he really loved me, he'd stay. He said that if I really loved him, I'd go with him anywhere, and trust him to care for me. In the end, I gave him his ring back and told him that if he wanted to live in a foreign country, he'd have to go without me."

"And so he went." Nan nodded wisely.

"Not straightaway. I didn't think he'd go at all, to tell the truth. For weeks I stayed at home waiting for him to knock at the door, but he never did.

"Then I heard that he'd sailed. He'd actually gone. I was heart-broken." Glenda's expression was sombre as she remembered.

"It happens to many of us," Nan said. "And you got over it in time, as we all do."

"Oh, yes." Glenda smiled, her mood of gloom lifting for a moment. "The following year I met John, and we married, and I was happy again. It was a good marriage, Nan."

"John was a fine man," Nan agreed. "You'd have to look far to find better."

"I was devastated when he died," Glenda confessed, her brow clouding again. "Even now I think of him almost every day."

"There's nothing wrong with that, my dear," Nan pointed out.

Glenda coloured a little and looked away from her friend.

She whispered, "But the thing is, I think of Alec, too. I always have done — even when John was alive. From time to time something would remind me of him, and I'd smile at the memory of him, and the laughter we shared, and his kisses."

She glanced at Nan, her eyes apprehensive.

"There," she said, "now I've told you. I daresay you're going to get very cross, and call me a wicked woman."

"I'm going to do nothing of the sort!" Nan replied. "A woman never forgets her first love. I never forgot mine, even though he was a funny little fellow.

"And I certainly wouldn't have forgotten a handsome young man like Alec Wilson."

She looked rather wistfully at the old photograph. "I wonder where he is now?"

HERE, in town," Glenda answered shortly.

"What?" Nan stared at her in disbelief. "I don't believe it. Alec's come home at last?"

"He's staying with his cousin, Annie, no more than a ten-minute walk from this spot," Glenda revealed. "I got a note from him this morning. He wants to come and see me."

"He's coming here, today?" Nan asked, her face flushed with excitement.

"No, tomorrow at four o'clock. He wanted to give me time to think about it. He said that if I decided not to see him I could phone Annie, and she'd give him the message."

"Of course you must see him," Nan assured her. "After all these years you've got to see him, if only to find out how he's spent his life."

"Oh, I know that already," Glenda said. "I don't see Annie often, but when I do, I always ask for news of him."

"And you've never mentioned him," Nan reproved her. "You never said a word. I often wondered what became of him. I expect he had a lot of adventures."

"Not really," Glenda replied. "He went into farming, and did quite well, I believe.

"He married when he was about thirty, and had four children — all grown up and living away now. His wife died the year before last."

"So, he's alone," Nan mused, "and thinking of you. That's what I told you — first loves are never forgotten."

"Oh, it's nothing like that." Glenda laughed in spite of herself. "If he comes round tomorrow, we're not going to throw ourselves into each other's arms like a couple of kids. After all, he's in his sixties now, and I'm fifty-eight and looking every second of it.

"We'll just sit and chat about old times, then say our goodbyes. I don't suppose he'll want to stay too long when he sees how I've changed.

"He'll remember me as I was — slim and dark haired and pretty. I don't know what he'll say when he sees the plain, plump, little grey-haired woman I've become. He's bound to be disappointed."

"You're not plain!" Nan protested. "You were always a nice-looking woman, and you still are."

"Tomorrow I must look my best."

"Of course you must," Nan agreed. "Take my advice and wear your cream jumper, and maybe just a touch of lipstick."

"No, I'm going to buy something new," Glenda said. "Something more pretty than practical."

"Well, it certainly won't do you any harm to spoil yourself for once," Nan told her. She stood up and started buttoning her jacket. "Now I must be off, or Dan will get home before I do."

"Do you think you could pop round tomorrow about three?" Glenda asked anxiously.

"To check that you look all right before he arrives?" Nan asked. "Of course I will, my dear. I wouldn't miss it for anything."

NAN arrived shortly after three the following afternoon.

When Glenda opened the door, Nan glanced at her briefly, saying nothing, and walked through into the living-room. She sat down on the sofa, then gave Glenda a long, appraising stare.

"Well, what do you think?" Glenda asked. She lifted her arms and turned slightly to the left and right. "I want your honest opinion."

Nan looked her up and down and clamped her lips tightly together.

Glenda was wearing a brightly-patterned cotton dress in gold and red, frilled at the hem, with high-heeled crimson sandals on her feet. Her face was heavily made-up, and the mascara was already beginning to run a little.

"Don't just sit there, Nan," she pleaded. "Surely you can say something."

Nan took a deep breath, then she said slowly, "In all my life I've never witnessed such a spectacle. If ever there was a case of mutton dressed up as lamb, you're it."

"I see," Glenda returned coldly. She turned away, tottering precariously on her high heels, muttering, "I thought it was rather a cheerful dress, actually."

"It's more than cheerful," Nan said, "it's hilarious."

All at once her face creased into a smile and she burst out laughing. "I'm sorry, I just can't help it! You look as if you've escaped from a circus!"

Glenda turned back to her friend, trying to keep her face straight, but it was no use. She started giggling uncontrollably, and fell into her armchair, helpless with laughter.

Nan was the first to pull herself together.

"This won't do," she said. "Alec will be here soon, and he can't find you looking like that.

"You dash upstairs and change. I'll have a cup of tea ready for you by the time you come down!"

★ ★ ★ ★

Glenda returned 20 minutes later. Her face was scrubbed clean, except a hint of pink on her lips. She was wearing the cream jumper and a plain, cream skirt, and she moved comfortably in her casual shoes.

"There, don't you feel better now?" Nan asked.

"I certainly do," Glenda replied. "I knew that dress was a mistake from the moment I bought it, but I thought it might have made me look just a bit younger."

"You look wonderful just as you are now," Nan told her. "All the excitement and laughter has done you good. You've got a sparkle in your eyes that I haven't seen for many a year."

Nan stood up and smiled at her friend. "I'll be on my way now. You just sit there and drink your tea, and don't worry about a thing. Alec's going to like the look of you — just wait and see."

THE doorbell rang at four o'clock sharp. Glenda's heart lifted and fluttered absurdly at the sound of it, and she went to the door. It was Alec all right, the same old Alec.

Glenda vaguely noted that the shock of dark hair was now white, and there were lines etched deeply into the sun-browned face.

But the things that mattered were still there — the lop-sided grin, the quizzical eyebrows, the warmth in the soft brown eyes.

"Alec!" She laughed out loud in delight. "You haven't changed a bit."

"And neither have you," he said. "You're still my laughing girl."

They smiled at each other in silence for a moment, then he said quietly, "I'm home, Glenda."

He opened his arms to her, and she went into them without hesitation. As they closed around her she closed her eyes and sighed, and on her face there was the smile of a young girl. □

# The Wonder of Water . . .

## THE FALLS OF FEUGH

*When the salmon follow their primitive urge to fight their way upstream, the Bridge of Feugh and its falls are a magnificent spectacle. Only half a mile south of the Deeside town of Banchory, the bridge is now unsafe for sightseers as it is narrow and carries so much traffic, but a new footbridge makes access easy. After viewing the salmon, a pleasant drive by car to Aberdeen follows the A943 along the south bank of the Dee.*

THIS is Terry Watson, from the information office in the town hall," the voice on the telephone said. "We have had a letter from an American who is coming to West Minsford — to trace his ancestors."

"Oh, how — how interesting," Gillian managed to gasp, wondering why in the world was Terry, a voice from the past, ringing to tell her this.

"I'm ringing," Terry went on, as if sensing her unspoken question, "because he says his great-grandparents lived in Forge Street. In fact, his great-grandfather was a smith and lived in the forge before going to America.

"They were both born and bred here, went to the village school, were married in the old church."

Gillian looked out of the front window, at the row of modern houses like this one, where she lived with her parents.

"My goodness!" she said. "Isn't he going to be disappointed when he sees the huge town that's grown round the old village?"

"Oh, I don't know," Terry

# Through Fresh Eyes

**by LINDA RITCHIE**

replied defensively. "It's a fine new town. The old church still stands and the vicar's digging out records.

"The village school is still in the grounds of the big, new secondary modern. The headmaster wants the American to go and visit."

"I see." Gillian went on, "I realise now why you've rung. Although this is just a modern house it's supposed to stand on the site of the old forge. And you'd like the American to visit us?"

"Yes, please. He does sound — very nice."

"Well, my parents aren't here at the moment. They're away visiting relatives, but I'm sure they'll be very happy to welcome the visitor from the States. When's he coming?"

TERRY hesitated, then said briskly, "It's tomorrow, I'm afraid — that's typically overseas visitor, isn't it? Just dropping from the skies!

"But, Gillian — if you could — if you would meet me with

him tomorrow evening . . . He's staying at the Old Bull where I've just booked him in."

Gillian didn't answer. She was remembering the last time she'd seen Terry, the quarrel, the finality of it all.

Evidently sensing her doubt, he continued in a less business-like voice, "I do realise, Gillian, that this is a bit — embarrassing for you.

"It is for me, too, you know! But I've been thinking, as we talked, if we could just treat the whole thing as a — a sort of business proposition, which it is, in a way.

"You do see — I couldn't *not* tell your family, couldn't *not* give you the chance to meet the man if you wished."

He stopped and waited until Gillian said at last, "OK, Terry, we'll handle it on a casual business footing. I know Mother and Dad will want to do their bit.

"Besides," she suddenly remembered, "we do have a section of an old wrought-iron gate which was made by one of the smiths who lived here. I bet your old American will be interested."

"Yes," Terry agreed, "and thanks, Gillian, for being so reasonable.

"Actually, he isn't an old American. He's on vacation from university where he's reading — wait for it — psychology. He'll be a bit of an egg-head analysing our every word.

"But he does sound quite human!"

Gillian promised to be at the Old Bull for dinner at six-thirty, and rang off, trying to convince herself that there'd be no time to feel uneasy.

There'd be so much to talk about — the history of the old village, all the changes, and the young American's plans.

She hadn't wanted, ever, to see Terry Watson again. It had all been so painful.

Isn't it odd, she thought, how you can get up in the morning to what you think is going to be just another day? You never know — you never think — that some unknown person on the other side of the world is going to bring the past crashing back into your life.

Now she told herself firmly that it was time to have her lunch, before going back to her job as sales assistant in the dress department of the town's biggest store.

WITHOUT any real enthusiasm, Gillian went through her wardrobe that night, deciding what to wear. She chose a simple, blue dress with a wide, black belt — and the beautiful dragon brooch modelled on one from Hadrian's Wall.

That brooch, in a manner of speaking, broke the ice, for as soon as they were introduced by Terry, Barry Eastwood asked about it.

"My brother brought it back after a trek along Hadrian's Wall," Gillian explained.

That led easily to talking about the wall and history, then back to local history.

From time to time, Gillian glanced at Terry. He looked different in some way, she thought, though he sounded just the same — apart from his sudden interest in history. She realised he must have been doing a lot of research.

True to what they had said on the phone, they were coolly polite to each other. They all ate a good meal with hearty appetites, and over coffee afterwards, Gillian told Barry about the iron gates.

"My parents are hoping you'll be able to come to see them — perhaps on Saturday?" she suggested.

Barry beamed. He turned to Terry. "Oh! We'd like that, wouldn't we?"

For the merest second Terry hesitated, with a brief, uncertain look at Gillian. Then he said briskly, "Of course. It's wonderfully good of your parents, Gillian."

Slightly puzzled, Gillian told herself that at least her mother and father would be there, and she expected they'd invite a few neighbours in as well.

That would be the end of it, anyway, and the last she'd see of either Terry or Barry.

IT was, in fact, a lovely day. The sun shone from a cloudless sky, and, as Gillian had expected, her parents had invited not only the neighbours, but also the headmaster of the school and his wife, with the vicar and his wife — a lively young couple new to the parish but intensely interested in stories about the old town.

Barry — tall, lively and a bit crumpled — made a splendid guest of honour.

Terry, Gillian noticed, was quietly chatting to the headmaster's wife and daughter, apparently not even noticing when Gillian's father showed Barry the old, wrought-iron gates.

Later, helping Gillian with the washing-up after tea, Barry said warmly, "You Brits really are marvellous! Everybody back home said I'd be overwhelmed with hospitality. I feel already as if I belong here, even though you have this modern town all around. Don't *you* think you can still feel the past, the history?"

"Oh, I do, especially in the garden here. The gate, too . . ."

"Yes," he murmured. "Did you know your father has said I can have it to take back home if I wish? I do think my great-grandfather might have made it."

"We'd like you to have it," Gillian told him.

"You are a dear," he said suddenly. Then, "Have you and Terry known each other long?"

Gillian hesitated, and looked out of the window at the young man who had once meant so much to her — until she realised they were much too different ever to be able to live together.

But the old charm was still there, she thought, and the memories could still hurt.

"I — hope you don't think I'm prying." Barry broke into her reverie.

"Of course not. I had just gone into what we call a brown study. What was it you said?" Gillian managed an easy laugh.

"I just asked you if you'd known Terry long?"

"Oh! Terry," Gillian said casually. "Well, I've seen him socially at town events, of course. But —" she hesitated and then added firmly and, she thought, with truth "— I don't really know him."

Nor did she, nor would she, ever.

WE'VE been wondering," she continued, changing the subject quickly, "how long you can stay, because Mother and Father said now you'd had a good look round the old oak beams at the Bull, we could put you up here.

"It's going to take time for you to look at all the school and church records, isn't it? Or can you photo-copy them?"

"Oh, I wouldn't ask to do that!" Barry looked round the kitchen and through the sliding doors into the big, homely lounge.

"It would be lovely to stay here," he admitted. "I feel so — so at home."

"Then that's settled!" Gillian said promptly.

"You mentioned records. Do you know anything about a place called the Public Record Office in London? I think there's one place where you can look up your ancestors, and another where you can trace their wills going back for hundreds of years."

"The wills are in a big building called Somerset House in the Strand. The births and marriage records are in a building just off the Strand but almost opposite," Gillian explained.

"Ah!" Barry said. "It's possible to go to London for a day from here, isn't it?"

"Certainly!" Gillian told him. "The journey takes about an hour and a half."

"Are those places open on Saturdays?" Barry stopped stacking the cups and saucers and put down his tea-towel.

"Never," Gillian told him.

"I was wondering if — if you'd come with me. Do you have a day off during the week?" he asked hesitantly.

Gillian looked up with shining eyes.

"Oh, yes, I'd enjoy that," she said. "The stores close every Monday, because they open all day Saturday."

"Right," Barry announced promptly, "then we're off to London on Monday!"

Gillian laughed. "Gosh, you don't waste any time, do you?"

"Of course not. I'm a Yank — but anyway I want to get some information before I check on the local records. And —"

"What's all this you want to do before local records?" Terry's voice broke into their talk. He put some cups and saucers on to a trolley.

"Gillian and I are going to London for the day on Monday," Barry said. Then to Gillian's consternation, he added, "Coming?"

Terry didn't hesitate. "You bet I am! I'll have to fix it with my boss, but of course —" he grinned "— a visiting Yankee comes under official duties!"

Gillian's heart sank, but there was no way she could avoid the outing now. She'd accepted Barry's invitation.

When Terry rang from his home later that night and asked her if she minded, she managed to say calmly, "No. Why should I? Anyway, as you said, it's part of your job."

"Well, I just thought afterwards maybe I'd be playing gooseberry. Barry's young and handsome!"

"Don't be so idiotic!"

"OK, then. I'll meet you at the station."

DON'T look so tense," Gillian's mother said, seeing her off at the gate on Monday morning. "Remember, it's just as embarrassing for Terry."

Yes, Gillian thought, I suppose it is.

The journey to London was, in fact, fun and very lively in a full compartment which included a couple of Australians.

It wasn't until they reached the Record Office that Gillian realised the day wasn't going to be quite as she'd imagined.

"Thanks a lot for bringing me here. And now," Barry said, looking at them with a very odd look, Gillian thought, "you two have a nice day. What if we meet this evening at that hotel down the road for a meal?"

Terry, Gillian realised, looked as dumbstruck as she felt.

But, equal to the occasion, he said, "OK, if that's what you want. Shall we meet at about half past five?"

"Fine!" Barry agreed, and with a wave of his hand he strode across the courtyard of Somerset House.

"Very odd," Terry murmured. "I suppose he's decided that what he wants to do is a bit private. He seems different today, somehow."

They stood watching the traffic streaming down the Strand. "Don't you think it's a bit — well — fishy?" he went on.

"Oh, no," Gillian said promptly. "He's so normal — everybody has taken to him. Well, as we have the whole day, I think I'll go and look round the shops."

"I've a better idea. It's too hot for shops, and I remember you once said you'd like to see the Festival Hall and the National Theatre.

"Let's cross the road, and walk there across Waterloo Bridge. I know there's a lot to see and at the theatre they have very good food bars. You can eat on the terrace facing the river," Terry finished persuasively.

I don't want to go, Gillian told herself. But an inner voice whispered that she did. She'd love to see the theatre and eat by the river.

Despite their differences, Terry had always been fun to do things with, when he wasn't off playing football or attending some other sporting event.

She turned to him with a smile. "I'd enjoy that."

For an instant he laid a hand on her arm.

"I'll try to make it a happy day for you — for us," he promised.

THEY toured the Festival Hall, then joined a party being shown over the National Theatre, before queueing up to take their lunch out on to the terrace facing the Thames.

They later took a bus down the Strand, and walked along the Mall to Buckingham Palace, then into St James's Park where they watched and fed the ducks.

"I'm glad we came," Terry said, just before they started back to join Barry. "It's — it's almost like old times, isn't it?"

When Gillian kept her eyes averted, he went on quietly and earnestly, "I know I was thick-headed and selfish, Gillian."

"I daresay I was, too," she whispered.

"Let's say we've both grown up a bit. You've made me think, Gillian. Can't we be friends again?"

No, Gillian thought, we can't.

She turned to look at him straight in the eye. "I don't think we need to be enemies, Terry. Let's just enjoy this day and leave it at that."

"It must be Barry. I was afraid of that."

"Don't be ridiculous! He's probably got a string of girlfriends back home!" She added bluntly, "Anyway, for goodness' sake, we've only just met."

When they entered the hotel, half an hour later, Barry was sitting in one of the easy-chairs in the foyer, deep in a travel magazine.

He seemed slightly evasive about his researches, but very interested in their day, after telling them he'd decided to return to London and stay a week or so.

LATER, in the train going home, Barry disappeared into the corridor soon after the train left the station, leaving Gillian and Terry alone in the otherwise empty compartment.

"There's something wrong with that young man," Terry said. "I'm sure of it."

"Well, he *looks* OK, but why on earth should he walk out on us, just like that?"

"Know what?" Terry said, standing up and looking determined. "I'm jolly well going to ask him! After all, it could be we've done something to offend him without realising it."

He didn't wait for Gillian to reply. He just swept out of the compartment, and down the corridor.

Gillian looked after him, startled. This was a new Terry, she thought. Once he wouldn't have bothered, wouldn't have cared — probably wouldn't even have noticed — that someone was acting strangely.

He's different, she thought. He really is.

Wryly, she wondered if perhaps she was, too. But it was no use.

As she'd told him when they split up, he needed a different sort of girl, a sporty girl who could —

Gillian remembered how he'd butted in then and said bitterly, "Who could cope with an only son who's been spoiled rotten."

Gillian remembered the look in his eyes when he'd said, "You made me think, Gillian."

She'd felt so stirred then by all the old charm — much more potent than Barry's, she thought ruefully.

She turned round as the door of the compartment slid back and Terry came in. He was grinning broadly.

"It's OK," he said, "nothing at all mysterious."

He paused, wondering how much, if anything, to tell Gillian of what Barry had actually said.

"Well, it's like this, Terry," he'd assured him. "I just had this instinctive feeling that there was something between you and Gillian — but it had gone wrong.

"I wondered if it could be anything to do with me, or whether I was rubbing salt into wounds just by being here."

"So," Terry had said to him, "you thought if you kept out of our way today we might get ourselves sorted out?"

"Yes, being away from your usual environment. You don't have to explain, to tell me anything. If I'm wrong —"

"Barry," Terry had thumped his back heavily, "you were right on target . . ."

WELL," Gillian said, "what is it? I'm waiting."

Terry leaned forward and took both her hands. "It was simply and only that Barry likes us both very much. He'd thought — realised that we — that I —" he stammered "— that I was very much in love with you and there was something —"

"Are you telling me," Gillian asked, "that Barry thought he was being a gooseberry?"

"That's right," Terry said, relieved.

He came and sat beside her and put his arms around her. "I told him he was bang on target — that we'd been in love and out of love and now we were in love again. And don't you dare to deny it!"

"What I've seen and learned today," Gillian said, "is that though we might be difficult to live with — we can't live without each other! Hi, where are you going?"

Terry had jumped up and opened the door. "I'm going to tell Barry he can come in and congratulate us!" □

# Secret Heart

LOVE is like a flower, it needs a
chance to grow,
A special kind of cosseting that only
the heart can know.
Sometimes it needs the salt of tears, as
warm and soft as rain.
If fading, it needs warmth, like sun, to
make it bloom again.

Yes, love is like a slender flower, its
beauty is the same.
It's like a haunting perfume when
someone breathes your name.
Just like a sweet bouquet, love's
radiance lends such grace
To anyone whose secret joy shows upon
their happy face.

*— Georgina Hall.*

ALONE in her bed-sit, Beth leaned her elbows on the window-sill and gazed down into the crowded street below. She was scarcely aware of the stream of traffic or of the hurrying feet of the passers-by. Her thoughts that summer evening were with Rod — and with an unknown girl called Sylvia.

Beth glanced at her watch. It was seven o'clock. In just half an hour, Rod would be calling for her. His blue eyes, serious when he wasn't smiling, would light up suddenly the moment he saw her, just as they always did. But would they be lighting up for *her*, she wondered. Or was she, after all, no more than a substitute, a second-best?

It had been Rod's sister, Tina, who had first mentioned Sylvia.

"Know something, Beth?" she'd murmured thoughtfully on a Saturday morning just a few days ago when the two girls had met for a coffee in town. "I'm glad Rod's got over Sylvia at last.

"You're very like her, of course," she'd continued quietly. "Maybe that's why —"

She'd broken off quickly then, as if she were scared of saying something tactless. The two girls had sipped their coffee in silence till Beth had felt she could bear the silence and suspense no longer.

LOOK – who *is* Sylvia?" she'd blurted out at last. As soon as she'd said it, she remembered the words of a song a song she'd learned years ago at school.

*Who is Sylvia? What is she?*

The rest of the words had faded from her mind, but one fact remained. The Sylvia in the song was someone special — as sweet and loving as she was beautiful . . .

"You mean — Rod hasn't told you?" Tina had stared at Beth in frank astonishment.

"Still, after all, it's a good sign, isn't it?" she'd added hastily. "It shows it's only you he thinks of now.

"I thought he might have mentioned her. They were engaged, you see, for several months."

But, no — Rod hadn't mentioned Sylvia.

Beth had glanced at Tina who, at 15 years old, was still very much Rod's "little" schoolgirl sister.

"A good sign, isn't it?" she'd suggested innocently.

But it wasn't, of

course, Beth had thought. It was full of an ominous significance. Rod would have spoken of Sylvia long ago if she hadn't been too special, too important . . .

It was then that Tina had quickly changed the subject and begun to talk about some disco she'd been to.

Beth wasn't listening — she'd been longing to be alone for a while to think. There was suddenly so much to think about.

She'd left the café and begun to wander through the crowded street, trying to come to terms with what she'd heard. She'd never been really in love till she'd met Rod — and somehow she'd always taken it for granted that she was Rod's first love, too. How naïve could she be?

THREADING her way among the milling crowd of Saturday shoppers, Tina had found herself thinking of that other Saturday morning, three months ago, when she and Rod had met for the first time.

It was in the local lending library — the two of them had been standing in the queue, waiting to have their books stamped, and somehow they'd started chatting.

"I see you're keen on poetry," Rod had said, glancing at Beth's book.

"I don't know a lot about it," she'd confessed. "But — what's the saying? 'I know what I like . . .' "

"Me, too." He'd smiled at her then, and she'd smiled back at him, annoyed with herself for blushing.

Then suddenly he wasn't like a stranger any more — he was someone she seemed to recognise quite clearly, as if she'd been waiting for him all her life.

He'd walked her home that day and they'd talked a lot. It seemed he'd left college just two years before and was teaching at the local comprehensive.

After that first, casual meeting, it became an accepted thing that the two of them met in the library on Saturday mornings. All through the week, Beth would find herself longing for these meetings,

# IN NO-ONE'S SHADOW

**by ELIZABETH FARRANT**

keeping her fingers crossed, half-scared that Rod mightn't turn up.

But he was always there, and as they talked together Beth had felt a wonderful sense of closeness, of belonging.

The night Rod kissed her for the very first time was a night she knew she'd remember always. He'd driven her out into the countryside and they'd parked the car in a narrow, little lane and gone for a walk in the lingering, summer twilight scented with flowers and new-mown hay.

"Beth," he'd whispered softly, "you know I love you?"

As their lips met, she'd responded to the tenderness of his kiss with a warmth which seemed to come from deep inside her. During the next few weeks, when their love had seemed to deepen with every day, she'd told herself she'd never been so happy.

Yet this evening, looking back, she found herself wondering for the first time about herself and Rod. How well did they know each other, after all?

All kinds of memories came back to her — of things she'd accepted quite easily at the time as a part of Rod's serious nature, but which now seemed full of a new significance. There were times when she'd caught his blue eyes watching her — thoughtfully, even a little wistfully. Then there were his spells of quietness every now and then, for no apparent reason . . .

Had he been tracing her likeness to this other girl, this girl named Sylvia?

Beth turned from the window and stared into the mirror, trying to see her face the way Rod saw it — as a substitute for someone else's face. Oh, quite a good substitute, she assured herself with a hint of bitterness.

It was then that Beth first became aware of the resentment mounting up inside her. She wanted Rod to love her for herself — not as a shadow of some other girl.

BY the time Rod called for her that evening, Beth felt she could bear the strain no longer.

He took her in his arms and held her closely.

"What's wrong, Beth?" he asked her, quick, as always, to sense her mood.

"Tell me about Sylvia," she said quietly.

She felt his arms slacken around her just a little. "Sylvia? She was — a girl I used to go around with."

His voice sounded strained, unnatural.

"That much I'd gathered," Beth retorted, aware of the brittleness in her own voice. "I also know that you got around to getting engaged to her, though you never so much as mentioned her to me."

The tears were welling up in her eyes.

"Why didn't you, Rod?" she demanded in a burst of desperation. "Because you still love her? Because you still want her back?"

There was a pause which seemed to last too long.

"Look, Beth — Sylvia's dead," Rod answered quietly.

There was another pause — an even longer one.

"I'm sorry," Beth muttered awkwardly.

It sounded so inadequate, she thought, yet what else was there for her to say?

"It was an accident," he explained in that same quiet, flat, monotonous voice. "She'd kept her old bike — the one she had at school. She loved to cycle out into the country.

"She was like that — Sylvia," he went on, half to himself. "There were times when she seemed to need to be on her own — she enjoyed the quietness and the peace of it all.

"That's how it happened — the accident, I mean. She was cycling to Applegate village one evening — it was one of her favourite haunts — and halfway down the hill she was hit by a lorry. She was killed instantly.

"She was a pretty wonderful person," he added.

Beth nodded. "I'm sure she was."

She glanced at her watch. "Look, Rod, I've just remembered — I can't go out tonight. There are things I must do . . ."

Now that she knew the truth about Sylvia she felt worse, much worse. Rod's image of Sylvia would always be the same. He'd always remember her as young and beautiful.

She, Beth, would change. The time would come when she wouldn't look like Sylvia any more. And how would Rod feel about her then, she wondered.

★ ★ ★ ★

Beth never knew what made her go to Applegate that evening, but she found herself doing just that. She caught a bus from the centre of the town, and half an hour later she was walking down the hill which Rod had mentioned, approaching the spot where Sylvia had died.

The village was small — just a huddle of stone-walled cottages at the bottom of the hill. She arrived there tired and depressed, wishing she hadn't come.

There was no chance of a cup of tea or coffee — the little cafés, mainly for visitors in the holiday season, had closed hours earlier. But the tiny village pub, of course, was open.

It was cosy and quiet, used mainly by friendly local "regulars." Beth asked for a lager and lime, but the woman behind the bar just stared at her blankly.

"I'm sorry, my dear," she apologised quickly when Beth repeated her order. "But I thought — I thought for a moment you were someone else. You know what silly tricks your eyes can play."

She handed Beth her drink, quite cheerful now, her plump face creased in smiles. The next moment her eyes were serious.

"You reminded me of a poor young girl who was killed on her bicycle on Applegate Hill just over a year ago," she explained. "She used to come in here — oh, many a summer evening — and sit by the window, looking out for her boy . . ."

Leaning her dimpled elbows on the bar, the woman prepared herself for a cosy gossip. "Tall, dark and handsome he was — this boy of hers. They made a lovely couple, as I remarked to my husband many a time.

"Mind you, the thought did sometimes cross my mind that theirs was what you might call a secret romance. It's not as if they ever arrived together . . ."

She broke off, startled, as Beth pushed aside her unfinished drink. "I'm sorry, I have to go. It's later than I thought — I must run for my bus . . ."

*Tall, dark and handsome.* Those words were echoing in Beth's mind as she hurried along the narrow village street. Rod, of course, was fair, with deep blue eyes.

So Sylvia — the girl Rod had loved and trusted so completely — had had a secret love?

All the way home in the bus, Beth stared through the window like someone in a dream. Rod should be told — it was surely only right that he should know.

And Beth couldn't suppress the other thought that flashed across her mind — once he did know, she wouldn't be Sylvia's shadow any more. She'd be Beth, the girl who really and truly loved him, the girl who would always come first.

WHEN Beth reached her door, she saw Rod standing there in the glow of the lamplight. He held out his arms and Beth ran into them, forgetting everything but the joy of his nearness, the sweet, familiar warmth of his embrace.

"My lovely Beth," he whispered tenderly. "I was worried sick when you rushed away like that this evening. Somehow — don't ask me why — I got this feeling that you weren't coming back to me. Promise you'll never, never go away."

He tilted her face to the light. "I've been waiting here for you for hours and hours. Where have you been?"

Beth felt as if she'd been on a long, dark journey into the past, but she didn't say so.

Instead, she just whispered, "I'll always come back to you, Rod."

He was holding her tightly now. "Well, mind you do — I love you too much to lose you. Know something, Beth? You're the loveliest thing that's happened in my life."

As they kissed in the yellow glow of the lamplight, Beth knew she would never tell about Sylvia — her secret was safe in the past where it belonged.

The bitterness and resentment had ebbed away. All Beth felt now was a genuine sense of sorrow for a girl so full of life who'd died so young.

She and Rod were facing the future together, and it had never looked more beautiful. □

I'VE got a gem of a job for you this morning, Millie!" Mr Doughty cried, jumping up from his littered desk.

Millie Jones put her bag down among the papers and the filing trays, and smiled at Mr Doughty.

This was what she liked about working at the Doughty Typing Agency: Mr Doughty's enthusiasm, the homely informality of his untidy little office, and the excitement of coming in like this on Monday morning not knowing what sort of a job would be waiting.

Millie supposed there must be disadvantages about working as a temp, but she had never been able to discover what they were. She had been with Mr Doughty for three years now, and she couldn't imagine ever going back to an ordinary office job.

"Mrs Ruth Ray, Data-Date Agency, Ten Cross Street," Mr Doughty announced, holding up a letter on blue paper. "Mrs Ray needs a temporary typist urgently, due to a sudden rush of clients."

He looked at Millie over his spectacles, thinking how small and neat she looked in her trim, grey suit.

"Computer dating," Mr Doughty said. "A fairly new idea, but

**by ELIZABETH ROBERT**

evidently very popular."

"Among some people," Millie retorted.

"Will you pop along to Cross Street and see what you can do?" Mr Doughty asked, suppressing a smile.

"Very well, Mr Doughty," Millie said briskly, checking her bag.

CROSS STREET was a long, narrow street of Victorian houses which had been converted into offices. In the hallway of No. 10, Millie found a board giving the names of the occupants.

There was a gentlemen's tailor, a firm of solicitors, and Studio Ten, where "photographic portraits of distinction were taken."

On the first floor, in the midst of all this respectability, was the Data-Date Agency, "prop. Mrs Ruth Ray, Find Your Mate Through Data-Date."

Millie had some difficulty finding Data-Date. The notice outside was quite small and discreet, then when she opened the door there it was — a desk with a typewriter and a vase of flowers, one or two comfortable chairs, and against the wall opposite the door the Data-Date computer.

Our dumb friend, Millie thought grimly, looking at the machine with dislike.

A girl came through from the far room and said, "Hello! I'm awfully sorry but I didn't hear you come in!"

She was tall and slim with red hair, and she wore a green, silky dress the colour of her eyes.

Millie thought she had never seen anyone so lovely.

"Millie Jones," Millie said, hoping her nose hadn't begun to shine. "I'm from the Doughty Typing Agency."

"Oh, marvellous! I'm Ruth Ray. I can't tell you how pleased I am to see you!"

She looked as though she really meant it.

"Well, you can get to work right away if you don't mind, Millie. It's all right if I call you Millie, isn't it? And you must call me Ruth.

"There's rather a pile of letters, I'm afraid, but if you could possibly get them off today I'd be awfully grateful . . ."

The computer suddenly gave a metallic click that nearly made Millie jump out of her skin, then began humming in a low baritone.

"Are you having trouble?" she asked nervously.

"Not in the least," Ruth assured her, giving the computer a severe look. "He's just feeling a bit overworked. We've been very busy this week.

"He'll be OK in a couple of minutes," Ruth went on. "He's very quiet when he settles down. You'd hardly know he was there."

She talks about the thing as if it were the family pet instead of a monster that interferes in people's lives, Millie thought grimly, then sighed and settled herself for work.

Ah, well, perhaps she was just old fashioned. People wouldn't come and consult a computer unless they wanted to, and perhaps there were those who really believed they could find romance with the help of a machine.

I couldn't do it, she thought as she inserted paper into the typewriter. However desperate I was I couldn't do it. It's so — so *calculating*. Besides, what have machines to do with love?

AT that moment, the office door opened and a young man appeared. When he saw Millie he started visibly

"Hello!" Millie said quickly. "Can I — we — help you?"

He stood with one hand on the doorknob, looked round and swallowed.

"It's all right," he said in a loud stage-whisper. "I'll come back another time, when it's more convenient . . ."

"Good morning!" Ruth said, coming in from the other room and giving the nervous young man her wonderful smile. "Are you Mr Picton, by any chance?"

"Well, as a matter of fact, yes, I am."

"Mr Picton!" Ruth's voice was warm and pleased. "How good of you to come in! Please sit down. This is Miss Jones, my confidential secretary. Millie, dear, could I have a Data Form please? You'll find them in the top drawer of the desk."

In seconds, Mr Picton was seated in a comfortable chair. A cup of coffee appeared as by magic, then Ruth sat beside him with an air of friendly interest.

Millie watched discreetly from behind the typewriter.

"Before we begin, Mr Picton," Ruth said gently, "I would like to reassure you that your interview will be entirely confidential.

"Most of our clients at Data-Date feel a little nervous at first, and that's quite understandable."

Mr Picton coughed and relaxed a little.

"I must also reassure you," Ruth went on, giving her lovely smile, "that if you change your mind about using the services of Data-Date, you have only to say so. You are under no obligation at all, at any

▶ *over*

## ST ANDREWS HARBOUR AND ST RULE'S TOWER

The building of St Andrews Cathedral began in 1160 on a site adjoining St Rule's Church. Although only the ruined gables and parts of the south wall now exist, the Cathedral was by far the greatest church in Scotland. St Rule's Tower, probably erected towards the end of the 11th century, is a notable landmark even from the Angus coast. In St Andrews the atmosphere is town and gown, with the scarlet-gowned undergraduates of Scotland's oldest university bringing a splash of colour to the ancient streets, especially when they take their traditional Sunday morning walk along the harbour walls.

ST. ANDREWS HARBOUR and ST. RULE'S TOWER : J CAMPBELL KERR

time. There will be no pressure exerted on you."

Mr Picton stretched out his legs and took a drink of coffee.

"Oh, well," he said. "Now that I'm here . . ."

Millie watched, enthralled. To say that Ruth treated her client with kid gloves would have been the understatement of the year.

Mr Picton blossomed. He had once won a cup for table-tennis, he confessed to Ruth.

"Interested in sport," went down on the Data Form, along with other details of interests and hobbies. When they reached the more personal questions, Mr Picton had finished his coffee and forgotten his nerves.

"I'm not — well — very tall, and it can be rather — um —" he murmured.

"I should guess from what you've told me, Mr Picton, that you admire the rather more petite young lady?" Ruth said, as if she hadn't heard.

When the Data Form was completed, Mr Picton seemed quite disappointed.

"Leave everything with me," Ruth assured him, smiling. "Don't worry, we'll be in touch. Data-Date is here to help — discreet and dignified."

She ushered Mr Picton out, and turned to find Millie smiling admiringly.

"Well, there you are, Millie," she said. "That's all there is to it."

"I think you're wonderful," Millie told her and blushed. "He's gone home feeling like a million dollars."

"Quite a lot don't come back," Ruth admitted cheerfully. "Filling in the Data Form and talking to someone is often all they need."

"But isn't that an awful waste of your time?" Millie asked in astonishment.

"Giving someone who's lonely a little attention is never a waste of time, is it?" Ruth said.

ON Wednesday morning, Millie arrived to find the cleaning lady running a duster over the filing cabinet.

"Good morning," Millie said. "Isn't Mrs Ray in yet?"

The woman shook her duster and sniffed. "No idea. Don't have much to do with her."

Millie's opinion about Data-Date had changed remarkably over the last couple of days. She had become more and more interested in the people who came through the door, and more and more fascinated by their variety.

She still didn't like the idea of the computer but that was really incidental, wasn't it, she told herself. The wonderful thing about Data-Date was Ruth talking to all these shy, lonely people and making them feel important and confident again. Our dumb friend in the corner was just window-dressing.

Millie glanced cautiously at the computer, but he appeared to be asleep. She was getting used to the clicking and the humming now, but she couldn't get rid of the uncomfortable feeling that he was sitting there watching her, especially when the small lights came on.

At half past nine, the telephone rang.

"Millie?" Ruth inquired. "The car won't start. Can you hold the fort until I get there?"

"Well," Millie said doubtfully. "Will you be long? I mean, is it something drastic?"

"Haven't the faintest," Ruth replied cheerfully. "I'll have to ring the garage."

"What shall I do if anyone comes in?" Millie asked. "Like a client? I'm not used to talking —"

"You'll manage wonderfully, Millie, dear," Ruth said. "You know how to fill in a Data Form, after all. I have complete confidence in you."

"Well — all right. But get here as soon as you can."

Millie hung up and found the cleaning lady listening.

"Well," she said with relish. "You've landed right in it, haven't you?"

Millie didn't answer. She thought about all the things Mr Doughty had told her about keeping calm and carrying on under adverse conditions.

"Best of luck," the cleaning lady said, collecting her things. "And if you take my advice you won't touch *that* thing!"

WHEN she had gone, Millie sat and looked at the computer. It was the first time they had been alone together.

"Don't be silly," she told herself. "It's only a machine, and probably not even switched on. Just ignore him."

But she was nervous and her typing not as perfect as usual. It wasn't only the computer squatting there like a sleeping tiger that made her jumpy, but the thought of what she would do if a prospective client walked in.

She got on with the morning's letters, though, and by half past ten had begun to breathe more easily.

She had a coffee and began to enjoy being in charge of the office, so much so that she approached the computer and gave him a friendly pat.

As her fingers touched the cold metal, the office door burst open, and she turned with a little shriek. It would be hard to say who was the more startled, Millie or the dark-haired young man standing in the doorway.

"Oh, sorry!" he said, recovering. "I wanted to see Mrs Ruth Ray."

"I'm afraid she's out!" Millie gasped.

He looked confused. "Oh?"

"She'll be in later."

She seemed to be having difficulty getting her breath and her heart was pounding in an alarming manner.

Millie told herself it was because he had burst in so suddenly, but it was really because he was looking at her very intently. He had hazel eyes with long, dark lashes and was without doubt the most handsome man she had ever seen.

It was only after the initial impact that the thought occurred to Millie — what was a man who looked like that doing at Data-Date?

"Would you like me to come back another time?" he asked.

Millie said, "No!" rather too quickly, and blushed.

"I'm sure I can help you," she went on, trying to collect her wits and look efficient. "Won't you come in and sit down? I'm Mrs Ray's confidential secretary."

"Are you really?" He closed the door.

He sat comfortably in one of the chairs and waited while she got a Data Form and found her pen. Then Millie sat down, too, and found those hazel eyes looking at her again.

"Before we begin, Mr — er —" she murmured faintly.

"Carsfield," he said. "Tony Carsfield."

"Before we begin, Mr Carsfield, I would like to reassure you that your interview will be entirely confidential. Most of our clients at Data-Date feel a little nervous at first . . ." Millie's voice tailed away uncertainly.

"Do they?" he said.

"I must also reassure you," Millie pressed on bravely, "that if you change your mind about using the services of Data-Date, you have only to say so. You are under no obligation at all, at any time.

"Shall we fill in a Data Form?" Millie croaked.

"If you'd like to," he said agreeably.

THEY made good progress, except that every time Millie asked a question about himself, he asked her one, too, which wasn't the way things were supposed to go at all.

It was quite amazing how they agreed about things — holidays abroad, Italian food, and equal opportunities for women — which weren't actually on the form but seemed to come up somehow.

"What kind of work do you do, Mr Carsfield?" Millie asked.

"I'm in computers."

There was a long silence. Millie compressed her lips and turned to

▶ *over*

## KIDWELLY CASTLE, WALES

The market town of Kidwelly, at the head of the Gwendraeth estuary in Dyfed, is dominated by its huge castle. A fortress was first built here in 1094 by Fitz Hammon, the first Norman conqueror of South Wales, then re-modelled by Edward I in the 13th century. Kidwelly holds the record of being probably the most fought-over castle in Britain.

KIDWELLY CASTLE, WALES : J CAMPBELL KERR

the more personal details.

He said he liked tall, slim women, preferably red-heads, but that wasn't too important so long as they were intelligent and well read.

The more he talked, the more depressed Millie became.

"Have you done this kind of work long?" he asked when they had finished.

"No, not very long."

"It must be very interesting."

"Oh, very," Millie said bleakly.

"And what about our dumb friend here?" he asked, getting up and going to look at the computer.

"Oh, please don't touch him!" Millie cried nervously. "If anything goes wrong, I shan't know what to do!"

"Do?" Tony said, surprised. "Why, you just pull the plug out. He's not a very up-to-date model," he added. "If you'll excuse the pun. Not a patch on the one I have at the office."

The computer gave an angry click and woke up.

"What's happening?" Millie squeaked, jumping up.

"Start of programme," Tony said, reaching round to where Data Forms were beginning to flick into a shallow tray. He picked out a few and looked at them.

"One moment!" Millie said. "You shouldn't be doing that!"

"Force of habit," Tony apologised. "I was just interested in the —"

AT that moment the door opened and there was Ruth, slightly out of breath and looking breathtakingly lovely.

"Tony!" she cried. "I didn't expect you until the weekend!"

"Did you know your computer's off-alignment?" Tony said. "Look at these margins —"

"Never mind the margins!" Ruth cried in delight. "Let me look at *you*!"

And she flung her arms round him and kissed him.

Well, Millie thought, he said he liked tall, slim women and preferably red-heads. He was probably talking about Ruth all the time.

Her eyes lit on the Data Form still lying on the desk, and realisation dawned.

"Excuse me," Millie said in a voice like ice. "I was wondering about your Data Form, Mr Carsfield?"

"Oh — yes —" He was embarrassed.

"Please don't worry about it," Millie continued picking up the form and tearing it carefully into bits. "I'm afraid I made a mistake. I didn't realised you'd come to see Mrs Ray socially."

"Millie," Ruth began, "you didn't think Tony was a client?"

She looked from one to the other. "Oh, Tony, you didn't get Millie to fill out a Data Form for you?"

She began to laugh.

"Yes, that's right," Millie said, dangerously calm. "He seemed to find it all very amusing, and now I know why.

"You'll be pleased to know, Mrs Ray, that Mr Carsfield likes tall, slim women with red hair." Her voice was beginning to tremble. "And of course they must be intelligent, too, not gullible or unsophisticated."

"Now look here, Millie," Tony put in.

Millie said in a freezing voice, "I beg your pardon, Mr Carsfield?"

"Now, Millie, dear," Ruth said soothingly.

Millie looked at her, and thought how much she had got to like Ruth these last couple of days, and how it was all spoilt now.

"It was a despicable thing to do!" Millie told Tony. "I suppose you thought it would be a bit of a lark to string me along then tell Ruth about it afterwards? Over a cosy dinner somewhere, I suppose?

"Well, Mr Carsfield, I'd like you to know that your amusing little prank has succeeded. I shall now go back to the typing agency where I work and try to forget I ever heard of Data-Date."

"Millie," Tony said, "you're wonderful!"

"No!" Millie retorted. "I'm small and plump and mousy and not very intelligent. If I filled in a Data Form, our dumb friend in the corner there would probably come up with someone like — like Mr Picton!"

"Who's Mr Picton?" Tony asked, mystified.

"Mr Picton is a rather nervous, lonely person who feels shy because he's not very tall, and who came here for help and understanding. He isn't heartless, or conceited or —"

MILLIE, dear," Ruth interrupted gently. "He's my brother."

"What? Who?"

"Tony," Ruth said. "He's my brother and I'm very, very fond of him. When you get to know him better, you'll find that he's really the kindest person in the world."

"I haven't the slightest intention of getting to know —"

"I'm so sorry, Millie," Tony said, coming and looking down at her. "It was a stupid thing to do, but I only did it because you looked so nervous and so sweet and I wanted to talk to you. Will you forgive me, Millie?"

There was a metallic click from the computer followed by a whirring sound.

"What's happening?" Millie asked faintly, but Ruth had disappeared and they were alone with our dumb friend.

"Tony?" Millie gasped. "He's making a peculiar noise — what do you think we ought to do?"

"I told you before," Tony said, kissing her. "Pull out the plug. It's only a machine."

"I know that," Millie replied, kissing him back. "But he's in the middle of a programme."

"So what?" Tony said. "We can't let a machine rule our lives, can we? Besides, what have machines to do with love?"

"Nothing, Tony," Millie agreed dutifully. "Nothing at all." □

by
GAYE
WILSON

# TOUR OF

I WAS not at all pleased when my mother discovered Apr Cottage. I'd wanted her to buy a flat nearer to mine, so that w could help each other out from time to time. It seemed the mos sensible thing to do now that she had sold the shop and retired.

But I'd reckoned without the romantic streak I'd always suspecte lingered in her subconscious, and she was determined that I shoul go and look over the place.

"You do realise," I pointed out, "I'm a civil engineer, not surveyor. That's what you need."

"A surveyor," she said flatly, "would condemn the place out o hand. They prefer nasty new buildings with about as much characte as a roll of linoleum."

I sighed.

"They're bound to cover themselves, Mother," I explained "Otherwise they could get sued right and left."

SHE smiled coaxingly. "I feel we can get by with your engineerin skill and my intuition."

I gave up then and swigged the remains of the sherry she ha handed me. "When do you want me to take you?"

"I don't want you to take me, David, I want you to go on you own. If I'm hovering in the background, all eager and enthusiastic, i could cloud your judgment, which I want to be unbiased."

She looked at me anxiously. "Do you understand?"

"I suppose so. You've got a point. Where's the form you got fror the agents?"

She passed it over.

"There's a picture on the back," she said. "It's my dream cottage."

"Drains are more important than dreams," I told her sternly. "I'l bet there are septic tanks."

"You're wrong!" she exclaimed in triumph. "There's a nuclea power station not far away, and the whole village has been put on t mains drainage."

I let this pass.

"I see it's thatched," I said, studying the form. "Have you any ide how much re-thatching costs?"

"No," she replied gaily, "but it's just been done. It won't need t be done again in my lifetime.

"Do look at the roof ridge — it's finished in part semi-circles an part diamonds. I would never have been able to choose between th two.

# INSPECTION

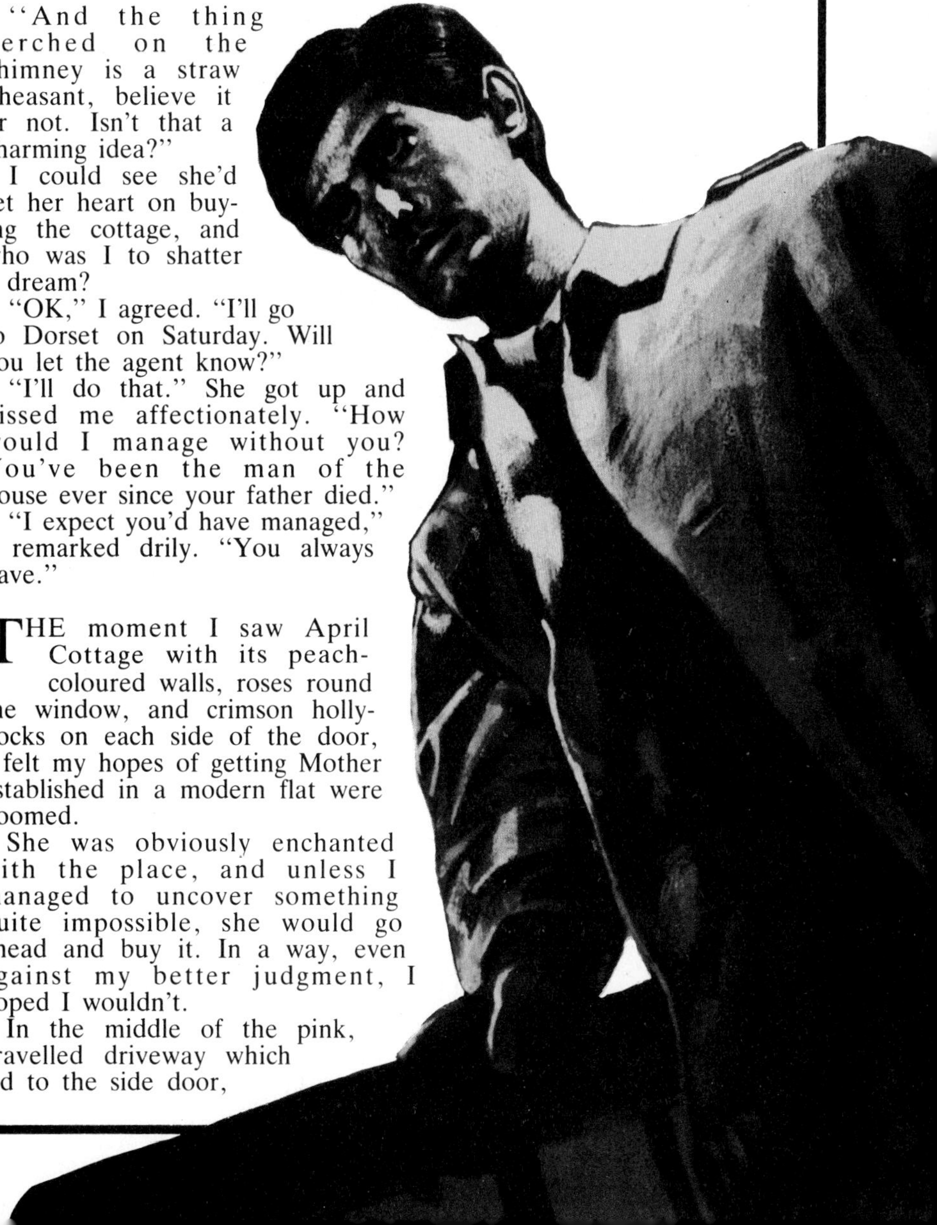

"And the thing perched on the chimney is a straw pheasant, believe it or not. Isn't that a charming idea?"

I could see she'd set her heart on buying the cottage, and who was I to shatter a dream?

"OK," I agreed. "I'll go to Dorset on Saturday. Will you let the agent know?"

"I'll do that." She got up and kissed me affectionately. "How would I manage without you? You've been the man of the house ever since your father died."

"I expect you'd have managed," I remarked drily. "You always have."

THE moment I saw April Cottage with its peach-coloured walls, roses round the window, and crimson hollyhocks on each side of the door, I felt my hopes of getting Mother established in a modern flat were doomed.

She was obviously enchanted with the place, and unless I managed to uncover something quite impossible, she would go ahead and buy it. In a way, even against my better judgment, I hoped I wouldn't.

In the middle of the pink, gravelled driveway which led to the side door, someone had planted a bright orange traffic cone. Kids realising the place was empty, I thought, and set about removing it.

The agent, a business-like man about my own age, arrived almost as soon as I did. We chatted for a bit and explored the outside, and then he handed me the key.

"I expect you'd like to have a quiet browse round on your own," he said. "Drop the key back to the office on your way home."

I wandered round the village first, as the weather looked doubtful. It was very picturesque, with church, school and duck-pond in all the traditional places. There was one shop with post office attached, and a bus timetable pinned up on a board outside giving the times of local buses to the nearby county town.

After I'd toured the village, which only took about 20 minutes, I went back to the cottage and got down to work. The walls, as I'd suspected, were anything but true, and there was some — apparently inactive — woodworm in the beams, which were so low I cracked my head on them.

But the layout was practical and the windows reasonable. I found a mouse's nest in the thatch, and a family of house martins in one of the eaves.

I jotted all this down in my notebook, trying to be fair and unbiased, and after a short trip round the rather wild garden, prepared to depart.

IT was then that the most extraordinary things began to happen! Whereas less than half an hour earlier all had been dreamily peaceful, now the activity in the lane outside resembled Piccadilly Circus — and there was a peculiar looking person waiting at the front door.

When I opened it, I actually felt my jaw drop! She was not the least bit peculiar. In fact, she was the most beautiful creature I'd ever set eyes on.

It was her outfit which was peculiar, for she looked as though she'd stepped straight out of an early Victorian picture-book with her be-sprigged gown, corkscrew curls and ridiculous bonnet!

". . . er . . . hello," I said.

"Are you the person who removed my traffic cone?" she demanded.

". . . er, yes. I wanted to park my car."

"You'd no right to do that!" she stormed. "That space was legitimately reserved for my stall."

"Your what?"

"My stall! Surely you've noticed it's Fair Day?" she cried. "Why d'you suppose I'm dressed up like this?"

"I've no idea." I grinned. "But you look smashing!"

"Flattery will get you nowhere," she said witheringly. "When are you going to move your car?"

I looked past her at the intense activity in the lane. "Where shall I move it to?"

She made a sound of sheer exasperation.

"I can't even guess," she said. "What about going back to wherever you came from?"

"Would that I could," I returned with mock humility, hoping to make her laugh.

"You couldn't — it's too congested, and anyway the lane's sealed off for the Fair. But it doesn't solve my problem."

Now that her anger was abating, she looked prettier than ever, biting her lips to stop them from trembling.

And quite suddenly my heart turned over (twice)!

"How big is your stall?" I said.

She indicated the dimensions with her hands.

"If I manoeuvre the car nearer to the side of the cottage, perhaps we could squeeze it in somehow," I suggested.

"We could have a try," she said. "I must sell some of my stuff. I've got to make some money so that I can buy materials for more."

"What sort of things do you make?"

"Pots," she said. "Hand-painted pottery."

"Right!" I rubbed my hands together. "What are we waiting for?"

SETTING up her stall in the tiny space available proved a mammoth task. She worked with a will, her bonnet askew, and I couldn't keep my eyes off her.

In the course of erecting the stall, I learned that her name was Holly, and that she was just starting her own small business. " 'Potty Holly,' they call me." She giggled, pushing a grimy hand across her forehead. "Thanks a million. Is there anything you'd like to choose to take home for your wife?"

"I don't have a wife," I told her. "But my mother simply loves hand-painted pots. She's thinking of buying April Cottage. That's why I'm here — to give it the once-over."

"Oh!" she said politely. "Choose something for your mother, then."

"You choose," I suggested.

She stretched out a slim, brown hand and selected a piece of pottery. "This is one of my better-selling pieces. D'you think she'll like it?"

She handed me a dainty little model of a fieldmouse clinging to an ear of wheat. It reminded me of the mouse in the thatch. I knew Mother would hate it.

"Would that be all right?"

"She'll treasure it," I lied. "How much is it?"

She blushed bright red.

"Please!" she protested. "It's a gift from me. You've been so helpful after — after I was so rude."

She smoothed her besprigged gown, adjusted her bonnet and smiled.

"Would you like to take a stroll round the Fair?" she suggested. "You might find something else to take home to your mother."

Observing that a small crowd was now assembling round her display, I agreed. She wrapped the mouse in a piece of pink tissue and handed it to me.

"Could you hang on to him until I come back?" I said. "He's a bit bulky for a jacket pocket."

"OK. See you later."

Her smile was utterly devastating!

BY now the lane was lined on both sides with spinning wheels, weaving looms and other craft-producing bits and pieces.

A rustic carpenter, attired in a holland smock with straws stuck in his hair, was busily putting the pieces of a Windsor chair together. Dairymaids, dressed like pantomime Bo-Peeps, patted golden slabs of farmhouse butter into intricate designs.

A farrier was shoeing a farm horse from a portable forge, and maidens in mob-caps were filling muslin bags with pot-pourri, and tying them with lilac ribbon.

A magnificent shire horse, colourful with red, white and blue ribbons, cantered up and down the lane with a wagonette full of cheering children behind him.

Outside the church, a troop of majorettes strutted and twisted to a Boys' Brigade band, which clashed badly with music from a dilapidated hurdy-gurdy a few yards farther down the lane.

It was all gaudy and gay and utterly refreshing, and I realised I was enjoying myself in a way I had never done before. After a leisurely inspection of the rest of the stalls and sideshows (and winning a hideous pink teddy-bear on the tombola), I stopped at a fresh herbs stall with the intention of adding to my mother's newly-formed herb garden.

I knew she was short of a particular one — rue — which, she had informed me knowledgeably, was the herb of grace.

"Do you have a pot of rue?" I inquired of the plump, cheerful woman dressed up as Mother Shipton.

"I did have some," she replied, searching amongst her pots. "It's either all gone, or I forgot to include it."

She gave me a smile full of apology. "I am sorry."

"Not to worry," I said, and prepared to move away.

I had made up my mind to present the teddy-bear to Holly of the Pots. It seemed an amusing thing to do, and I was looking forward to meeting up with her again with ridiculous eagerness. I felt like a kid on his first date.

But the woman motioned me back.

"If you would just hold on to my stall for a few minutes," she said, "I could pop across home and get you that rue. I must have left it in my greenhouse."

"Please don't bother," I began, for there was a big, black cloud gathering over the church, and I feared the rural craft fair hadn't much longer to survive.

"No trouble," the beaming reply came. "Just hang on there — I'll be back in less than a jiffy."

I really enjoyed selling those herbs. I was pretty hazy as to which was which, but the customers knew and helped themselves, paying the prices marked on the pots.

At last there was little or nothing left, but still no sign of Mother Shipton. Her idea of a "jiffy" certainly wasn't mine! Other stall-holders had noticed the ominous cloud, and there were signs of hasty packing up all around me.

IF it hadn't been for the cash bowl in the middle of the stall, I would simply have walked away, but I could hardly leave the afternoon's takings wide to the world.

I had to possess my soul in what patience I could. Eventually, she did return, but not before the heavens had opened and I was uncomfortably wet.

"I'm so sorry," she panted, thrusting a bundle of rhubarb into my astonished hands. "I got held up, but I got your rhubarb. Forty pence, please."

I forebore to explain that rhubarb was the last thing I needed, in case she decided to dash off again, so paid her the 40 pence. Then, tucking the pink teddy-bear under my jacket, I headed for April Cottage at top speed.

Of course, the pottery stall had gone, and so had Holly Pots, as had most of the other stalls. Apparently, a lorry had collected them all, according to a couple of litter-gatherers still working in the lane. Altogether, it was a bad ending to what had been an eventful day.

My disappointment was deep, the only consolation being that when my mother was established in her dream cottage, I would be able to visit the area whenever I wanted.

This thought cheered me quite a bit, and I had visions of myself becoming a weekend countryman.

The drive home was dismal, but at least there was a meal waiting for me when I finally arrived.

Mother dropped her brick before my first mouthful of soup!

"I've changed my mind about the cottage," she said. "I'm sorry you've had a wasted journey."

It was the last straw, and I was too tired and dispirited to argue. I knew it would have been useless anyway.

We ate our meal in silence. I'm sure Mother knew I was upset for she kept giving me nervous glances and generous second helpings.

"The agent rang," she announced as I helped her carry plates through to the kitchen. "You forgot to return the key. He says he's got clients wanting to view tomorrow, and what can you do about it?"

"Bother," I muttered, "so I did. I'll have to drive down there again in the morning."

My mother sighed . . .

DRIVING through the New Forest the next morning in glorious sunshine found me with mixed feelings. I was disappointed about the change of mind, and even played with the idea of selling my flat and buying the cottage for myself.

It would probably be suitable for summer renting, I reasoned, in which case I could even keep the flat. This was all a bit of a pipe-dream, not really me at all.

I reckoned I'd fallen in love! How utterly idiotic. I'd known plenty of girls, but none had affected me the way Holly Pots had.

*Perhaps* she was already married, I thought with a feeling of horror, but I was pretty certain she hadn't been wearing a ring of any description.

*Perhaps* the house agent would be able to help me in some way. I wondered in which part of this fairly large county she would be starting her small business. I could hardly comb every town and village!

*Perhaps*, I thought (narrowly missing an L driver), she hadn't given me another thought. She certainly hadn't liked me to begin with, but afterwards, when she'd waved me off to visit the Fair, there'd been a certain light in her eye.

And she'd said, "See you later," as though she meant it . . .

I wondered why she hadn't waited. I hadn't been all that late getting back from Mother Shipton. Even if she wanted to get in touch with me, I hadn't told her my name nor where I lived. There hadn't been an opportunity.

I reached the agent's office well before lunch.

"I'm sorry about the key," I said. "It was the sudden storm — everything finished so rapidly, it just went out of my head."

"Well, I certainly appreciate your bringing it down this morning. I've several clients coming to view this afternoon. Sunday is always a busy day. Did your mother mean what she said over the phone?"

"I'm afraid so," I said.

He grinned. "I half expected it. You get used to romantically-minded elderly ladies changing their minds.

"Oh, and by the way, a woman from a gift shop in Frensham Road phoned here early this morning. I think she was inquiring about you."

"How come?"

"She had an order for something from someone she met at April Cottage, but she didn't have an address."

"Did you say Frensham Road?" I asked so quickly that he stared.

"That's it . . ."

"Opposite the Council offices?"

"That's right."

"Excuse me," I said, "I've suddenly remembered. I have to see a . . ."

"Man about a dog?" He grinned.

"No, a woman about a mouse," I said. □

# A MOST IMPORTANT DAY

**by KATE MORRISON**

SATURDAYS rarely began quietly in the Mullin household. By nine o'clock, the washing-machine was humming and Jill Mullin had started on vacuuming the living-room carpet.

Her husband, Charles, could be heard mowing the back lawn or hammering together a new frame for his sweet peas.

The loudest noise came from their son Derek's room where his hi-fi waged its regular battle for supremacy against the drone of the vacuum cleaner.

Kim had grown up in this hubbub, and usually slept through it all with little trouble. Even her brother's radio in the adjoining bedroom did not disturb her as a rule.

But this Saturday was different. She had been awake long before the first sounds had broken in the house.

Blonde head resting on the pillow, she gazed dreamily at the window and the square of cloudless sky beyond.

Already a shaft of sunlight was filling the room, and Kim felt as if it was welcoming her to this new and special day. Even if it had been raining, it would have still looked beautiful to her.

In a few hours she would be with Jack, and the prospect sent a thrill racing through her body. On first waking, a cold panic had gripped her. Was it just a dream?

But as reality came back to her, she remembered Jack asking her for the date, and the exhilaration returned. It was

true. They were going out together, and the world was a bright and wonderful place.

THE one problem would be the reaction of her family. Derek she could predict and was well prepared for. He would tease her, make some silly joke, all of which she could handle.

Dad was the problem, his reaction not so easily brushed aside. In his over-protective fashion, he would almost certainly not be too enamoured with the idea.

There would be mutterings about Kim's head being full of romantic nonsense, stuff like that. But he would not stop her going on this date — Kim had made up her mind about that.

And she could count on her mum's support.

She heard her mum's voice, raised above the blare of music.

"Derek! Nine o'clock! And turn that noise down!"

Derek complied and a temporary peace settled over the house.

Kim basked in the silence, which somehow helped concentrate her thoughts on her coming date with Jack Williams.

Soon after, her mum shouted again, this time with a touch of impatience, "It's quarter past. This is the last time I'm going to call you."

Kim smiled. Poor Mum. Every Saturday she said it, and repeated her "last call" warning at least three or four times before Derek finally emerged for breakfast.

It was an all-too-familiar Saturday routine. How Derek was ever in time for his rugby games was beyond Kim.

Perhaps he did it deliberately, she mused lazily, to keep his team on tenterhooks before making his last-minute entrance. Really, although he was two years older than she was, sometimes her brother acted so childishly!

Anyway, let the rest of the family carry on in their usual ways. For Kim the world had taken on a whole new and magical meaning.

Oh, she had had her eye on Jack for some time now, but so had quite a few other girls. Well, he was so good looking, and athletic, too.

The wonder was that he had even noticed Kim when he could have his pick of girls.

In a burst of delighted eagerness, she threw aside the bed covers and sprang to her feet.

NOW came the difficult part, choosing what to wear and deciding about her hair. Should she leave it long and loose, or perhaps sweep it high, on top of her head?

She had just tied the cords of her dressing-gown around her slender waist when there was a slight knock on the door. Derek opened it and stuck his tousled red head through the opening.

"Ah, you're up, Sis. Look, I was wondering — can I borrow your leather jerkin for today?"

"My new one? You must be joking!"

She ended the discussion by ushering Derek out and pushing the door shut with her back.

Kim studied her wardrobe earnestly, and a frown crept over her pretty face.

There was nothing new except for the leather jerkin which had caught Derek's eye. The yellow, print frock was the other latest thing, but somehow that suddenly looked too girlish.

★ ★ ★ ★

Jill Mullin looked round from the cooker. Her eyes, matching Kim's in colour and shape, widened slightly.

"You're up early, dear. Going somewhere special?"

Kim shrugged her shoulders as she sat down at the table and grabbed at the toast.

"Could be," she declared, with deliberate vagueness.

Her dad stopped short as he entered. The surprise on his face was obvious.

"Don't usually see you at this time on a Saturday, Kim. What's up?"

"Why is everybody making such a big thing about me getting up early?" she demanded.

Dad grunted and took his usual place at the table, unfolding his newspaper and glancing at the headlines.

"What are you doing up at this time?" Derek's voice asked.

"Since everybody is so interested, it just so happens that I have a date this afternoon," Kim said casually, deciding it was best to be open about the whole thing.

As she fully expected, all three were looking at each other as if she had suddenly announced she had joined the space programme!

It was left to Derek to break up the awkward moment as he flopped into a chair.

"A date! Wowee! Hear that, Mum?"

"That's enough, Derek," Mum ticked him off. But Kim had heard her do it with much more conviction.

"What do you mean — a date?" There was no mistaking the edge in her dad's voice.

This was it, Kim thought.

MUM, bless her, Kim thought, came to the rescue.

"I thought everyone knew what a date was," she cut in with a little laugh. She followed it by slapping a plate of sausage, egg and bacon in front of Dad, making him jump a little. "It means Kim is going out with a boy!"

Kim looked up at her mum. Their eyes met and they exchanged smiles.

But Dad was still not appeased.

"I know what a date means," he growled. "What I want to know is why she's going on a date? She's only fourteen, for goodness' sake, still only a child."

"I am not a child!" Kim slapped her half-finished slice of toast on to a plate, to emphasise her protest.

"You are to me!"

"But she isn't dating you, Dad!" Derek chuckled, which earned him a glare from both parents.

"I don't think our daughter is planning to elope just yet, Charles," Mum said evenly, taking some of the tension out of the atmosphere building up in the kitchen. "Who are you going with, Kim?"

"Jack Williams."

"Jack Williams!" Derek almost leaped from his chair. Now he suddenly looked wide awake.

"Who's Jack Williams?" Dad wanted to know.

"Just the best prop forward in our seniors' rugby team," Derek

## The Wonder of Water . . .

### A STEALL BAN

*This spectacular waterfall is in upper Glen Nevis. It is reached, after parking in the car park at the end of the road from Fort William, by walking through the Steall Gorge and emerging into a hanging corrie. It is a walk which can be made by any reasonably fit person, but care should be taken to wear strong shoes or boots. For the hardy, an extra dimension can be added by viewing the waterfall in winter when it is frozen, the ice spreading like a veil across the face of the mountain.*

declared, clearly impressed. "How come you've got a date with him, Sis?"

"Because he just happens to have asked me," Kim informed him coolly, then dropped her bombshell. "He's taking me to Murrayfield to see the big match."

From the stunned silence, Kim could tell that they were all overwhelmed by the news. She felt pleased with herself.

"You lucky thing!" Derek exclaimed. "How did he get the tickets?"

"From his dad." Kim was really enjoying her brother's stunned envy and astonishment.

"I like the international games," she asserted with as much casualness as she could muster. "And Jack says the atmosphere at Murrayfield is magic. You don't get that on television."

"Suddenly, she's a rugby supporter!" Dad threw up his hands and sighed heavily.

"I'm sure it must be very exciting, dear," Mum said. "Are you going through by train?"

"No." Kim paused, savouring this last bit. Her blue eyes went round the table, watching for the reaction on each face. "Jack's dad is taking us in his car."

Dad looked less worried.

"So his dad is taking you," he observed with a satisfied nod. "That's different. Bringing you home, too, I suppose?"

"Well, he'll be dropping us at the Randolphs' house."

"What's on there?" Mum asked.

"Just a party."

A PARTY!" Dad's eyes narrowed warily. "What other surprises have you got for us this morning, young lady?"

"That's just what it is, Dad. A surprise party, for Keith's sixteenth birthday."

Charles Mullin seemed about to say something, caught his wife's look and settled for a forkful of food.

"Will you be late, dear?"

"I don't know, Mum. Never can tell with these things."

"Well, I don't want you coming home late on your own," her dad warned.

"Don't worry, Dad," Derek put in with a wicked grin on his face. "I'll see Sis home OK."

"You!" Kim gaped at him.

"Didn't I tell you?" Derek waved his arms in exaggerated innocence. "Guess this is a day of surprises for everybody. I'll be at Keith's party, too. He is in my class, after all."

Dad cleared his throat. He suddenly looked pleased as he retrieved his newspaper.

Kim glared across at Derek who was grinning widely.

Then, remembering how much Derek liked her new leather jerkin, she began to relax. Perhaps she would let him borrow it after all. At a price, of course! □

JENNY GREAVES and Robin Trent paused yet again to admir the smart new lettering on Robin's shooting-brake.

*R. Trent. Electrical Engineer.*
*Telephone: —*

They exchanged smiles as he opened the door and helped her int the front seat.

"Where to, madam?" he asked teasingly. "I am yours to command."

"Well." Jenny hesitated. "We're having an open day at the schoo next week. I'd like lots of branches. Twigs and things to decorate th room."

"Mmm, and I think you have a special place in mind," Robi prompted.

Jenny giggled. "I have, but I can't remember the name of th wood. I know it was a special place when I stayed with m grandparents.

"I always felt it was a magic wood. It had moss on the ground an a little stream running through. I've thought about it a lot lately. I must be with being with the children. Made me think about my ow childhood."

Her voice tailed off and Robin glanced down at her with a smile Jenny had recently started teaching in an infants' school, and love every minute of it.

"I do need a bit more to go on, love."

"Well, Grandma's cottage was just outside the village of Simpton It might be too far for a picnic."

"Simpton? I remember that name. I camped near there with th Scouts. It's about forty miles away. I think we can manage that a right. If I find the village, can you find the wood?"

AN hour later they pulled up outside a fringe of thick, dar conifers.

"I'm sure that's it. But it looks different," Jenny said. "Ther were proper trees."

Robin laughed. "Darling, those are proper trees! Remember, it's long time since you were here. The trees have grown and so hav you. Come on, hop out and we'll explore."

Once they were through the outer edge of the wood, Jenny spirits rose. Deeper still, she turned to Robin with shining eyes.

"It's just as I remembered. And I still think it's magic!"

# WAIT FOR THE HEALING

by MARY LEDGWAY

They stood, arms entwined, looking round. The trees — ash, elm, rowan, oak — were beautiful in their fresh spring green. The blue sky, dappled by the light movement of the trees, shone through the maze of branches. The turf, sprinkled by clumps of wild flowers, was soft beneath their feet, and moss covered the stones and old tree stumps.

Their kiss was long and sweet, then Robin took her hand.

"Come on, let's find this stream of yours. I'm feeling peckish and the food will be easier to carry once we've eaten it."

The stream, though, was not as Jenny remembered.

"Some stream," Robin murmured, as they stood by the deep gorge watching the water swirling over rocks, carrying debris and forming small, foaming whirlpools.

"It wasn't like this when I was little," Jenny said, disappointed. "I remember now, Grandad did once tell me there were sluice gates higher up and that the stream overflowed when they were opened. That's what must have happened."

They ate cheese and french bread and drank ice-cold apple juice. They talked and held hands, and time slipped by.

"Goodness!" Jenny exclaimed at last. "If I'm going to get my greenery, we'd better make a move. You take the high branches and I'll take the low ones. Here's a pair of secateurs."

Soon they both had armfuls of fresh, leafy sprays.

"Jenny, love, you're getting carried away again," Robin said with a wide smile. "Come on, now, we'd better be getting back. We promised to go to Neil's engagement party tonight, remember?"

But the hurry didn't stop him leaning over and kissing her. In spite of the barrier of branches each held, the kiss was full of promise.

The same thought was in both their minds.

"Yes, love. One day it'll be our turn," Robin promised. "Just give me a year to build the business up, and we'll see."

HE looked down at her — long, brown hair falling round her shoulders, deep, blue eyes, and a smile that melted his heart every time he saw it. Jenny was not strictly beautiful, but she was all he wanted in his girl, and he loved her dearly.

He was determined to have something to offer her, though, when they married. The thought of the business he was gradually building up reminded him of a message his mother had given him as he was leaving home — a call in the better part of town, and if he could get some work there it would be a help.

He glanced at his watch. "We'll have to hurry, love. There's a call I promised to make before the party."

"We can't really be late, Robin. You're making the presentation from the tennis club," Jenny reminded him.

"I'll make it," he promised.

The traffic, though, was heavier than he had anticipated, and once back on the roads nearer home he glanced anxiously at his watch.

"Think I'll take a short-cut through Barnes Edge. It will save at least fifteen minutes."

"Robin, no! You know what the road was like the last time we walked there. There's a warning —"

"Don't worry, I'll drive carefully."

"But all the rain and the tree-felling has —"

Jenny didn't say any more. Robin was already turning off the main road.

They were nearly at the end of the short-cut when it happened. Their front, nearside wheel caught the corner of a large stone that had fallen off a neglected wall, and the car swerved.

Jenny screamed as she saw the wall coming crashing towards her, then all was dark.

FOR the young teacher, the next few days were a blur of pain. She was vaguely conscious of gentle hands easing her. She knew that when the pain was too much to bear, there would be a slight prick and the pain would recede.

She knew her parents came and went, but throughout all the agony she was aware of Robin's presence, his voice comforting her, urging her to get well, his hand holding hers, the touch of his lips as he bent over her.

She couldn't hear her own words, mumbled as she lay tossing, reliving the agony of the crash.

"No, Robin — please don't go. It isn't safe, Robin! You're going to kill us! Robin —"

Robin heard the repeated screams, the condemnation in her voice, saw how he had injured the girl he loved.

For the sake of a few, brief minutes he had thrown away a lifetime's happiness. Jenny would never be his — now.

Then the day came when Jenny woke up and the pain was bearable. Robin's face, haggard, older, came into focus, and she smiled.

"Oh, Robin! You look so tired."

"You're better today, love. We've all been so worried," he told her, stroking her hand.

Jenny looked down at her leg, clumsy in its plaster.

"It'll heal, Jen. Take a bit of time, but it was a clean break."

"And my head?" She touched the bandages.

"Just cuts — but they had to cut your hair. You hurt your ribs, but they'll heal," Robin assured her.

Then the nurse arrived at Jenny's bedside, smiling.

"So you're back with us, young lady! About time, too. Now drink this and then have a good sleep.

"There!" The nurse turned to the young man. "She's sleeping naturally now. That's what she needs. You look tired — I think you should go now, and follow suit."

Robin nodded. "Yes, I'd better go now."

He looked down at Jenny, touching her gently, not daring to kiss her in case he disturbed the sleep she so badly needed. " 'Bye, Jenny, love."

There were tears in his eyes as he turned away. He had done all he could for Jenny, he told himself sadly.

WHEN Jenny opened her eyes again, her mother was there. She looked round for Robin, then turned to the older woman.

"Robin will be resting. He looked as though he'd been up for hours."

"He had," her mother told her. "And I've strict orders not to stay too long."

The following day her mother handed her a note.

"Robin asked me to give this to you," she said gently.

*I know you won't be able to bear me near you. The accident was all my fault. I'm going away, but I had to know you were going to be all right first,* Jenny read.

There was more, but all she could understand was that Robin had gone.

When the afternoon's visitors had left, Jenny fingered the bandages on her head, and asked another patient to reach her her handbag.

The pocket mirror had been removed, as had her compact. But whoever had removed them had missed the long thin one in her comb case.

Slowly, Jenny turned back the edges of the bandage that reached almost to her eyes. It didn't take her long to trace the cut running from her right ear almost to her hair-line, or the one from her left eye finishing below the curve of her chin.

Jenny let the mirror slip to the floor. So that was it, she thought bleakly. She was disfigured for life. She had never laid claim to beauty, but now . . . No wonder Robin had walked away.

She read the letter again, but was too distraught to read the love that lingered between the words, the heartbreak between the stilted phrases.

She didn't cry — she just lay back on her pillows and was silent. When she pushed her evening meal away untasted, the nurse looked at her thoughtfully. Catching sight of the mirror beneath the bed, she understood.

The elderly doctor who came at the nurse's request sat on the edge of the bed and looked at his patient . . .

"So you're feeling sorry for yourself, young lady. Well, I suppose it's understandable. But, Jenny, you should really be feeling thankful.

"When you came in we were so afraid of brain damage," he explained. "Fortunately the cuts were mostly superficial and even the others hadn't gone too deep. I know we had to cut your hair, but —"

"Stop it!" Jenny's outburst surprised even herself. "You don't have to pretend. My face is scarred and will always be scarred.

"No wonder Robin doesn't want me. I should think he never wants to see me again! How can I face people? Go back to school?"

Then the tears came and the kindly doctor let her cry a while before leaning over and speaking earnestly. "Jenny, you probably won't believe me, but what I am saying is the truth. We never lie to patients. Those cuts will heal. A year from now you'll hardly notice them — they won't even need plastic surgery.

"You'll dance again. Oh yes, you will," he insisted as Jenny glanced at her ungainly leg. "You're young, at twenty-two you have your life in front of you. Just lie a while and think how easily that life could have been ended, or reduced merely to being alive.

"Tomorrow we'll be taking that plaster off, and in a day or two you'll be starting physiotherapy. The sooner we get you mobile the better. And, Jenny, if that young man of yours has walked out on you, he's not worth bothering about," he finished.

JENNY did laugh again — and sooner than she expected.

Leigh Grinsdale, the young physiotherapist, was very gentle as he massaged her wasted leg. But when he made her walk, he was not moved by either her pleas or tantrums.

"You can do it," he told her firmly. "Just keep trying. And walk — don't waddle like a duck!"

The joke was poor, not worth the gale of laughter with which Jenny greeted it, but it was either laughter or tears. Leigh joined in and so the pattern was set.

Jenny and Leigh worked together well, and in less than three weeks Jenny was ready to go home.

All her stitches had been removed. She was still horrified when she looked at herself in the mirror, but she had thought over the doctor's words and realised she had indeed had a lucky escape.

Robin's mother had been to see her. Now Robin had sold the business he had been so proud of and had used the money to join his uncle in Australia, as the older man had often asked him to.

Jenny was too proud to ask for his address.

Her hair had begun to grow again, just a fine down on her head. She had a wig to wear in public, but knew that her scars would heal better if they were not covered up.

Jenny took a long, dispassionate look at herself in a mirror. The scars stood out, red and livid. She still walked with a limp, and her hair was little better than a stubble around her head. She couldn't blame Robin for walking out, but if only he had told her, talked to her . . .

When Leigh Grinsdale rang and suggested an outing, Jenny accepted. At least he knew what she looked like, and anything was better than moping at home.

Gradually her hair grew, and in September she went back to school. The children greeted her warmly and appeared to notice nothing wrong in her appearance.

By Christmas the scars had faded sufficiently for Jenny to accept Leigh's invitation to the hospital dance.

Leigh had kissed her before, light kisses that Jenny accepted as a sign of friendship, but when, on the way home from the dance, his kisses grew more urgent, when he whispered how much he cared, she knew she didn't return his feelings.

Gently she told him she didn't feel the same way, and when he said he would still like to take her out, she shook her head.

"No, Leigh. It's best if I walk out of your life. Someone else will walk in then," she added gently.

Leigh telephoned a time or two, but she kept her resolve. She guessed rightly that his feelings had not gone deep enough really to hurt.

## *The Blessing Of Love*

I'M blest by love, so I'll not sigh for
things I'll never gain,
For envy only leads down the path
of bitterness and pain,
Content with family, home and friends,
my cup of joy fulfilled,
This is a life of happiness as Heaven
surely willed.

From early morning's bustling hour to
evening's gentle close,
The ties of love enfold each day and
blossom like a rose,
If I live to a hundred years, in love with
life I'll be,
So long as love for ever walks, hand
in hand with me.

— *Georgina Hall.*

WINTER passed and it was spring Bank Holiday again. Jenny couldn't help remembering the happiness and the tragedy of the last one.

"Mum, do you think I could borrow your car? Just for today."

"But, love, you haven't driven on your own since —"

"Please, Mum? I'll be careful, I promise."

So Jenny drove out again to Simpton, and walked alone through the thick fringe of trees into the clearings she had once thought were part of a fairy-like world of magic.

This time even the stream was as she remembered it. Shallow, clear, the sound of it burbling over its bed of stones was like a gentle lullaby.

Jenny sat a while, then turned back into the woods. There was the tree she and Robin had picnicked under.

Suddenly it was all too much. Jenny leaned against the tree trunk, buried her face in the shelter of her folded arms and wept.

She had tried so hard to forget Robin, to make another life for herself, but she knew she still ached for him as much as she had ever done.

Lost in grief, Jenny didn't hear the sound of footsteps on the grass, didn't hear her name spoken slowly, hesitantly.

Only when she felt a hand on her shoulder did she turn. Through a blur of tears she saw Robin's face, anxious, afraid.

She didn't stop to think. Robin had come to the woods, just as he had said he would last spring Bank Holiday . . . Pride and hurt feelings didn't count.

Jenny threw herself into his arms, and great, shuddering sobs racked her body as she felt them close round her.

FOR a while, neither of them moved. Then Jenny partly released herself and looked up into his eyes.

"Why?" she asked. "Why, Robin?"

"Oh, Jenny! The accident was all my fault. You warned me, but I didn't take any notice. I caused you all that pain, that suffering.

"I didn't think you would be able to bear me near you, let alone go on loving me —"

Gently, his fingers traced the outline of a scar.

"And I thought it was because of that!" Jenny took his hand in hers and touched the other scar. "I thought it was because you didn't want a wife who had to hide part of her face."

"Oh, Jenny! I could never stop loving you," he assured her, his voice thick with emotion. "I went to Australia, but you were still there with me.

"Will you give me another chance, Jenny? Let me prove how much I really love you?"

The sun was dipping in the sky before they left the wood. Robin would have to start again, but he had saved a little while he was away. And they would start again together.

Jenny's eyes were full of dreams. Her wood was magic after all. □

# Say It With Flowers

by
**BETTY HAWORTH**

DON'T know what time I'll be home tonight, love," Philip Scott said, picking up his brief-case. "If I'm going to be late I'll give you a ring."

"Oh, Phil!" Valerie Scott's voice was dismayed. "We're going to Craig and Amy's. Surely you haven't forgotten?

"They asked us for supper, and to see the video of Sandra's graduation. You can't have forgotten that!"

She saw his look of irritation, quickly suppressed.

"No, of course I hadn't forgotten! But I'm meeting Madden at six, and I can't just rush away —"

He stopped and she gave him a searching look.

"You can't rush away to have supper with friends? The point is, Phil, you promised."

"Look, Valerie." Philip's face was set in the familiar expression. "I'd really like to be there, but we've got to get our priorities right. This contract with Madden is absolutely vital!"

His mouth tightened. "The plain truth is, if I don't get it, there'll be no holiday abroad next summer — and we'll have to do without other things as well."

Valerie didn't answer.

"They're old friends, Valerie," he finished. "They'll understand."

"Why can't Madden see you during normal office hours?" Valerie burst out angrily. "Why has it always got to be in the evening? Surely —"

"Look, love," Philip said again. "I haven't time to go into all that now. I've tried to explain, but you don't seem to —"

"You'll be eating out then?"

"Try to understand," he pleaded, checking his brief-case. "We can see Craig and Amy another time. I don't suppose they'll mind showing the video again!"

She didn't respond to his smile.

"They're very proud of Sandra, if that's what you mean," she said sharply.

Outside the front door, he clasped her hand and bent to kiss her but she turned away.

WAITING at the third set of red traffic lights, Philip drummed his fingers impatiently, glancing at his watch.

Valerie had been right. Madden was being unreasonable over this contract, and had kept Philip dangling nearly a month now.

"Give me another day or two, Scott," he'd said in his suave way. "One or two points I'd like to check with you — what about drinks tomorrow evening?"

There was no reason why he couldn't sign — the contract was solid, down to the last comma — but still he put Philip off.

On Friday he'd said, "We'll meet somewhere on Monday at six to finalise matters, Scott. My secretary will ring you some time during the day. All right?"

Philip had agreed once again. Now here he was, still hanging on, and he'd probably have to wait all day for that darned phone call!

Ann Turley saw him coming across the car park, and thought how tired and pre-occupied he looked. She put the kettle on for coffee, and when Philip walked in it was ready.

" 'Morning, Mr Scott! Gregory's rang about five minutes ago to see when you could —"

"Later, Ann," Philip said, and went into his office.

She waited a few minutes then went in.

"You'll have to stall Gregory's for today," Philip said, opening his desk diary. "You can do that, can't you?"

"I expect so," Ann replied. "I'm doing it rather a lot at present."

He ran his hand through his dark hair impatiently.

"I've got to get this Madden contract settled," he said.

"I know it's not my place to say so," Anne burst out, "but I think Madden's just being awkward, Mr Scott! If you want my opinion, he's enjoying keeping you waiting!"

Philip drank his coffee in silence.

"There's a lot at stake in this," he told her at last. "I don't think you realise the implications."

She flushed at his criticism, but said nothing. It was unfair of him to say that. She had been involved in the contract from the start, to say nothing of the juggling of appointments and the soothing of other clients. It had been hard work.

"Call when you're ready," she said quietly.

Philip began looking through the pile of letters on his desk. He bent to pick up one that had fallen out of the pile, and found himself looking at a single sheet of paper: "Don't forget twenty-first."

IT was his own writing, underlined, and he stared at it for several seconds before putting it down. His mind was completely blank.

He hadn't a clue what the message meant — he couldn't even remember writing it.

He got up abruptly and went out. "Ann? Have I anything special on the twenty-first?"

"I've put everything in the diary, Mr Scott."

"No, something else —"

"You mean something personal?" she asked.

"There's a note here." He held it out. "The twenty-first . . ."

"That's today."

He stared at her, nonplussed.

"Shall I check the diary again?" she offered.

When they returned to his office, his desk diary showed it was the first quiet day for weeks. Apart from some letters and the expected phone call from Madden, there was nothing urgent.

"Lunch appointment?" Ann suggested. "Anniversary? Dentist?"

He looked lost, standing with the mysterious paper in his hand. Ann knew if he hadn't been so tired and overworked this wouldn't have happened.

"I'm sorry I can't help." She shook her head. "Why not ring Mrs Scott? Better than worrying all day!"

When she'd gone, Philip stood looking out of the office window. The plane trees across in the square were in full leaf, and the sun was casting dappled shadows on the pavements.

People were shopping and stopping to gaze into the windows, enjoying the morning in unhurried pleasure.

Philip remembered how he and Valerie used to go shopping together like that. He remembered the drives in the country at weekends and meals out. He remembered how he'd promised Valerie that he'd never let his job get on top of him, for her sake as well as his.

He remembered her face that morning.

"Ann —" He was pulling on his coat, aware of her surprised face. "I'm just going out for an hour. If Madden rings, tell him I'll be back straight after lunch. If he gets awkward —"

"I'll deal with Mr Madden!" she said firmly.

PHILIP bought roses, dark red and long stemmed with a beautiful scent. It was ages since he had bought Valerie any flowers, and roses had always been her favourites.

When they were first married he couldn't afford them, but Valerie used to laugh and say, "When you're a successful businessman, you can buy me red roses all the time!"

He drove home eagerly, knowing Valerie would be surprised. He'd say, "Come on, love, I'll take you out to lunch!"

That was something they hadn't done for a long time, either.

When Philip put his key in the front door and called that he was home, there was no reply. He stood in the hall with the roses wrapped in their fancy paper, and knew the house was empty.

"Shopping," he decided aloud, looking at his watch.

He sat in the armchair in the sitting-room, watching for Valerie's trim figure coming along the road from the shops. The hands of the clock moved round slowly and the house was quiet.

He woke suddenly from a doze and saw that it was after twelve. The sight of the roses lying on the table made him oddly anxious.

Valerie hadn't said anything about going out today. But then, she never did tell him her plans for the day any more — and he never asked.

He dialled the office and spoke to Ann.

"No calls," she told him. "Everything's under control."

Philip got into the car, and drove over to his mother-in-law's neat bungalow a few miles away. It was a long time since he'd been there, and he noticed the new paint and the small alterations to the garden at once.

Valerie's mother was a widow but she seemed to cope with everything very well on her own. At least, she never asked Philip for help.

"Philip! This is a nice surprise!" Her face changed. "There's nothing wrong — Valerie —"

"No — we're fine!" Philip said quickly, hiding his disappointment. "I just thought I'd call and see how you are."

He looked down at the roses he'd brought with him, and held them out awkwardly.

"How lovely!" Mrs Carter exclaimed, casting a thoughtful look at her son-in-law. "And how kind! Roses are my favourite flowers!"

She made coffee and began to arrange the roses in a tall vase.

"Having a day off?" she asked.

Philip roused himself and watched her clipping the long stems.

"Well — not really. I was going to take Valerie out to lunch, but —"

"Oh, what a shame!" Mrs Carter stood back to admire the roses. "And you'd forgotten it was her swim day!

"She really loves her day with the Beech school children, doesn't she? And even the most badly-handicapped ones enjoy the water. Didn't you go at one time, Philip?"

"Yes," he said. "But I got so busy . . ."

WELL," Mrs Carter said briskly, "Valerie won't be back for a while, so if you'd like to have some lunch, you're very welcome."

"I haven't a lot of time . . ." Philip looked at his watch and got up.

"Valerie tells me you have an excellent secretary." Mrs Carter was watching him quizzically.

Philip thought about Ann, calm and utterly reliable. He remembered her support over the years when he was building up the business, the things she did without being asked, the way she smoothed the rough patches in the day. How indignant she had been that morning about Madden!

"I have a treasure of a secretary," Philip agreed slowly. "But I'm afraid I take her for granted."

"You could buy another bunch of roses," Mrs Carter suggested.

"I bought those for Valerie really," Philip blurted out, "because I've been neglecting her a bit lately, too!" ▶ *over*

The Wonder of Water . . .

**EAS COUL AULIN**

*This, the highest waterfall in Britain at 658 feet, is near the head of Loch Glencoul. To reach the waterfall on foot is arduous, but an excellent view can be obtained from a hired boat from Unapool. This is in the heart of some of the most remote country in Scotland. The name means "Maiden's Tresses."*

"I guessed as much!" Mrs Carter chuckled. "They aren't the sort of flowers a man buys for his mother-in-law!"

Philip looked at her guiltily and they both laughed.

"You look jaded, Philip," she told him affectionately. "It would do you good to have some time off."

"It's impossible. There's an important contract in the offing and they're playing hard to get."

She hesitated.

"It's an old problem," she said. "But you've got to decide what's more important."

She went out and left him in the little sitting-room. It was cosy, with well-worn furniture and bright cushions. There was a photo of Valerie's father on the bookcase and another of Valerie in plaits and school uniform.

Mrs Carter had put the roses next to Philip and Valerie's wedding photo, and he thought back to that day and all the plans and dreams they'd had. Most of them had come true: a home of their own, comfortable lifestyle, holidays abroad, things they would have considered luxuries when they were first married.

Odd how they didn't seem to get the same satisfaction out of life now as they had then.

AFTER lunch Philip helped with the washing-up.

"You keep busy, don't you, Mum?" he said. "I admire the way you cope on your own."

She flushed with pleasure at the unexpected compliment.

"It's not always easy, but I do my best."

"If there's ever anything I can do," Philip offered awkwardly. "I mean, jobs around the house . . ."

"That's good of you, Philip," she said, "especially when you're so busy. Thank you."

"I mean it," he told her. "Don't forget."

He mowed the lawn and mended the lock on the garage door. Occasionally, he wondered about that note he'd found, but it didn't seem as important now as it had that morning at the office. The twenty-first was nearly over, anyway.

At four o'clock he drove back to town, pleased with his afternoon's work. He chatted with the girl at the florist's for a few minutes, gathering up all the rest of the roses.

Ann gasped with delight when he laid a bunch on her desk.

"Oh, they're beautiful, Mr Scott! Did you find out about the note?"

"No," he said cheerfully. "I just thought I'd hedge my bets and buy roses for all the women in my life today!"

"But you really shouldn't —"

"It's a very small thanks, Ann," he told her. "I just wanted you to know how much I appreciate all you do."

She blushed and began fussing with the papers on her desk.

"Mr Madden hasn't rung, Mr Scott, and it's getting very late. Shall

I ring him and find out where he wants to meet you tonight?"

"Ring him by all means, Ann," Philip agreed, picking up the rest of the roses. "And tell him I shan't be able to keep our appointment after all."

She stared at him in astonishment. "But — he said he was ready to sign up —"

"Tell him to get in touch with me during office hours," Philip went on levelly. "Tell him I'm having dinner with old friends tonight."

Ann's eyes sparkled. "Very well, Mr Scott, I'll give him your message!"

VALERIE was getting ready for her evening out when she heard Philip's key in the lock.

"What's happened? Is something wrong, Philip?"

He looked up and saw her at the top of the stairs, her face anxious.

She came down slowly, a dozen questions in her eyes. He held out the roses, sweet and dark in their wrapping.

"Happy birthday!"

She took the flowers with a little gasp of pleasure. "But it's not my birthday! You know it isn't!"

"Happy anniversary!" he said.

She began to laugh, responding to the laughter in his eyes.

"And it's not our anniversary either! Philip, what on earth —"

"Happy Monday, then," he said.

She flung her arms round him. "I thought you were seeing Madden tonight."

"No," he told her. "I'm having dinner with friends. And if you don't let me go, we'll be late."

"Thank you," she said, and kissed him.

Philip got ready with a feeling of pleasant anticipation. There would be news to catch up with tonight, one of Amy's delicious suppers, and the pleasure of sharing their pride in Sandra's graduation day.

He had been spending too much time at the office recently, and Valerie was right to be upset. It had been a good day today, putting things right with the people who really mattered to him.

It was just that business was so cut-throat these days, and there was always the risk of something unforeseen happening to destroy everything he'd built up over these last years.

"Valerie, have you ever wondered how you'd feel if we were hard up again? I mean — if we had to give up . . ." Philip stopped, shrugging slightly.

Valerie was getting her fur jacket out of the big wardrobe.

"This?" she asked. "The house and all our possessions? The holidays abroad and all the luxuries we accept as our right?"

She came and looked up at him, her eyes understanding.

"You're the most important thing in my life, Philip," she said simply. "I enjoy the luxuries and I'm grateful for them, but the important thing to me is that we should be together.

"I'm sorry about this morning. I know how hard you work and I know you do it for me. But material things don't mean that much to a woman — not if she's honest about it."

The sound of the phone made him start, and he went downstairs with a mounting feeling of foreboding.

"Scott? It's Madden. Your secretary gave me your number. You don't mind me ringing you at home?"

Philip only hesitated for a fraction of a second. "Of course not, Madden, but I'm going out in a few minutes."

Valerie was coming downstairs, her eyes fixed on his face. Silently he held out his hand and took hers.

"Sorry you had to break our appointment." Madden's voice was smooth.

"Perhaps you could meet me tomorrow?"

"Sorry," Philip said. "I've a full diary tomorrow — in fact, I'm pretty busy all week. And next week I'm taking some time off."

Valerie's hand tightened in his. The pause that followed seemed to go on for ever.

"Right!" Madden's voice was affable. "I'll sign the contract this evening and send it round by messenger tomorrow morning. Will that be convenient?"

"Fine," Philip assured him. "I'm glad it's all settled."

HE put the phone down and smiled at Valerie.

"Now we can celebrate," he told her.

"I knew it would be all right!" she said, hugging him. "Won't everyone be pleased!"

"Everyone?"

"Of course! Mother, and Ann, and Craig and Amy — all the people who care!"

Philip thought back on the day and smiled.

"Oh, and Phil — you won't forget the twenty-first, will you? Amy's bound to mention it tonight."

"The twenty-first?" Philip asked casually.

She looked at him hard. "You did promise —"

"It's the twenty-first today."

"No, silly! Sandra's twenty-first! I told you ages ago — don't tell me you'd forgotten?"

"Of course I hadn't forgotten!"

"You're sure?" She looked at him doubtfully. "They'll be so disappointed if we're not there."

"Look, love," he said, with infinite patience, "stop worrying! I won't forget."

"It isn't in your diary," she agreed in a small voice, and he began to laugh.

"No, it's not," he said, kissing her and opening the front door. "It's on a piece of paper, underlined, in a prominent position on my desk at work. Now can we please go and celebrate?" □

# SYMBOL OF HOPE

by
ISOBEL
OSBORNE

DICK tried to repress a shudder as Lynne peeled off the last piece of wrapping from the newly-delivered package.

"I do hope you'll like it," she said anxiously.

"It could have been worse." Dick grinned. "It could have had a red pointed cap and a beard, and been clutching a fishing rod!"

"I wouldn't have inflicted a *gnome* on you," Lynne protested. "This is a cherub. I think he's meant to be Eros or Cupid or something . . ."

"What's the round thing for?"

"It's a birdbath, silly. It sits on top of his curls and his hands hold it up. It will encourage the birds."

"Oh!" Dick said. Not for worlds would he have wiped the animation from his young wife's face. It had been so long since he'd seen the old, bubbly Lynne.

"Where shall we put it?" he inquired with forced enthusiasm.

"I thought in the bare patch in the middle of the pansy bed. Nothing grows there because of the buried tree trunk.

"We'll be able to see it from the kitchen window there. Do you think it needs a plinth to raise it up a bit?"

Dick winced inwardly, but agreed stoutly, "Yes, you're right. Let's pop down to the garden centre and get one right away."

LYNNE couldn't relax until her new toy was set in place. She hovered round excitedly while Dick cemented it upon its plinth. Then she stepped back and clasped her hands together.

"He's perfect!" she cried. "We must give him a name. What shall it be?"

"What about Percy Thrower Junior?" Dick suggested.

"OK," she agreed after a moment's hesitation.

"So that's settled," Dick said. "Hi, Percy!"

He picked up his spade and leaned on it. "Now that's finished and his Concrete Majesty has been installed, is there any hope of a bite of supper? I'm starving."

As they ate their meal, she changed her chair to get a better view of the pansy bed, and Dick noticed that the strained look which had so dismayed him had disappeared (at least temporarily).

He would have put up with a colony of cherubs — or even red-capped gnomes with fishing rods — to have the old Lynne back, for her recent miscarriage had weakened her, not only physically, but spiritually, too. She seemed to have lost the bright spring of hope which had kept them both going for the last five years.

During the next few weeks, he watched her tending the pansies surrounding Percy, and eventually got over his dislike of the little garden ornament.

He couldn't resist, however, draping his old college scarf around its neck one windy morning, and was delighted when she laughed.

WHEN Christmas came, a robin who lived in the yew hedge opposite used the birdbath as a skating rink. They had a lot of laughs at his antics, but when the pansies started to unfurl their purple and yellow flags, something dreadful happened.

It was a Saturday morning, Lynne had gone shopping, and Dick was about to cut the lawn. Suddenly he heard a crash and was just in time to see a youth throwing half bricks at Percy. Enraged, he managed a swipe at the fleeing marauder.

"What d'you think you're doing?" he yelled.

He decided not to mention the incident to Lynne, and hoped she wouldn't notice Percy's slightly damaged nose!

After a while, he forgot about the incident with the boy — until the morning he found Percy totally destroyed! His concrete curls, together with the birdbath which had rested upon them, lay in pieces amongst the pansies. His plump torso now cracked, scratched and leaning askew, looked both grotesque and pathetic.

Dick went down on his knees in a futile effort to fit some of the bits together, but it was hopeless. He was pretty sure he knew who was responsible for the scene of destruction.

When Lynne returned from her shopping trip, he had loaded some of the debris into a wheelbarrow. He dreaded her reaction when she discovered what had happened, and hoped to lessen it by a bit of tidying-up. Suppose Percy's accident brought back the mood of depression which had only recently lifted?

He was shocked by his feelings of rage against the perpetrator of the crime. What was wrong with the youth of today that they could take pleasure in hurting and destroying?

BEFORE Dick could sort out his angry feelings, Lynne came walking up the garden path.

"Hi!" she called cheerily. "What are you doing?"

Then she saw what had happened and stopped short.

"What happened? Was it an accident?" she stammered. "Was it vandals?"

"I'm almost sure it was," Dick replied. "If it had simply toppled, there wouldn't have been the pieces of brick amongst the rubble. I'm so sorry, darling. Poor old Percy."

Then Lynne did an extraordinary thing. She walked slowly round the ruined pansy bed, and said, "It doesn't matter, Dick. After all, Percy was only a piece of concrete."

He stared. "But he meant a lot to you. You wove dreams around him — I saw it in your face."

Lynne's voice was suddenly wobbly. "Oh, Dick, I've been selfish. Don't look so stricken. It doesn't matter, honestly."

"You mean — you're not upset?"

She sniffed, smiled and shook her head.

"I'll buy you another Percy," he promised. "I'll buy you one made of stone this time. How about that?"

"No, thank you, Dick. You see we — we don't need another Percy. We're going to need the space in the pansy bed for something different. The earth's hard but it gets the sun, and we can keep an eye on it from the kitchen window."

Dick gave a deep sigh and scratched his head. "My mum always says I don't understand women, and I reckon she's right. What have you got in mind?"

She beamed at him before she answered. Then she said in a trembly voice, "A pram, darling. I — I've just seen Dr Lewis. I didn't dare tell you until I was sure!"

He understood everything then, and suddenly the world was a brighter, happier place. He could even sympathise with the lad who toppled Percy. People who are happy don't do things like that.

He looked at Lynne. Her face was transformed. He had never realised before how beautiful she was, and his heart gave a mighty lurch at the depth of his love for her.

He put down the piece of concrete he was still holding and pulled her into his arms.

"I always felt Percy would bring us luck," he declared untruthfully.

Her happy tears made a damp patch on the front of his sweater.

"I always felt that, darling," she whispered. "But it's sweet of you to admit it." □

CLARE sighed and picked her lunch things up. The repair man hadn't come. She should have been expecting that — they never did, at least not when they said they would.

They waited till the minute you gave up and left the house, then slipped a frosty message through the letter-box informing you they'd called and got no answer.

Still, she reflected, crossing to the sink, this *was* a little different. The old oak in the garden had come down at three a.m. and torn the guttering off the roof, then smashed the landing window as it hurtled earthwards.

She didn't mind about the guttering. That could wait a day or two. It was the howling gale upstairs that bothered her, not to mention the convenient gap it opened for intruders.

She'd rung the glazier first thing. He had already gone, but his

by
CERI
EVANS

father promised that he'd get a message to him.

Abandoning the dishes, Clare phoned the office. "I'm sorry, but I'm stuck, still waiting for my window to be fixed. Looks like I won't be in this afternoon."

There was a heavy sigh at the other end. "You're not the only one. A tree came down in Peter's garden, too, across his car. And Bill's wife's gone into labour prematurely. In fact, there's just me and the tea boy."

"I'm sorry," Clare repeated.

"Me, too," her boss said gloomily. "We've that report to finish by tomorrow. You know, I sometimes think the only way to run a business and succeed is just to emigrate — preferably to somewhere with a decent climate."

He sighed again. "That was quite a storm last night."

Clare plunged her hands into the washing-up distractedly. She knew how crucial deadlines were in landing jobs, and hated letting Malcolm down. If nothing else, her own security depended on his ability to make a go of things.

SHE pulled a plate out of the bowl, reached for the tea-towel, and felt the china slipping. There was a crash, a scattering of pieces.

It brought her quite absurdly close to tears. Not that a plate was either here or there.

It was just there were too many broken things around her life already — the window and the guttering, and her engagement.

She gazed down at the finger where the diamond had been.

She swept the floor. By rights, she thought, she ought to spend this unexpected afternoon at home constructively. For starters, the kitchen floor needed scrubbing thoroughly. But, she had no heart for it. Her

# AFTER THE STORM

heart was broken, wasn't it?

Or was it? Sitting at the table later sipping coffee, Clare wondered about that. It wasn't something that she'd really dared to think about too hard.

Perhaps now all the family palaver had died down, she ought to spend a bit of time examining her inner self. It couldn't hurt that much, surely, not after three whole months. Besides, the storm had somehow cleared the air and left her feeling suddenly relieved, released.

Perhaps it wasn't quite so much a day for cleaning up as clearing out. There were so many things to go through, things she'd hidden in the back of cupboards, tucked in drawers, because they'd made her think of Andrew and she couldn't bear the hurt. Today, perhaps, she would find strength enough to face them.

She washed her cup and walked determinedly upstairs. She glimpsed the old oak, lying in the garden. It was beyond retrieval now, just like her past with Andrew. No point in crying over either of them . . .

IT was after four before the van pulled up.

"Bill Mullins at your service," the young man said cheerfully.

"I've been expecting you all day," Clare answered.

She'd meant the words to sound reproachful, but his twinkling smile had robbed them of their bite and left nothing but a little sadness in her voice.

"I'm sorry. But there's such a mess. The side roads are all flooded and there's debris everywhere. It really was quite a storm."

She nodded. "Yes, of course. I didn't think. I haven't been out yet to see what's happened."

"I wouldn't bother, not if I were you." He grinned. "You're better off at home till things get straight. Now, where's this window?"

Clare led the way upstairs and he surveyed the damage.

"Soon have that fixed," he said. "Pity that we can't do something for the tree, though. Must have been a fine sight in its prime."

"It was."

He worked in silence for a while, then turned and looked at her. "This is a lovely house."

"It's going on the market soon," Clare told him. "It's far too big for me. Besides, it needs an awful lot of renovation."

"A bit of tender loving care, maybe," Bill suggested.

"It was all right when there were two of us," she began, then bit her lip. You couldn't tell a total stranger . . .

He raised an eyebrow in inquiry and suddenly she simply couldn't *not* tell. She'd glimpsed the pile of letters and old photographs that spilled around the waste-paper basket in the bedroom, and the words came spilling out as well.

Bill worked on in silence, not looking at her as she spoke, which made it easier. There seemed to be no tense embarrassment between them as there would have been with friends. No questions, no reproaches. No saying that she should have been more careful making a commitment, waited till she'd known Andrew better before investing all that emotion in a doomed relationship. And all that money, too — half of the mortgage . . .

Of course, she didn't tell him Andrew had cheated on her, kept promising the wedding and postponing it, spent long weekends away with another girl. The old desire for revenge vanished as she talked. What was more, she didn't want the young man's pity. His sympathy was one thing, but his pity . . .

"There," he said eventually, standing back to show his handiwork, "all done."

"All done," Clare echoed, knowing all was done indeed.

THERE would be healing in her heart from this time on, she thought, and she led him back downstairs.

"You'll let me make you tea?" she asked as she wrote a cheque.

"That's very kind, Miss —" He peered at the cheque "— Miss Walters."

"Clare." She smiled. "And it's the very least that I can do before you have to battle with those roads again."

Glancing at his watch, Bill sighed contentedly.

"It's going on for six already. Time I was knocking off, and tea would be a welcome end to a hard day."

She poured and offered him the sugar. His hand was gentle when he passed the bowl back, warm and strong.

"I'm sorry things went wrong for you," he murmured.

"I'm not — not any more," Clare said. "Perhaps it wasn't meant to be. We would have ironed the problems out somehow if we had really wanted to.

"The only thing that grieves me is the house. I've grown attached to it." She sighed. "Still, I can't afford to buy his share and, even if I could, I couldn't do it up, not as I'd hoped."

Her plans for renovation tumbled, too, though this time Bill made suggestions for projects Clare never dreamed of. It turned out he had his eye on an old place himself and had such ideas for it.

"Sounds wonderful." She sighed. "But not for me, not here."

"There will be other people, other places, other times," he murmured, as he touched her hand by way of comfort, then poured out another cup of tea.

His words went echoing through her mind, consoling her.

It was only the soft fall of twilight through the garden that alerted them to time.

"It's late," he said, "Maybe we'll talk some more?"

Clare watched him from the landing window as he drove away. There was the faintest shadow of a smile about her lips. Maybe they *would* talk more. Maybe she would accept Bill's dinner invitation.

Tomorrow, when she'd thrown the last of all the rubbish and the memories away, she would be able to think clearly again, of other places, other times, another person — the healer in her life. □

CHANGES, changes! I don't like changes! Why can't things stay just as they are?"

Irene Hay asked herself that again and again during the summer of Trudy's wedding.

Life goes on and changes are part of the moving pattern, something you have to accept, Irene's commonsense told her. But these days her commonsense wasn't winning the argument.

Some traumatic changes were indeed taking place in Mrs Hay's life.

Of course it was wonderful that her daughter — her only child — was marrying so happily. But the news that Trudy and Harry would be living in Germany was a blow. Harry was a soldier, serving in BAOR.

The other traumatic change was about Irene's job. Something happened there which she never thought could happen.

Fifteen years ago, Irene had been left on her own to bring up their small daughter when Ron Hay died with tragic suddenness one spring day at his work as a gardener.

It was a tragedy, but the young widow had little time to feel sorry for herself. Finding a way to earn a living was Irene's problem. She and Ron had married young and she had no well-paid career to fall back on.

Then she spotted a card in Purdie's window. Purdie's, whose gracious shop dominated the High Street, specialised in bakery and confectionery. In a discreet corner by the door Irene read: *Lady Assistant Wanted.*

She was taken on. A year later Mr Purdie promoted her to chief counter-hand, and three years after that Irene became his shop manageress.

This was a blessing. It meant more money in her pay packet, and an easing of the scraping and contriving for Trudy and herself.

MRS HAY enjoyed her work. Purdie's speciality was celebration cakes, and making the most of window displays was one of her main tasks.

Every Thursday, Irene stayed on alone after the shop closed,

# All Change For Love

cleared the big corner window, brushed it gently and put down fresh sheets of shining paper.

Next, she scattered a few flower heads and placed a silver vase with one fresh rose, two crystal goblets and an imitation bottle of champagne.

Then came the cakes.

A three-tiered wedding cake always took pride of place then, three pale blue or pink birthday cakes, a snow-white christening cake, anniversary cakes with touches of gold or silver icing, and maybe a special presentation cake whose flat surface was set out as a miniature bowling-green, or curling-rink, or tennis court.

Irene had an artistic eye, and was proud to note week by week how her cake window halted High Street shoppers in their tracks.

She was in charge also of counter-fare: pretty platters heaped with pancakes and scones, glass stands holding chocolate delicacies, fruit fancies and vanilla slices.

Purdie's were known, too, for their hot pastries. At eleven o'clock

**by**
**LAURA**
**CALDWELL**

each morning, one of the bakers would emerge from the back-shop bakery balancing a tray of savoury pies and bridies, sizzling hot. Their mouth-watering aroma wove its way out into the street causing queues to form, especially on frosty, winter days.

Trudy's handsome wedding cake was a gift from old Mr Purdie to mark his appreciation of Mrs Hay's loyal service.

Irene was content. It never occurred to her that Purdie's might change.

Then one afternoon, just a few days before Trudy's wedding, Mr Purdie took Irene aside to tell her, "I've had a good run, lass. Now it's time to go. This bakery was started by my grandfather, then Father took over, then it was my turn. Three Joe Purdies in a row, but I'm the last."

Irene was dismayed.

"The fine, old, family businesses are vanishing, Irene. They're hard to sell. I've been forced to accept an offer from one of the big flour firms. They'll be putting in a manager, of course."

The old man heaved a sigh, then cheered up. "No fear for my staff, though. It's part of the bargain you're all to be kept on."

TRUDY and Harry got a perfect summer day for their wedding. Just before the bride and 'groom got into the car to leave, Trudy turned and tossed her bouquet among the crowding guests. It was as if the flowers had been aimed straight into her mother's arms!

A lump came into Irene's throat as she clasped the lovely roses.

Everyone cheered. Someone called, "Lucky for you, Irene! Wedding flowers bring romance. Your turn next!"

How absurd, Irene thought. Anyway, the flowers should have gone to one of Lynn's pretty young guests, not to a plump, middle-aged widow!

She was relieved when the last guest departed, and she was free to make her way alone to the far end of the High Street, where the flat above McBain's paper shop was home.

As she put her key in the door, Mr McBain came out.

He smiled. "You're back then! How did it go, Irene?"

"Oh, a beautiful wedding, but —"

Her landlord waited, his kind brown eyes concerned, for Irene was looking very pale.

She was tempted to say, "I'll have to get used to living alone for the first time in my life, Neil. And I'm afraid. Things are changing at Purdie's, too."

But all Irene said aloud was, "I feel a bit tired, that's all. Too much excitement." She managed to smile.

Neil McBain commented, "That's bonnie flowers you have there."

"Trudy's bouquet. Though why I got it —"

"Why not, lass? Why not?"

When she went upstairs, the little flat was quiet.

Irene plunged the roses into a basin of water, deciding to keep one bloom and take the rest to the Cottage Hospital in the morning.

She made a cup of tea, then wandered into her daughter's old room where the fragrance of Trudy's favourite scent lingered. A framed snapshot had vanished from the dressing-table. Taken one summer long ago on a beach, it showed Trudy as a leggy schoolgirl arm in arm with her mum.

The elderly teddy-bear still flopped on the bed. There was a scrap of paper pinned to his threadbare chest: *Dearest Mum, Thank you for everything. Take great care of yourself. Please look after Honey-bear for me. Love always and always — Trudy. XXX.*

Irene Hay joined Honey-bear on the bed, and the tears came.

A MONTH after the wedding, on a thundery Thursday evening, Irene dressed the celebration cake window with her usual care. Then she hurried outside to view the display from the street.

She moved to go inside again, but a hand on her shoulder halted her. "Good evening, Mrs Hay."

It was Cecil Cranford, the new shop manager, a handsome man with casual charm.

The new boss had taken over, and to Irene's immense relief no change had yet taken place in the shop. A fresh show of cakes went

into the main window once a week, the hot pastries came out of the bakery each morning at eleven.

Mr Cranford kept his hand firmly on her shoulder and asked with a smile, "Well, what do you make of this, Mrs Hay?" He swept a critical eye over her display.

"Make of it? My window? It does attract shoppers, especially on a Saturday." She added with pride, "Of course Purdie's always have been famous for celebration cakes."

"Purdie's? Naughty! You mean the new owners, I take it?"

Irene flushed. What she didn't realise was that, with her rose-pink cheeks, very blue eyes and the curling strands of damp hair at her white neck, she looked astonishingly attractive.

Cecil Cranford clasped an arm about her rather too closely and steered her into the shop. "Time for us to have a little chat, I think."

He sat her on a chair while he himself lounged in a very relaxed way against the counter, then began, "Time marches on, Mrs Hay. It's Irene, isn't it? You don't mind?

"I'll explain. The image of the village bakery in the High Street is fast becoming dead as the dodo. Agreed? A window crammed with outsize cakes has lost its appeal. We demand a rather more sophisticated image. Few sugary titbits, lots of the new savoury packages . . ."

Irene, completely dismayed, ventured, "But Purdie's — sorry — have savouries too, their hot pies and bridies —"

"Bridies! I never heard the word till I came here!" He laughed. "My sweet Irene, today's shoppers have a European way of looking at the food we eat — pastas, patés, pizzas.

"You're looking positively bewildered!" He leaned towards her. "I tell you what, let me take you out for a real European meal. I could do with cheering up in your wretched Scottish rain!

"I've discovered a very good country-house place near the coast. We can talk — make a happy night of it." His pale fingers reached to touch a strand of Irene's hair. "Do you know something, Irene? You have the prettiest hair."

But Mrs Hay, 50-year-old widow, mother of a married daughter, loyal servant for 25 years to Purdie's, wanted to hear no more.

She jumped to her feet, grabbed handbag and umbrella, then turned to announce crisply, "Keep your new-fangled ideas — and your hands — to yourself, Mr Cranford! I want none of them!"

She pulled open the door and, without a backward glance, slammed it shut behind her.

It was only when Irene was halfway home to her flat that she slowed her rushing footsteps, overwhelmed with dismay. Oh, what had she done? Just slammed herself out of her job!

THAT same evening, Neil McBain shut his shop early. There was a steady downpour, and scarcely anyone about. He would stay on and have a real tidy-up.

The truth was, Neil's shop was a bit of a muddle and a mess, especially the window. He peered at it now and felt twinges of shame. The space was crammed with piles of notebooks, boxes of small toys, shaky pyramids of cans of soft drinks. A doll had fallen forward, its golden curls spread across the glass.

Four big, glass, sweet-jars occupied the shelf above the window-display — these could do with a dust, for a start. Neil stretched to fetch one down, his fingers moved awkwardly, caught the shelf, tipped it forward and sent everything crashing!

He gazed in horror at the devastation. Sweets spilled across the fallen pyramid of cans, the golden-haired doll lay buried under a mountain of pens and notebooks. And the noise would have wakened the dead!

Indeed, the sounds of the crash brought Irene Hay to a halt as she made to cross the street.

She stared in disbelief at McBain's shop. Were vandals inside? With galloping heart, she hurried to the shop door. The door was locked, the "Closed" notice prominent.

Irene hammered on it, first with her fists, then her umbrella. She called, "Neil! Neil! Are you there? Is anybody there?"

After a long, nail-biting silence, she heard keys turn, and the white face of the newsagent peered out.

Through in the back shop, Mrs Hay made a pot of strong tea.

Neil McBain was slumped on an old sofa.

"I'll have to give up, Irene. This place is getting beyond me," he said.

Irene was filled with pity.

"Nonsense," she murmured.

"Not stuff and nonsense at all," Neil responded quite angrily. "That window was a shambles — even before the smash."

Irene smiled a gentle smile. "I know. I often longed to get my hands on it. I've a real flair for window-dressing. Of course you know I do Purdie's cake-display every — every —"

She stopped suddenly — Purdie's celebration-cake window! But that had come to an end.

"Neil! Oh, Neil —"

Neil McBain was very concerned at the sudden change in Irene's composure. "My dear, what is it? What's wrong, Irene?"

He reached out loving arms.

ONE evening six weeks later, Irene sat at the table in her pretty living-room, writing to Trudy in Germany.

"I'll begin straightaway with my wonderful news. Yesterday, Neil and I were married! I know you won't be at all surprised considering the hints in my recent letters! It was in the manse and the minister gave a beautiful service.

"A honeymoon? Maybe sometime. Meantime, we've both been very busy doing up the shop. Lots of shining white paint inside, and buttercup-yellow outside with black lettering: N. and E. I. McBain, Stationers and Booksellers. I've persuaded Neil to stock books as well as papers and magazines.

"I wish you could see our window. It's one of my jobs to set it out freshly every second Monday. Though I say it myself, it's a triumph.

"Changes, changes — funny how I dreaded them so much. I never dreamed they could bring me all this happiness. It's so wonderful, dear Trudy, to have someone special to care for and love."

Neil looked up smiling from his paper. "Who's this you're writing to, lass?"

"Trudy and Harry."

Neil came to stand beside his wife. "Here, let me have it. I want to tell our daughter how happy her mum's making me, and that we'll be going to them at Christmas for a fantastic German honeymoon!" □

LIZ's mother and father made it all sound so easy.

"Just keep reminding your gran of what a burden a big garde can be to a pensioner," Mr Fulton said.

"And make sure you take her to see Malcolm's Court on the Ope Day," Mrs Fulton added. "The Warden says she'll be there t explain how the place is run. She sounds such a nice woman!"

"The great thing is to make sure Gran doesn't think she's bein pressurised," Mr Fulton said. "Gentle persuasion is what you need

**by ELSIE JACKSON**

ust enough so that she'll put her name down for a flat."
"Are you sure — " Liz started unhappily.
"Yes," her parents said firmly.
Now, as Liz stood at the bedroom window, watching her gran ıake her way down the garden path with the aid of her walking-tick, Liz saw that they were right. She had missed her annual visit to Gran Fulton's last year, because she had been working as a teaching ssistant in France. And in two years Gran had really aged.
"It was that attack of shingles that did it," Mrs Lindsay, Gran's indly neighbour, had told Liz that morning. "It knocked the stuffing ut of poor Maggie. We were really worried about her for a while."
At that point, Liz remembered, Duncan had walked in unxpectedly, his hands covered in oil from his old car. She had been aken aback because she had thought he was at work.
Although Duncan had obviously known Liz was in his mother's itchen, his face had flushed, too, when he said lightly, "Hi there, iz. How's life at university?"
"Not so bad," she had answered, managing a smile.
Her heart had been racing, just as it used to do when she was 16 nd she met Duncan Lindsay unexpectedly in the street.

# Gentle Persuasion

"Not working today?" she had asked.
"I'm on holiday," he told her. "I'm having a week at home. Next veek I'm off to Minorca with some friends."
"Lovely," Liz had said politely.
"Tom and I are off at the same time," Mrs Lindsay had chimed in. 'But we're not ones for venturing abroad. North Berwick is more our up of tea."
"Have you been away yet?" Duncan had asked Liz.
She had told him briefly about her camping holiday in Normandy, t the same time thinking how strange it was to be having this formal onversation with a young man who had asked her, two years ago, to narry him.
She could still remember the hurt in his eyes, when she had said, 'No." She remembered, too, her own feeling of inadequacy as she truggled to explain to him that she wasn't sure of her own feelings.
Since then they had kept in touch only by Christmas cards, any ews of Duncan coming to Liz through her gran. He had one or two irlfriends, but there seemed to be no-one on the horizon at the

present, Gran had told Liz yesterday.

"Is there anyone on yours?" Gran had asked sharply.

"No," Liz had admitted. She had felt like adding, "But don't start dreaming up a romance between Duncan and me again, Gran. That was over a long time ago."

LIZ jumped as the kitchen door suddenly slammed shut. She could hear the kettle being banged down on the cooker, and cups and saucers being set out noisily on the table.

"What on earth has upset Gran?" she wondered aloud, hurrying downstairs.

Gran *was* upset, too! Liz could see it the moment she stepped into the kitchen. Her cheeks were bright red and her eyes were sparkling behind her spectacles.

"What's happened?" Liz asked in bewilderment.

As far as she knew, her grandmother had only been in the garden. What could have happened out there to leave her in this state?

"Liz, I've never been so offended!" the old lady began.

"Who by?" Liz cried, more and more puzzled.

"By Edith Lindsay," her grandmother said. "You know how they're all going away on holiday next week? Duncan, too?"

Liz nodded.

"Well, I've just heard Edith asking that young Mrs Rae if she'll keep their house-key and go in and water her plants. Asking Mrs Rae who's only lived next door to her since Easter! And I've done it for the last twenty-two years!

"I know it's twenty-two years, for the first occasion was when she went into hospital to have Duncan, and Tom went to live with his mother for a week."

"Oh, Gran! I'm sure there must be a good reason," Liz said in dismay.

Her heart sank when she saw how genuinely angry and insulted her grandmother was. It did not bode well for their visit to Malcolm's Court that afternoon.

Gran had agreed to go to the Open Day, but in a half-hearted way. If she was in a bad mood before they even set out, the place wasn't likely to make a very good impression on her.

"What sort of reason?" her grandmother demanded crossly. "I can't think of one."

"Perhaps Mrs Rae offered to keep the key, and Mrs Lindsay would be anxious not to rebuff her, with her being a newcomer," Liz suggested.

"It didn't sound like that, from the conversation I heard," her gran replied, but there was a trace of uncertainty in her voice.

Liz traded on this.

"I don't suppose it would," she said firmly. "Mrs Lindsay is a very tactful woman."

"Hm," Mrs Fulton muttered non-committally. "Still," she added after a moment, "I shall let Edith Lindsay know I heard her making



▶ *over*

# *Lammas Fair*

THEY granted us a charter
so we could hold a Fair,
Where folk could come and barter
Out in the open air.
Pedlars came, with dusty feet
A-shouting, "Goods for sale."
Gipsies told the future,
Landlords sold their ale.
There were games to play,
And fairings,
My friend bought one for me.
There was brandy-snap
And apple pies,
I had one for my tea.
There were games of skill
And games of chance
And games of Do and Dare.
There was lots of fun
For everyone
At the Lammas Fair.

— *Jean Harris.*

her arrangements with Mrs Rae."

"Best wait till you've simmered down." Liz smiled, putting an arm round her gran's shoulder. "In the meantime, let's have our cup of tea, then we can be off to Malcolm's Court. It's a lovely sunny afternoon."

Her grandmother nodded, then gazed regretfully out of the back window for a minute.

"I should really be working in the garden." She sighed. "Look at those weeds in the borders. I can't seem to keep up with them any more."

"If Dad and Mum didn't live three hundred miles away, they'd come and help you," Liz told her.

"I know that, love." Her grandmother patted the girl's hand.

"As it is, it's an awful lot of work for you to battle with on your own," Liz pointed out. "Don't you think so, Gran?" she added quietly.

"I do on my bad days!" Her grandmother chuckled, pouring out the tea.

Liz decided to leave it at that for the time being. She mustn't put any pressure on Gran at this crucial moment before she had even seen the sheltered-housing complex, otherwise she was quite likely to refuse even to look at it.

MRS McLELLAN, the warden of Malcolm's Court, was a plump, cheerful little woman. Mr Fulton had spoken to her at length on the telephone, so she knew the reason for Liz bringing her gran along to the Open Day.

Liz listened gratefully as the warden emphasised those features of the unit that would be important to someone like Gran Fulton — the fact that residents could be as "private" or as "sociable" as they wished. No-one was ever pressed into "joining in" if they didn't feel like it.

"And of course all the residents furnish and decorate their flats as they wish. There aren't any rules and regulations about that." Mrs McLellan smiled as she showed them round the show flat.

"Well? What did you think of Malcolm's Court?" Liz asked her grandmother quietly, as they stood at the bus stop waiting for a bus to take them home.

"It was all right," her gran said warily.

Then when Liz didn't speak, she went on more enthusiastically, "I liked their kitchens. They were a good size, and beautifully streamlined. Didn't you think so?"

"Yes, I did," Liz agreed, careful not to sound too eager. Gran must not feel she was being persuaded into taking a step she would later regret.

"And that underfloor heating must be a boon in winter," Maggie Fulton went on thoughtfully.

"M-m-m," Liz said, taking her grandmother's arm as the bus came into view.

She purposely didn't talk about Malcolm's Court during the journey. She wanted to let her grandmother sort out all her impressions in peace.

Then, when they turned the corner of the street where her grandmother lived, Liz's heart gave a lurch — Duncan Lindsay was coming towards them.

"Hi!" he called. "I've just been at your door. I wondered if you would care for a game of tennis this evening, Liz?"

Liz felt her cheeks grow hot. "Well, I haven't a racket with me, or shoes," she said regretfully.

"I can lend you a racket, and there are always plenty of spare shoes lying around in the clubhouse," Duncan told her, his dark eyes anxious.

"Oh, go along," Mrs Fulton urged her with a chuckle. "You've had a boring afternoon. You must have a bit of fun in the evening."

"It wasn't boring at all," Liz protested.

But she smiled at Duncan. "All right. Thanks, I'll come," she told him. "When do you want to leave?"

"Around seven?" Duncan suggested.

"Fine," Liz agreed.

Maggie Fulton stood at the window watching the young couple walk along the road at five minutes past seven.

"Just like old times," she murmured with a smile. Then suddenly her brow clouded.

"I didn't ask Duncan about Mrs Rae keeping their key," she whispered. "I'll do it when they come back. I won't be happy until I've got to the bottom of that."

THE old magic was still working for Liz and Duncan. Liz knew it by the time they had finished their first set. It was as powerful as electricity, this attraction between them.

Yet, even as she acknowledged that it was still there, she was as uncertain about her feelings for Duncan as she had been two years ago. She still didn't know whether she really loved this dark-eyed, curly-haired young man, or whether it was merely a strong physical attraction tempered by a romantic "holiday" mood.

"I still feel the same about you, darling," Duncan whispered, suddenly putting his arm round Liz as they walked home along the twilit avenues of the small town. "I've never met anyone else to compare with you. As soon as I saw you yesterday, I knew nothing had changed."

"Oh, Duncan!" Liz let her head fall on his shoulder for a moment.

"You're right," she said softly. "Nothing has changed. I still feel as uncertain as ever. If you were to ask me what you asked me two years ago, I'd still have to give the same answer."

"But you haven't met anyone else?" Duncan asked sharply.

Liz shook her blonde head.

"I'd wait for you, you know," Duncan said, staring into her eyes. "Until you finish your degree . . ."

"Don't!" Liz put a finger gently on his lips. "Don't let's get too serious too soon. Let's enjoy each other's company for a bit."

"But we only have a week," Duncan pointed out.

"A lot can happen in a week," Liz told him gently as she squeezed his arm.

When she reached her grandmother's house, she asked him in for supper. It was the least she could do, she felt.

She had completely forgotten about Gran's outburst over Mrs Lindsay leaving her key with Mrs Rae. She was soon to be reminded of it, though.

"I hear that Mrs Rae will be watering your plants and looking after your mail next week," Mrs Fulton remarked as she poured out the tea.

"Yes, that's right," Duncan said unsuspectingly. "Mum thought it would be too much for you now, Mrs Fulton."

"Now?" Gran demanded. "What do you mean, Duncan?"

"Well, now that you're older," he told her uneasily.

"I see. Well, how considerate of her," Gran said in an icy tone.

Liz's heart sank as she looked at her grandmother's rigid little figure. As soon as Duncan had gone, Gran turned to Liz, indignation blazing in her blue eyes.

"Too old!" she exclaimed. "Did you hear him? What cheek! There's nothing worse than being written off before your time, Liz. I'll show them all who's too old! I'm as able as I was twenty years ago.

"And to think I was considering putting down my name for a flat in Malcolm's Court! They really would write me off then!"

Liz groaned inwardly. Duncan had not meant any harm, but by his unfortunate remark he had undone all Liz's good work of that afternoon.

Gran would never be steered towards Malcolm's Court now. Her pride had been too badly hurt.

LIZ was hanging out the washing the following day while her gran prepared lunch. She had almost finished when her grandmother appeared at her side waving a wet tea-towel.

"Hang this up too, love," she told the girl. "I just washed it through while I was waiting for the chip-pan to heat up."

"All right," Liz began, when a loud bang behind her made her jump.

"It's the wind," Gran said. "It's blown the door shut."

She hurried over to the kitchen door, then Liz heard her gasp.

"What is it?" the girl called.

"Oh, Liz! I had the catch down on the door. We're locked out!" her grandmother cried.

"Don't worry," Liz said calmly, as she walked over to join her gran. "We'll get in somehow, even if we have to find a locksmith. It's not a crisis."

"But, Liz! That's just what it is," her grandmother replied in a shaky voice. "I've left the pan of fat on the cooker heating up for the chips."

"What!" Liz gasped.

Suddenly she heard someone whistling in the next garden, and looked across to see Duncan out working on his car.

"Oh, Duncan!" the girl shouted in a panic. "Come quickly! We're in real trouble!"

Duncan was beside them in a second. When he had heard what Gran had done, he ran round to the side of the building.

"The bathroom window's open," he called. "I can shin up the drainpipe and get in that way."

"But it's not safe," Gran shouted in a quavering voice. "I've been meaning to get that pipe renewed for months."

"I'll have to risk it," Duncan said. "We're running out of time."

He was beginning to climb even as he spoke.

Oh, no! Liz thought, looking up in horror at the swaying pipe. He'll break his neck if he falls.

It was as though a hand were squeezing her heart. Suddenly, she knew that she lovd Duncan Lindsay with her whole being, and that if anything happened to him, she would feel the end of the world had come.

"Oh, darling! Don't fall! Please don't fall!" she whispered.

Just as the young man reached the window-sill there was an ominous, cracking noise and the old pipe broke away from the wall. But Duncan was already halfway through the small window.

A minute later he opened the kitchen door, the pan of smoking fat now sitting safely on the work surface.

"Oh, Duncan!" Liz threw herself into his arms.

"It's all right, love," he assured her, kissing her hair.

"I was so afraid I'd lose you," she said, pulling him to her.

"You won't do that," Duncan whispered. "Not ever, sweetheart."

GRAN wrote a letter to the warden of Malcolm's Court that evening.

"It's not that I feel old," she told Liz, "but I've got to face facts. My memory lets me down at times. That could have been a very nasty accident this morning, if Duncan hadn't been so quick and plucky."

"He's not the only plucky one — "

" — in the family? Is that what you were going to say?" Gran asked with a twinkle in her eye.

"No, I was not," Liz said, going across to give her grandmother a little hug. "I won't be able to say that until at least next year. We're going to wait until I have my degree before we get married."

"Good," her grandmother announced. "I'll be in my new flat by then, I hope. I'll be able to cook a first-rate wedding breakfast in that lovely kitchen."

"I shall hold you to that, Gran Fulton," Liz said.

And she did. □

WORKING on a market stall until midnight was not an ideal wa for a girl to spend the Saturday before Christmas, but Lorr had no choice. Her father was in hospital with a broken thig after slipping on a patch of ice, and now her mother was confined t the house with a severe attack of laryngitis.

"If you could take along the Christmas orders to save disappointir people," her mother had croaked, "I'm sure that nice couple wh sell the pottery would join our stall with their own.

"Or there's that young chap, Robert, who sells wooden toys. H could make room on his counter for our orders."

"Will you please do as the doctor told you, Mother, and rest you voice." Lorna tried to be firm. "I can easily manage."

Evidently she had sounded firmer than she meant to, because he mother sighed and whispered reproachfully, "I didn't mean that yc weren't capable. It just seems a shame . . . with everything else."

Hastily rubbing at the corner of her eyes, she said, "My eyes ar watering because I shouldn't be trying to speak."

"I know, Mum." Lorna had been sympathetic, although there wa a familiar indignation niggling at the back of her mind.

She wanted to say to her mother fiercely, "Will you stop pityir me and acting as if you're afraid you'll upset me!"

But Lorna had to bite her tongue and say nothing, because all th awkwardness was entirely her own fault. She had told her paren that she didn't want to talk about her break-up with Gavin Sinclai

"Please," she had begged them, as she struggled to hold bac tears, "please don't ever mention his name to me again."

Naturally, because they were the nicest, most understandir parents a girl could have, they had respected her wishes. Neverthele it was becoming more and more of a strain, especially as she wa spending so much time alone with her mother while her father was i hospital.

It wasn't pleasant to admit to to herself, but she had been secret dreading this long day helping her mother on the stall. They ha arranged that each of them would go separately to visit her father i hospital, but even then there would be hours and hours of he mother extra-carefully avoiding the subject of Lorna's heartbreak with Lorna, herself, strangely unable to bridge the constant gaps an tense pauses.

FORGET all that, Lorna ordered herself sternly as she unpacke boxes and bags of knitted garments. You are here to do a jo of work, so just get on with it.

"How would you like to buy some lovely holly and mistletoe t decorate your stall for Christmas?" The salesman was a freckle-face boy accompanied by his little sister, who looked almost exactly lik him.

Lorna could not resist their winning smiles.

All their greenery was piled into an old pram, and Lorna left th two youngsters to select some branches for her. Then she realise

**by PEGGY MAITLAND**

hey were taking a long time about it — because a quarrel had leveloped between them.

She stepped round the counter to try to mediate. In doing so she accidentally knocked a knitted tea-cosy to the ground.

She bent down quickly to pick it up.

The little girl burst into noisy tears and accused her brother, "See

# Her Own Christmas Miracle

what you've made the lady do!"

"There's no harm done." Lorna brushed at the cosy and smiled at the children, asking, "What's the matter? Why were you quarrelling?"

"We want to buy that pink jumper." The boy pointed behind Lorna. "It's for our mum, and we have enough money."

"No, we don't!" the girl cried. "If we buy that, we won't have enough money left for Grandma's gift!"

Lorna discovered that the children were called Chris and Cindy, and that their parents had a bookstall in the market. Indeed, she would have been given all their family history if she'd had time to listen.

It took all her ingenuity to help solve their problem by wrapping up the pink jumper, which they paid for, then wrapping up a pale blue scarf to be put aside until later, when they had earned enough money to buy it from the sale of their holly.

"I wanted something pretty for Grandma. The scarf will be lovely." Cindy smiled cheerfully as they moved on with their pram load of holly.

LORNA had not realised that the scene had been watched and overheard by the woman at the pottery stall.

She introduced herself as Mrs Macrae, then said with a smile, "I just wish all the world's quarrels could be sorted out so nicely. Just a bit of give and take makes all the difference."

Then she asked, "Where's your mother? Is she coming along later? I haven't seen your father yet, either."

Her eyes widened in dismay as Lorna explained why she was in sole charge.

"What a chapter of misfortune your family's been suffering," Mrs Macrae said. She called to her husband, "Would you listen to this, John!"

Lorna's face was hot with embarrassment, then she truly wished that the ground would open up and swallow her as the older woman said in commiserating tones, "It was such a shame about you and your boyfriend — you must be missing him more than ever now."

Lorna kept her head lowered and carefully rearranged some cards on the counter.

But this encouraged Mrs Macrae to say, "He helped you to design and make the cards, didn't he?"

Lorna nodded.

"He drew the pictures and you wrote the verses — your mother told me that you made a wonderful team." Mrs Macrae sighed.

"But we weren't planning to go into business," Lorna was provoked into replying. "We were simply helping out."

"I know." Mrs Macrae did not take offence and she went on, "Not many of us here planned to go into business. My husband took up pottery as a hobby when he was made redundant.

"When his teacher said he had a talent, he began to make stuff to sell — and here we are, every Saturday. It's surprising how your life can change, isn't it?"

"Yes." Lorna was more relaxed now. "My parents were the same, except that they bought a knitting-machine."

Glancing round the busy market hall, she added, "I think this market is a marvellous idea."

"Almost everything sold here is hand-made — we are all artists and craftsmen." Mrs Macrae smiled. "But then, you're an artist yourself."

"No, I'm an office worker," Lorna replied, and was glad to be able to turn away immediately as a customer approached.

She was certain that Mrs Macrae would somehow get around to asking more personal questions.

I don't know why I'm so determined not to talk about my quarrel with Gavin, she reflected. Anyone would think I was afraid — or ashamed — and I'm not. I was totally in the right . . .

So what? A voice inside her head was scornful, jeering. If you're so perfect, why do you feel so guilty and miserable? Why do you still keep picturing that hurt look on Gavin's face?

A steady flow of customers kept her from having to dwell on her thoughts, but she was constantly aware of a forlorn ache in her heart.

AT lunch-time there was a lull and Mrs Macraw offered kindly, "I'll look after your stall later, if you want to visit your father in hospital."

Lorna was hesitant about accepting. Then her mind was made up for her, as some other stallholders came to her with flowers and fruit and sweets for her parents, and such a flood of good wishes that Lorna felt quite overwhelmed.

At four o'clock there was another lull in trade, and Lorna reached for her jacket.

"I think I should go home first to see if my mother needs anything," Lorna told Mrs Macrae, "then I'll give my father a quick visit. I won't be too long, though."

"Take your time," Mrs Macrae said. "As you can see, our stall is almost cleaned out — we've been really lucky, so maybe we'll go home early."

"Good for you." Lorna smiled, but as she drove out of the car park, she was thinking that she herself didn't have a hope of leaving before the hall closed at midnight. Still, sales had been steady — she would have a good enough report for her parents.

She had expected the house to be in darkness, but all the lights were on. She stood on the pavement, frozen for a moment as she wondered what had happened. Then she saw her father at the sitting-room window, and her heart lifted.

Douglas Crawford was hobbling around on crutches, his face beaming as he told his daughter, "They decided to let me out for Christmas!"

Turning to his wife, who was muffled in scarves but smiling, he said joyfully, "We'll have a real family Christmas after all."

Lorna returned to the car for all the gifts and cards from their friends at the market.

"Everyone has been asking about you. They all miss you and send their best wishes to you," she told them.

Her parents were pleased and touched.

There was a suggestion of a tear in Mrs Crawford's eye as she said, "Last year at this time they were all strangers to us, and now they are such dear friends. I really look forward to seeing them every week."

Lorna sat for about 20 minutes telling them proudly all that she had sold so far.

She emptied her cash bag happily, saying, "I left some money for change with Mrs Macrae, so I'd better get back and see how much she's managed to add."

Lorna noticed that her parents exchanged a swift look, then her

## The Wonder of Water . . .

### LYDFORD GORGE

*Close to the village of Lydford, once a town where the Anglo-Saxons minted coins, the Gorge is almost roofed over by trees, while wild garlic grows in abundance by its sides. The Gorge is almost a mile long, with the river running over boulders, through dark pools, forming cascades and rapids. According to local history, an outlaw family named Gubbins lived here while alternately scandalising and terrorising the townsfolk.*

mother said in her husky voice, "There's a card for you, dear, and a parcel."

She paused. "I put them upstairs in your room."

LORNA'S heart gave an enormous lurch.

She had to swallow hard before she could ask, with intuition, "From Gavin . . . ?"

Her mother nodded and the atmosphere was heavy with tension.

Suddenly, Lorna recalled her awkward conversation with Mrs Macrae, and her thoughts crystallised with a new and loving clarity. She had been so wrong to try to shut her parents out of her unhappiness — and she had not succeeded. Now she realised that they had been sharing her heartache in silence, which it was up to her to break.

She said shakily, speaking the first thought about Gavin which came into her head, "I didn't buy anything for him, not even a card."

She bit her lip as her eyes filled with tears.

Mrs Crawford put her arm around Lorna's shoulders. "It's not too late. Look, I have some spare cards."

Lorna chose the plainest card with the most ordinary message, *SEASON'S GREETINGS*.

As she scribbled her name, she thought sadly, after all that we meant to each other, how did it happen that we were divided by such a trivial quarrel?

She did not realise that she had asked the question aloud until her mother answered, "One angry word always seems to borrow another."

"And you and Gavin are both inclined to be hot-tempered," her father pointed out.

Lorna told him, "This is only a card, it doesn't mean —"

"No, but it's a gesture of peace and goodwill," Mrs Crawford whispered. Then she said, "Aren't you going to open your card?"

"I'll open it when I get home at midnight," Lorna replied. "I must dash now. I want to put this card through Gavin's letter-box while I have the courage. It's only a short detour."

★ ★ ★ ★

Lorna arrived back at the market to be told by Mrs Macrae, "Your outing certainly did you some good! You've got lovely colour in your cheeks and your eyes are sparkling!"

Quickly, Lorna told her the good news about her father getting out of hospital, and she added, "My mother is so much better. I hardly recognised her from this morning — although she still has to whisper."

Lorna knew that she was chattering but she also knew that it was because she wanted to guard and keep the secret hope which was lighting up her heart.

Gavin's home had been in darkness when she slipped the card through the door. She wondered if she would have been so brave if there had been a chance of anyone opening the door. She wondered what they would have said to each other if she had met him . . .

"Lorna!" Mrs Macrae's laughing tone cut across her thoughts. "You were away in a dream. You haven't been listening to a word."

"Sorry," Lorna apologised, "you were telling me about a blue scarf."

"The blue mohair scarf," Mrs Macrae repeated. "These two children came to say they didn't want it after all. So I took the liberty of putting it back on the counter — and it was snapped up right away! And I've sold two cardigans and a waistcoat, not to mention umpteen Christmas cards."

Lorna thanked her profusely, but at the same time she was concerned about the children's reason for deciding against the scarf.

Perhaps they hadn't made enough money to pay for it, she thought. If I had been here, I would have reduced the price. It would be a shame if Cindy were disappointed — she had set her heart on that scarf for her grandmother.

Although she was kept quite busy, Lorna frequently noticed Cindy and Chris playing amongst a crowd of children.

She tried once or twice to catch Cindy's eye, but it was Chris who came to say to her in a quiet moment, "I hope you weren't annoyed about the scarf."

"Not at all," Lorna assured him. Then she asked hesitantly, "Did you find another present for your grandma — something nice?"

The boy nodded importantly. "Something very useful." He lowered his voice and Lorna automatically leaned towards him to catch his next words, "We bought her a magnifying glass."

Suddenly there was a burst of laughter around them and children's voices chanting, "Kissing under the mistletoe! Kissing under the mistletoe!"

"I was not!" Chris protested, blushing furiously.

Lorna looked up, and was surprised to see that there was a sprig of mistletoe fixed to the crossbar above their heads.

"I didn't know that was up there!"

She added her laughing denials to the boy's, but the other children refused to believe them and now a vociferous challenge went up. "Kiss her again! Kiss her under the mistletoe!"

SUDDENLY, Lorna's smile faded. She had not seen Gavin approaching, yet her heart told her she had been watching and waiting for him.

"Hello, Lorna."

"Hello, Gavin."

The children sensed an extra feeling in the air. Their laughter was infectious.

"Kiss her under the mistletoe! Kiss her under the mistletoe!" they shouted, louder than ever.

Lorna and Gavin smiled at each other for a fleeting second, then Lorna leaned across the counter and her lips met Gavin's in a kiss of sheer enchantment. □

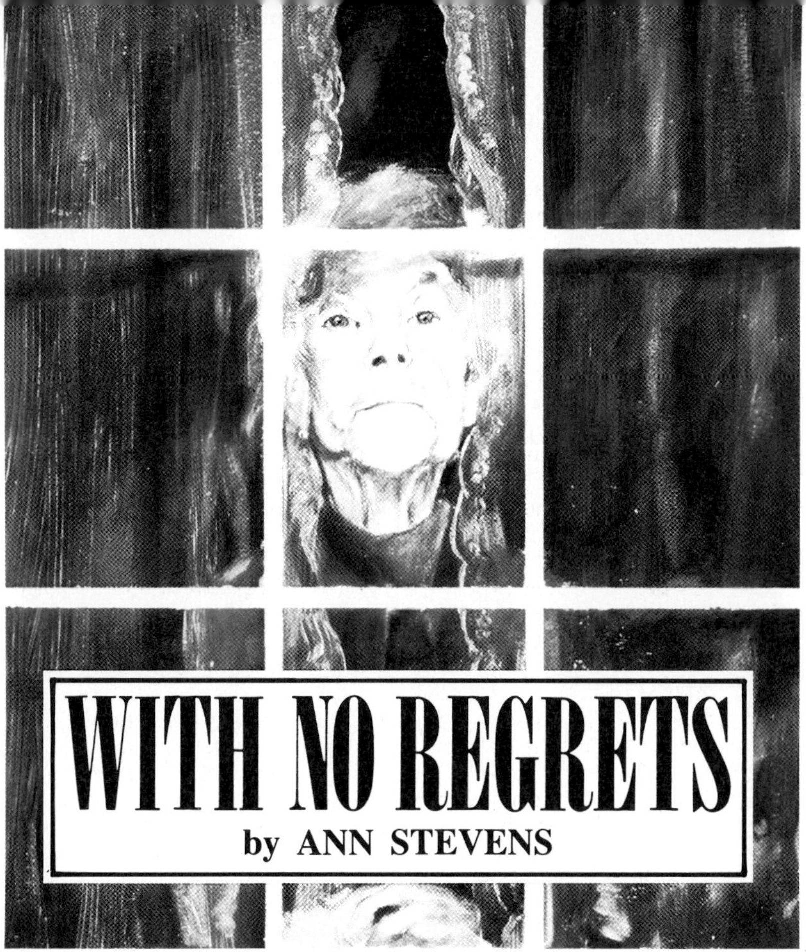

# WITH NO REGRETS

**by ANN STEVENS**

ELEANOR woke early on Linda's wedding day, and saw that the sun was shining and that just a whisper of a breeze stirred the muslin curtains at her window. Stiffly, she eased herself out of bed, got dressed and went to look out at the morning.

She had never got used to sleeping downstairs, and pulled aside the curtain cautiously. But there was no-one about.

The square was still and deserted, the morning sun glinting on parked cars and glazing the dew on the grass of the gardens behind the railings in the middle.

Contentedly she let the curtain drop and sat down carefully at her dressing-table.

Linda's wedding day! Linda was her youngest grandchild and the last of them to be married. How proud Edward would have been today.

She picked up the photograph of a good-looking, elderly man, clean-shaven except for the moustache he had sported all his life. Dear Edward! That moustache had been the most dashing and exciting thing about him, but he had made her happy.

Angela, the mother of the bride, had been his favourite of their four children, and Linda was so very like her mother had been on her own wedding day.

She looked tenderly down at her husband's picture, speaking to him as she often did.

"It's a beautiful day, Edward. I just knew it would be! What a pity you can't be with us . . ."

She sighed, setting down the silver frame and looking round the room. She had moved downstairs a year ago, when her legs refused to climb the steep stairs any more.

This room had been their dining-room, and sometimes she imagined it still echoed with the laughter and chatter and clatter of their happy family meals. Now it was quiet and empty, filled only with the scent of the roses standing beside the photograph.

She lowered her face to the silky petals, drinking in their perfume. Then she broke off a perfect, half-open, creamy bud. She would wear it on the lapel of her green silk coat.

"This will be the last wedding I go to," she had told herself as she took a taxi to make the carefully-considered purchase of the green coat and dress, and the matching silk toque to cover her thinning white hair. "I may be eighty-five, but I won't let Linda down. After all, I am the grandmother of the bride!"

She made herself a light breakfast and took a shower, being very careful not to slip. Mary, her housekeeper, wasn't coming in today. Eleanor had wanted to have this special morning to herself.

COMFORTABLY wrapped in her robe and slippers, she sat once more at her dressing-table, applying powder and the softest touch of green eye-shadow and a pale lipstick. She smiled at herself in the mirror, then at Edward.

"Not so bad for eighty-five, eh? And you weren't so bad yourself were you . . ." She reached out to touch the smiling face, a lump rising to her throat.

How she missed him, even after eight years. But now was not the time for grieving — there was one more thing she had to do. She had

## PRESTON MILL, EAST LOTHIAN

This 17th century mill stands on the banks of the River Tyne near East Linton. Owned by the National Trust for Scotland since 1950, it is Scotland's oldest mechanically working mill. The machinery is driven by water from the mill-pond, whose banks provide a nesting-place for Muscovy ducks. The conical roof of the kiln with its wind vane is known locally as "the long arm of friendship."

PRESTON MILL, EAST LOTHIAN : J CAMPBELL KERR

to find the gloves.

Eleanor had plenty of gloves, and she could have afforded to buy plenty more. But some irrational sentiment had told her that Linda's wedding day deserved a special gesture of reverence and love.

Reaching into the deepest recesses of her wardrobe drawer, gently pushing aside the bundles of letters and Valentine cards, children's drawings and little, unused but treasured gifts, she came at last to the cardboard box which had lain there undisturbed for years.

The tissue-paper, crisp with age, parted with a brief, evocative scent of lavender. She lifted out one of the gloves carefully, smoothing it gently and laying it against her hand. Her fingers were still slim and straight, though the skin was no longer white, but creased and darkened with age like the tissue-paper.

The glove was cream, of the softest suede with three little pearl buttons at the wrist.

Thoughtfully, remembering, Eleanor stroked the supple fabric, feeling it warm and soft as a living thing in her hand. Her movements became rhythmic, dancing to the tune of a waltz which had intruded into her mind.

"The Blue Danube!"

Wearing the cream, suede gloves on her pretty, white hands, she had danced to that tune on her 20th birthday when Edward had proposed to her. He had given her the gloves for her birthday — and later, after speaking to her father, he had given her the diamond which still sparkled on her finger.

Rousing herself briskly, she lifted the second cream glove from the box and began gently smoothing them on to her hands.

"Look, Edward," she said to the empty room. "See how they still fit! You always said I had pretty little hands. You will be coming to the wedding with me, after all!"

The Saturday traffic was building up, and Eleanor sensed the buzz of life outside and the passing of time. Removing the gloves, she slipped into the green dress and coat and adjusted her hat, pulling a few soft, white, wispy curls across her forehead.

She leaned to the mirror to inspect herself and nodded with approval.

"Not so bad," she said with satisfaction. "Linda will be proud of me. Now for the finishing touch . . ."

She went to close the glove box, but as she did so, a flash of blue in the crumpled paper caught her eye. Before she knew it, she had lifted out the other pair of gloves and was staring at them, her eyes bright with sudden recollection.

THE gloves were of blue silk, with velvet ribbon at the cuffs ending in a bow. They had been given to her on her 17th birthday by Geoffrey, who had easily persuaded her with his Irish blandishments to remove the white, cotton ones her mother had chosen and wear his blue ones instead.

She had been wearing a green dress on that day, too, she

remembered. The blue gloves had looked terrible!

Eleanor smiled to herself as she remembered her mother's horror and her sisters' protests, but she hadn't cared, for those blue, silken hands had been enclosed in Geoffrey's all evening and, during the last waltz, he had kissed her!

She stared down at the scraps of blue in her hands, her heart beating wildly and erratically. She might be an old woman, but she could still remember, no, still *feel* the excitement.

The years rolled away and she was 17 again, circling in Geoffrey's arms, feeling his kiss, her first kiss, warm on her lips.

But her father hadn't approved, and when Geoffrey had called on her he had been sent packing.

Eleanor had thought her heart was broken — until she met Edward. And she had had no regrets.

She heard herself murmur, "So lucky. I was so lucky!"

She stared at her flushed face in the mirror, noting the shine in her eyes and the eager, parted lips. Then she picked up the other gloves and thoughtfully, for a long moment, she looked down at them — two blue, two cream.

"So long ago . . ." She sighed.

She heard the car draw up outside the house. Swiftly and decisively she laid the discarded gloves on the dressing-table beneath the roses and Edward's smiling face, picked up her bag and with one final, proud, excited glance in the mirror, set off for her last wedding.

LINDA was standing with her tall, new husband, Martin, greeting the guests at the entrance to the reception.

Eleanor smiled at her granddaughter through over-bright eyes and kissed her flushed and happy face.

"You look just beautiful, Linda! I'm so proud of you . . ."

She moved on to be hugged by Martin, and her daughter Angela and son-in-law Bruce.

Gratefully, suddenly tired, she allowed herself to be shown to a chair, given sherry, and left to watch the antics of the pageboys who were teasing the bridesmaids. The smallest bridesmaid was her great-great-grandchild. Whoever would have thought it possible all those years ago?

Eleanor carefully removed her gloves, and accepted a vol-au-vent from a silver tray offered to her.

In a brief lull in the arrivals, Linda turned to Martin and said, "Gran looks terrific! But I hope it's not too much for her."

Martin was grinning. "She looks in fine form to me. Though — well, I suppose at her age, it doesn't really matter if you wear bright blue gloves with a green dress!" □

Printed and published in Great Britain by D. C. Thomson & Co., Ltd., Dundee, Glasgow and London. 

**ISBN** 0-85116-523-0

BLACK ROCK COTTAGE, RANNOCH MOOR : J CAMPBELL KERR